From the pyramid below, a blue lance of light reached up to paralyze him, select the control-suit from the other components, and send it tumbling to the planetary surface below like a swatted insect.

But the suit had been designed to protect its occupants, whether he himself was operative or not. At fifteen hundred feet, the drag chute broke free, looking like a silver cloth candle-snuffer in the sunlight; and at five hundred feet the retro-rockets cut in. The suit tumbled to earth among some trees two kilometers from the pyramid, with Harry inside bruised, but released from his paralysis.

From the pyramid, a jagged arm of something like white lightning lashed the ground as far as the suit, and the suit's outer surface glowed cherry-red. Inside, the temperature suddenly shot up fifty degrees; instinctively Harry hit the panic button available to him inside the suit.

The suit split down the center like an overcooked frankfurter and spat Harry out . . . .

IN THE BONE

BONE

THE BEST
SCIENCE FICTION OF
GORDON R.
DICKSON

GORDON R. DICKSON

ACE SCIENCE FICTION BOOKS
NEW YORK

IN THE BONE: THE BEST SCIENCE
FICTION OF GORDON R. DICKSON

An Ace Science Fiction Book / published by arrangement with
the author

PRINTING HISTORY
Ace Science Fiction edition/March 1987

ISBN: 0-441-37049-7

Ace Science Fiction Books are published by
The Berkley Publishing Group,
200 Madison Avenue, New York, New York 10016.
PRINTED IN THE UNITED STATES OF AMERICA

CONTENTS

CONTENTS

TWIG

For four hours Twig had been working up her courage to approach the supply post. Now in the pumpkin-colored afternoon light of the big, orange-yellow sun, she stood right beside one of the heavy rammed-earth walls. From the slice of dark interior seen through the partial opening of the door not two meters from her, came the sound of a raucous and drunken tenor—not a young tenor, but a tenor which cracked now and then on the dryness of a middle-aged throat—singing.

> . . . 'As game as Ned Kelly,' the people would say;
> 'As game as Ned Kelly,' they say it today . . .

It would have been something, at least, if the accent of the singing voice had been as Australian as the ballad of the old down-under outlaw who, wearing his own version of armor, had finally shot it out with the police and been slain. But Hacker Illions had never seen the planet Earth, let alone Australia; and his only claims to that part of Sol III were an Australian-born mother and father, both over twenty years dead and buried here on Jinson's Planet. Even Twig knew that Hacker had no strong connection with Ned Kelly and Australia, only a thread of one. But she accepted his playing the Aussie, just as she accepted his foolishness when drunk, his bravery when sober and his wobbly but unceasing devotion to the Plant-Grandfather.

Hacker had been drinking for at least the four hours since Twig had arrived at the supply post. He would be in no shape to talk sense to now. Silent as a shadow, light as a flicker of sunlight between two clouds, Twig pressed against the coarse-grained earth wall, listening and trying to summon up the courage to go inside, into that dark, noisome, hutchlike trap her own kind called a building. There would be others in there beside Hacker—even if only the Factor of the supply post itself. There might even be others as drunk as Hacker, but worse-minded, men who might try to catch and hold her with their hands. She shivered. Not only at the feel in her imagination of the large, rough hands; but with the knowledge that if they did seize her, she would hurt them. She would not be able to help herself; she would have to hurt them to make them let her go.

Sinking down into a squatting position beside the earth wall, Twig rocked unhappily on her heels, silently mourning inside herself. If only Hacker would come out, so that she would not have to go in after him. But for four hours now, he had not left the building. There must be some place inside there where he could relieve himself; and that meant he would not have to leave the building until he ran out of money or was thrown out—and the posse must now be less than an hour from here.

"Hacker!" she called. "*Come out!*"

But the call was only a whisper. Even alone with Hacker, she had never been able to raise her voice above that whisper level. Normally, it did not matter. Before she had met Hacker, when she had only the Plant-Grandfather to talk to, she had not needed to make sounds at all. But now, if she could only shout, like other humans. Just once, shout like the human she actually was . . .

But her aching throat gave forth nothing but a hiss of air. The physical machinery for shouting was there, but something in her mind after all those years of growing up with only the Plant-Grandfather to talk to would not let it work. There was no time left and no choice. She pulled taut the threads that bound the suit of bark tightly about her body. Hacker had always wanted her to wear human clothes; they would give her more protection against ordinary men, he said. But anywhere except in a closed box like this building, no other human could catch her anyway; and she could not stand the dead feel of the materials with which other humans covered their bodies. She took a deep breath and darted in through the half-open door.

She was almost at Hacker's side before anyone noticed her, so light and swift had been her dash across the floor. None of them there saw her passage. Hacker stood, one of his elbows on a waist-high shelf called a bar. It was a long bar that ran along the inside wall of the room with space for the Factor to stand behind it and pass out glasses and bottles. The Factor was standing there now; almost, but not quite, opposite Hacker. Facing Hacker, on Hacker's side of the shelf, was a man as tall as Hacker, but much heavier, with a long, black beard.

This man saw her first, as she stole up beside Hacker and tugged at his jacket.

"Hey!" shouted the black-bearded man; and his voice was a deep and growling bass. "Hacker, look! Don't tell me it's that wild kid, the one the Plant raised! It is! I'll be damned, but it is! Where've you been keeping her hid all this time?"

And just as Twig had known he would, the black-bearded man reached out a thick hand for her. She ducked behind Hacker.

"Leave her alone!" said Hacker thickly. "Twig—Twig, you get out of here. Wait for me outside."

"Now, hold it a minute." The black-bearded man tried to come around Hacker to get to her. A miner's ion drill dragged heavily down on a holster fastened to the belt at his waist. Hacker, unarmed, got in the way. "Get out, Hacker! I just want to look at the kid!"

"Leave her, Berg," said Hacker. "I mean it."

"You?" Berg snorted. "Who're you but a bum I've been feeding drinks to all afternoon?"

"Hacker! Come!" whispered Twig in his ear.

"Right. All right!" said Hacker with drunken dignity. "That the way you feel, Berg . . . Let's go, Twig."

He turned and started toward the door. Berg caught him by the looseness of his leather jacket and hauled him to a stop. Beyond the black beard, Twig could see the Factor, a fat, white man, leaning on his elbows on the shelf of the bar and smiling, saying nothing, doing nothing.

"No, you don't," said Berg, grinning. "You're staying, Hack. So's the kid, if I've got to tie you both up. There's some people coming to see you."

"See me?" Hacker turned to face the black beard and stood, swaying a little, peering at the other, stupidly.

"Why, sure," said Berg. "Your term as Congressman from this district ran out yesterday, Hacker. You got no immunity now."

Twig's heart lurched. It was worse than she had thought. Hacker drunk was bad enough; but someone deliberately put here to feed him drinks and keep him until the posse caught up, was deadly.

"Hacker!" she whispered desperately in his ear. *"Run now!"*

She ducked around him, under the arm with which Berg was still holding him, and came up between the two men, facing Berg. The big man stared at her stupidly for a moment and then her right hand whipped in a backhand blow across his face, each finger like the end of a bending slender branch, each nail like a razor.

"What?" bellowed Berg jovially, for her nails were so sharp that he had not immediately felt the cuts. "You want to play too—"

Then the blood came pouring down into his eyes, and he roared wordlessly, letting go of Hacker and stumbling backward, wiping at his eyes.

"What are you trying to do? Blind me?" he shouted. He got his eyes clear, looked down at his hands and saw them running with his own blood. He roared again, a wild animal furious and in pain.

"Run, Hacker!" called Twig desperately. She ducked in under Berg's arms as he made another clutch on her, lifted his drill from its holster and shoved it into Hacker's belt. "Run!"

Berg was after her now, but even without the blood running into his eyes, he was like a bear chasing a hummingbird. Twig was all around him, within reach one moment, gone the next. He lumbered after her, a madman with a head of black and red.

Hacker, woken at last to his danger and sobered, was backing out the door, Berg's drill in his hand, now covering both the Factor and Berg.

"Leave off, Twig!" Hacker cried, his voice thin on the high note of the last word. "Come on!"

Twig ducked once more out of the grasping hands of Berg and flew to join Hacker in the doorway.

"Get back, Berg!" snarled Hacker, pointing the drill. "I'll hole you if you come any farther!"

Berg halted, swaying. His mouth gapped with a flicker of white teeth in his black and crimson mask.

"Kill you . . ." he grunted hoarsely. "Both. Kill you . . ."

"Don't try it," said Hacker. "Less you want to die yourself first—from now on. Now, stay, and that means both of you, Factor. Don't try to follow. —Twig!"

He slipped out the door. Twig followed. Together they ran for the forest.

Twig touched with her hands the first trees they came to, and the trunks and branches ahead of them leaned out of the way to let them pass, then swayed back together again behind them. They ran for perhaps a couple of kilometers before Hacker's breath began to labor hoarsely in his lungs and he slowed to a walk. Twig, who could have run all day at the speed they had been keeping, fell into a walk beside him. For a little while he only struggled to get his breath back as he went.

"What is it?" he asked at last, stopping so that he would be able to hear Twig's whispered reply.

"A posse, they call it," she said. "Ten men, three women, all with drills or lasers. They say they'll set up a citizen's court and hang you."

"Do they?" grunted Hacker. He stank mightily of alcohol and ugly anger. But he was most of the way back toward being reasonably sober now; and Twig, who loved him even more than she loved the Plant-Grandfather nowadays, had long since gotten used to his smells. He sat down with a thump, his back against a tree trunk, waving Twig down to sit also.

"Let's sit and think a bit," he said. "Plain running's not going to do any good. Where are they now?"

Twig, who was already sitting on her heels, got up and stepped forward to the tree against which Hacker was sitting. She put her arms around the trunk as far as they would reach, laid her cheek against its dear, rough bark, closed her eyes and put her mind into the tree. Her mind went into darkness and along many kilometers of root and by way of many children of the Plant-Grandfather, until she came to the littlest brothers, whom other humans said were like a plant called "grass" back on Earth. Less than forty minutes walk from where she and Hacker were, some of the littlest brothers were feeling the hard, grim metal treads of human vehicles, pressing down to tear and destroy them.

"Peace, littlest brothers, peace," soothed Twig's mind, trying to comfort them through the roots. The littlest brothers did not feel pain as the variform Earth animals and humans like Twig felt it; but in a different way they felt and suffered the terrible wrongness that was making them not to be in this useless, wasteful fashion. Those being destroyed wept that they had been born to no better purpose than this; and, down below all living plants on the surface of Jinson's Planet, the Plant-Grandfather echoed their despair in his own special way. He was weary of such destruction at the hands of alien men, women and beasts.

"Peace, Grandfather, peace," sent Twig. But the Plant-Grandfather did not answer her. She let go of the tree, stepped back from it and opened her eyes, returning to Hacker.

"They're riding in carriers," she told him. From the grass, the trees looking down on the passing carriers, she could now describe the open, tracked vehicles and the people in them as well as if her human eyes had actually seen them. "When they first started, there were eight of them, and they were only walking. Now there are five more who brought the carriers. They can catch up to us in half an hour if we stay here. And the carriers will kill many trees and other children of the Grandfather before they come to us."

"I'll head for the High Rocks district, then," said Hacker. The frown line was puckered deep between the blue eyes in his stubbled, bony face. "They'll have to leave their vehicles to follow me on foot; and there's little for them to tear up and hurt. Besides, there they'll chase me a month or weeks and never catch me. Actually, you're the one they really want to catch so they can make you tell where they can find the Grandfather; but they daren't try that while I'm alive to tell the law. We've still got some law here on Jinson's Planet; and supraplanetary law beyond that. That reminds me—"

He fished with two fingers in a shirt pocket under his jacket and came out with a small slip of writing cellulose. He passed it over to Twig.

"While I was still down at Capital City with the Legislature," he said, "I got the Governor-general to send for an ecology expert from the Paraplanetary Government, someone with full investigative powers, legal and all. That's his name."

Twig squatted down once more and unfolded the cellulose strip which had been bent double to fit the small shirt pocket. She was proud of her reading ability and other schooling, which Hacker had gotten for her with a teaching machine he had carried upcountry himself; but the original printing on this sheet had been in blue marker and Hacker's sweat had dimmed it to near unreadability.

"John . . . Stone," she read off aloud finally.

"That's the man," Hacker said. "I had it fixed so the whole business of sending for him was secret. But he was supposed to land two days ago and be on his way upcountry here to meet me now. He shouldn't be more than a day's walk south of here on the downcountry trail. He's been told about you. You go meet him and show him that piece of paper. Bring him up to date about what's going on with the posse and all. Meanwhile I'll lead that crew around the High Rocks and down to Rusty Springs by late noon tomorrow. You and Stone meet me there, and we'll be waiting for the posse when they catch up."

"But there's only going to be two of you, even then," protested Twig.

"Don't you worry." Hacker reached out, patted the bark covering her shoulder and stood up. "I tell you he's a supra-planetary official—like someone from the police. They won't risk breaking the law with him there. Once they know he's around, none of these croppers that want to burn out new farming fields from the Grandfather's woods will dare try anything."

"But when he goes again—" Twig also rose to her feet.

"By the time he goes," said Hacker, "he'll have recommended a set of laws for the legislature that'll stop those forest-burners for all time. Go south now, Twig; and when you find him stay with him. If that posse's out after me, it's out after you, too, if it can just find you."

He patted her shoulder again, turned and went off through the trees, moving at a fast walk that was a good cross-country pace—for anyone but Twig.

Twig watched him go, wanting badly to go with him, to stay with him. But Hacker would be right, of course. If what was needed was this John Stone from another world, then he was the one she must go and find. But the unhappiness of every-thing—of everything all around here and to all the things she loved—was overwhelming. When Hacker was gone, she dropped face down on the ground, hiding her face against it, spreading her arms as if she could hold it.

"Plant-Grandfather!" she called, letting her mind only cry it forth, for it was not necessary to touch one of the plant children when she called the Grandfather. But there was no answer.

"Plant-Grandfather!" she called again. "Plant-Grand-father, why don't you answer?" Fear shook her. "What's the matter? Where have you gone?"

"Peace, little running sister," came the heavy, slow thought of the Grandfather. "I have gone nowhere."

"I thought maybe people had found you there under the ground," said Twig. "I thought maybe they had hurt you—killed you—when you didn't answer."

"Peace, peace, little runner," said the Grandfather. "I am tired, very tired of these people of yours; and maybe sometime soon I may actually sleep. If so, whether I will wake again, I do not know. But do not believe I can be killed. I am not sure anything can be killed, only changed for a while, made silent until it is remembered by the universe and regrown to speak once more. I am not like your people who must be one form only. Whether I am root or branch or flower makes no dif-ference to me. I am always here for you, little runner, whether I answer you or not."

Twig's tears ran down her nose and dampened the earth against her face.

"You don't understand!" she said. "You *can* die. You *can* be killed. You don't understand. You think it's all just sleep-ing!"

"But I do understand," said the Plant-Grandfather, "I understand much more than any little runner, who has lived only a moment or two, while I have lived long enough to see mountain ranges rise and fall again. How can I die when I am more than just the thing of woody roots these people would find and destroy? If that is gone, I am still part of every plant thing on this world, and of my little runner as well. And if these things should someday be gone, I am still part of the earth and stone that is this planet; and after that, part of its brother and sister planets, and after that even all worlds.

Here, alone, I taught myself to speak to all my plant brothers and sisters from the largest to the smallest. And all the while, on a world so far away it is lost even to my view, your people were teaching themselves to speak. So that now I and you speak together. How could that happen if we were not all one, all part of each other?''

"But you'll still be dead as far as I'm concerned!" sobbed Twig. "And I can't stand it! I can't stand to have you dead!"

"What can I say to you, little running sister?" said the Grandfather. "If you will make it that I am dead, then I will be dead. But if you will let it be that I cannot be killed, then I cannot be killed. You will feel me with you forever, unless and only if you shut out the feeling of me."

"But you won't help yourself!" wept Twig. "You can do anything. You took care of me when I was a baby, alone. There was only you. I don't even remember my mother and father, what they looked like! You kept me alive and grew me up and took care of me. Now you want to take yourself away, and I'm not to care. And you don't have to give up, just like that. You could open the ground in front of these people and let the hot rock out. You could empty the rivers they drink from. You could send seeds against them with pollen to make them sick. But you won't do anything—nothing but lie there until they find and kill you!"

"Doing what you say is not the way," said the Plant-Grandfather. "It is hard to explain to a little runner who has only lived a moment, but the universe does not grow that way. Along that way of damage and destruction, all things fail and their growth is lost—and so would mine be. You would not want me to be sick and no longer growing, would you, little running one?"

"Better that than dead."

"Again, that thought which is no thought. I cannot make you unsad, small runner, if you insist on sadness. I have put to use many of our brothers and sisters, from the littlest to the largest, to keep and care for you as you grew, alone and away from your own people, because I wished that you should come to run through this world and be happy. But you are not happy; and I, who know so much more than a small runner, know so little of a greater knowledge which I have yet to learn, that I do not know what to do about this. Follow your own sadness, then, if you must. I am with you in any case, though you will not believe it—with you, now and forever."

Twig felt the Plant-Grandfather turning his attention away from her. She lay sobbing her loneliness to the earth under her for a little while; but in time her tears slowed and she remembered the errand on which Hacker had sent her. She got to her feet slowly and began to run toward the south, letting the wind of her passage dry the wetness upon her face.

It did not come at once, but slowly the poetry of her own motion began to warm the cold lump of fear and sorrow inside her. If Hacker was right about what the man John Stone could do, then everything could be all right after all. Suddenly remembering that it would be well to check on the posse, she turned sharply from her original route to angle back toward the supply post. She came right up to the edge of the trees surrounding the clearing in which the post stood, and sure enough, the vehicles and the men and women were there. She looked out at them without fear, for like most of her people they saw and heard poorly in comparison to herself; and, in addition, the trees and bushes had bent around her to screen her from any discovery.

She was close enough so that she could hear clearly what they were saying. Apparently one of the vehicles had broken a tread and needed fixing. Some of the men there were working on its left tread, now like a huge metal watchband come uncoiled from around the drive wheels on that side beneath the open box of the vehicle body. Meanwhile those not working stood about arguing in the now westering, late afternoon sunlight.

". . . bitch!" Berg was saying. He was talking about her. The blood from his facial cuts had stopped flowing some time since, and what had leaked out had been cleaned away. But he was flushed about the forehead and eyes where the cuts had parted the flesh. "I'll hang her in front of Hacker himself, first, before we hang him when we get them!"

"You'll not," said one of the women, a tall, middle-aged, bony female in a short, brown leather jacket and country leather pants showing a laser in a black holster over her right buttock. "First she's got to talk. It's that Grandfather plant-devil that really needs killing. But then she comes into a proper home somewhere."

"Proper home—" shouted Berg, who might have gone on if another woman—shorter and heavier, but wearing a dress under her once-white, knee-length weathercoat and boots—had not snapped him off short. This one wore no visible weapon, but her voice was harsher and more belligerent even than that of the taller woman.

"Shut it, right there, Berg!" said this woman. "Before you say something you'll be sorry you ever thought of. There's plans been made for that girl among the decent croppers' families. She's been let run wild all these years, but she's a child of man and she'll come to be a good grown woman with loving rules and proper training. And don't go getting ideas about getting your hands on her after we catch her, either. It's us wives along on this posse who'll be making her tell where that Grandfather devil hides, not none of you men."

"If you can . . ." growled Berg.

The heavier woman laughed, and Twig shivered through all her body at the kind of laughter it was.

"Think we couldn't make *you* talk?" the heavy woman said. "And if you, why not a kid like her?"

Twig drew back until the leaves and the bushes before her hid the vehicles and their passengers from sight. She had learned all she needed to know anyway. The vehicles were now held up; so there was no danger of their catching up with Hacker before he reached the High Rocks—a hill region peppered with rounded chunks and blocks of stone where the vehicles would not be useable. Not that there had been much chance of their catching Hacker anyway—but now, at least, she was sure.

She turned and began to run once more southward in search of the man John Stone, as the sun lost itself among the trees and began to descend into twilight.

Once more, she ran. And once more the intoxication of her own running began to warm away the shivers that had come on her from the overheard conversation. Now, running, no one could catch and hold her, let alone do terrible things to her to make her say where the root-body of the Plant-Grandfather rested in the earth.

The sun was down now; and the big white moon of Jinson was already in the sky. It was full, now, and seemed—once her eyes were adjusted to it—to throw almost as much light as the twilight sun; only this was a magic, two-tone light of white and gray without color. In this light the trees and bushes leaned aside to let her pass, and the littlest brothers underfoot stretched like a soft gray carpet before her, making a corridor of moonlight and shadow along which she fled so lightly it was as if she went without touching the earth at all.

There was no effort to her going. She put on speed and earth, bushes, trees and moonlight swam about her. Together, they made up the great, silent music of her passage; and the music swept her away with it. There was nothing but this—her running, the forest and the moonlight. For a moment she was again only a little runner—even the Grandfather and Hacker were forgotten, as was the posse with its other humans. It was as if they had never existed. She danced with her world in the white-and-black dance of her limitless running; and it was she and the world alone, alone and forever.

Twig had run the moon high up into the night sky, now, and he rode there, made smaller by his isolation in the arch of the star-cap that fitted over the world when the sun had gone; and she began to hear through her mind, which was now fine-tuned to the plant brothers and sisters whom she passed and who made way for her, that the individual she ran to find was close. The brothers and sisters turned the corridor they were making ahead of her to lead her to him. Shortly beyond the far moonlight and shadow she saw a different yellow light that brightened and dimmed. She smelled on the night wind the scent of dead branches burning, the odor of an animal and a human man.

So she came to him. He was camped in a small clearing, where a stream Twig could easily jump across curled around the base of a large moss-patched boulder before going off among the trees again. A small fire was on the far side of the stream; the man was seated on the other side of it, staring into the flames, so still and large with his dark outdoor clothing and clean-shaven face that he seemed for a moment only another mossy boulder. Beyond him was one of the large hooved riding beasts that her people called a horse. This smelled or heard Twig and lifted its head and snorted in her direction.

The man lifted his head then, looked at the horse and away from the animal toward Twig.

"Hello," he said. "Come in and sit down."

His gaze was right on her, but Twig was not fooled. In no way could he see her. She was among the trees, a good four meters from him; and his eyes would be blinded by the light of his fire. He was simply going on what his animal had told him.

"Are you John Stone?" she asked, forgetting that only Hacker could understand her whisper at this distance. But the man surprised her.

"Yes," he said. "Are you Twig?"

Astonished, now, she came forward into the light.

"How do you know?" she asked.

He laughed. His voice was deep-toned, and his laugh even deeper—but it was a soft, friendly laugh.

"There ought to be only two people know my name up here," he said. "One would be a man named Hacker Illions; and the other might be a girl named Twig. You sound more like a Twig than a Hacker Illions." He sobered. "And now that I see you, you look more like Twig."

She came closer, to the very edge of the stream, hardly a jump away from him, and peered down into his large, white, handsome face. His blond hair was not long, but thick and wavy upon his head, and under light eyebrows his eyes were as blue as a summer lake. He had not moved. Behind him, his horse snorted and stamped.

"Why do you just sit there?" Twig asked. "Are you hiding something?"

He shook his head.

"I didn't want to frighten you," he said. "Hacker Illions left word not to move suddenly or try to touch you. If I stand up, will that scare you?"

"Of course not," said Twig.

But she was wrong. He stood up then, slowly, and she took a step backwards instinctively; because he was by far the biggest man she had ever seen. Bigger than she had imagined a man could be, and wider. At his full height, he seemed to loom over everything—over her, and the fire and the boulder, even over the horse behind him that she had thought was so large. Her heart began to beat fast, as if she was still running. But then she saw that he was merely standing still, waiting; and there was no feel of menace or evil in him, as she had felt in Berg, in the Factor of the supply post, the women of the posse and others like them. Her heart slowed. She felt ashamed of herself and came forward to jump the stream and stand right before him.

"I'm not frightened," she said. "You can sit down again."

She sat down cross-legged herself on the ground facing him, and he settled back to earth like a mountain sinking into the sea. Even now that they were seated, he towered above her still; but it was a friendly towering, as a tree-brother might loom over her when she nestled against the trunk below his branches.

"Does my horse bother you?" John Stone asked.

She looked at the big beast and sniffed.

"He has metal on his feet, to cut and kill the little living things, just like vehicles do," she said.

"True," said John Stone, "but he did not put that metal on by his own choice. And he likes you."

It was true. The animal was lowering its huge hammer-shaped head in her direction and bobbing it as if to reach out and touch her, although it was far out of reach. Twig's feelings toward it softened. She held out an arm to it, thinking kind thoughts, and the beast quieted.

"Where is Hacker Illions?" John Stone asked.

All her anxiety came flooding back into Twig in a rush.

"At the High Rocks," she said. "There are people after him . . ."

She told John Stone about it, trying to do the telling in such a way that he would understand. So often when she talked to people other than Hacker they seemed to understand only the words as words, not the meaning behind them. But John Stone nodded as she talked, and he looked thoughtful and concerned, as if understanding was honestly growing in him.

"This Rusty Springs," John said at last when she was done. "How far is it? How long will it take us to reach it from here?"

"For an ordinary human walking, six hours," she said.

"Then if we leave just before sunrise, we should be there when Hacker gets there?"

"Yes," she said, "but we ought to start right now and wait there for him."

John looked up at the moon and down at the woods.

"In the dark," he said, "I'd have to travel slowly. Hacker left word for me you didn't like to travel slowly. Besides, there are many things you can tell me that are easier to hear sitting here than traveling. Don't worry. Nothing's going to stop us from getting to the Rusty Springs on time."

He said the last words in a calm, final way that reminded her of the Plant-Grandfather speaking. Twig sat back, somehow reassured without being convinced.

"Have you eaten?" John Stone asked. "Or don't you like the same sort of food as the rest of us?"

He was smiling a little. For a second Twig thought he might be laughing at her.

"Of course I eat people-food," she said. "Hacker and I always eat together. I don't have to have it; but it's all right."

He nodded gravely. She wondered uneasily if he could tell what she was not saying. The truth was that for all his knowledge, the Plant-Grandfather had no real understanding of a human sense of taste. The fruits and nuts and green things on which he had nourished her as a child had been all right—and still were, she thought to herself—but the people-foods to which Hacker had introduced her were much more interesting to the tongue.

John began opening some small packages and preparing food for them, asking questions as he worked. Twig tried to answer him as well as she could. But even for a person as special as John, she thought, it must be hard to understand what it had been like for her.

She could not even remember what her parents had looked like. She knew, because the Plant-Grandfather had told her, that they both died of sickness in their cabin when she was barely old enough to walk. She herself had wandered out of the cabin and had been touched, mind-to-mind, by the Plant-Grandfather; and because she was young enough then that nothing was impossible, she had heard, understood and believed him.

He had directed her away from the cabin and the burned-over fields her parents had intended to plant, into the woods, where trees and branches wove themselves into a shelter for her from the rain and wind, and where she could always find something to eat growing within arm's reach. He had kept her away from the cabin until she was much older. When she had finally gone back there she had only glimpsed white bones on the cots in the cabin, hidden under a thick matting of growing green vine the Grandfather had advised her not to disturb. With those bones she had felt no kinship, and she had not been back to the cabin since.

Hacker was something else. By the time she had encountered Hacker, three years ago, she had already become the small runner the Grandfather had named her. Hacker had originally been a cropper like the ones now hunting him. A cropper—as opposed to a farmer who had homesteaded his acres of originally open land and had fertilized, ploughed and planted them year after year in a regular cycle—was someone who made a living by farming no more than two years in a row in any one place.

Most of the good land, the open land, on the world's one continent had been taken over by the first wave of emigrants to Jinson's Planet. Those who came after found that the soil covered by the plant-children of the Grandfather (the existence of whom they never suspected) was a thin layer over rock, and relatively unfertile—unless it was burned over. Then the ashes were rich in what was needed to make the soil bear. But two succeeding years of planting sucked all those nutrients from what had been the bodies of plant sisters and brothers into produce, which was then carried downcountry and away from the wooded areas forever. To the cropper, however, this was no matter. He only moved on to burn out a new farm someplace else.

Just before the spring rains, three years ago, Hacker had moved into the territory where Twig ran. An ideal time for burning over an area, so that the coming showers would wash the nutrients from the ashes into the soil below. But Hacker came, pitched his camp and let the days go by. He did not burn, and he did not burn. Finally it was summer and too late to crop that year. Twig, who had watched him many times, unseen from a distance, drew closer and closer in her watching. Here was a cropper who was not a cropper. He helped himself to the fruits and nuts the Grandfather had made the plant-children put forth for Twig, but other than that he did not take from the woods. She could not understand him.

Later she came to understand. Hacker was a drunk. A cropper who might never have been any different from other croppers except that, following one fall's sale of produce, he got into a card game and won heavily. Following which, in one sober moment he was to appreciate all his life, he took the advice of a local banker and put his money away at interest, drawing only enough for supplies to go upcountry and burn out a new cropping area.

But when he had gone upcountry once more, he had taken along a luxury of supplies in the way of drinkables. He had pitched his camp; but instead of setting to work to burn land clear immediately, he had delayed, enjoying his bottles and his peace.

Here in the woods, alone, he did not need to pour the drink down in the quantities he required in civilization. A nip now and then to blur his surroundings pleasantly was all it took. And besides, there was plenty of money still down there in the bank, waiting for him, even if he did not bring in a cash crop this year.

In the end, he did not.

In the end, he began to change. Among the woods, he needed alcohol less and less, for here there were none of the sharp and brittle corners of the laws that normally poked and pricked him, driving him into rebellion. He was not an observing man; but little by little, he began to notice how the seasons came and went and how every day the woods responded to the changes of those seasons in a thousand ways. He became aware of leaf and bush and plant stem as individuals—not as some large, green blur. And in the end, after two years without cropping brought him to the point where he had to get to work, he could not bring himself to burn this place where he had lived and been content. He blazed the trees there to claim the area for himself and to keep other croppers away, and he moved on.

But the next place he chose made him part of it also; and he found he could not burn it either. He moved again, this time to Twig's territory; and there, unconsciously fishing with a hook baited with his own differentness, he caught Twig's curiosity and hauled her in.

The day came when she walked boldly into his camp and stopped a few feet in front of him, no longer shy or fearful of him after months of observation.

"Who are you?" she whispered.

He stared at her.

"My God, kid," he said. "Don't you know you aren't supposed to run around without any clothes on?"

The wearing of clothes was only the first of many things they found they needed to reach an understanding upon. Twig's point was not that she was unaware of clothes and the fact that other people wore them; rather she did not like the feel of them on her body. Twig, in fact, was not ignorant. The Grandfather had seen to it that as she grew she learned as much about her own people as her maturity allowed her to absorb. He had also seen to it that she visited the woods fringing nearby croppers' farms and had a chance to watch her own people at work and hear them talk. He had even decided that she must practice talking as much out loud as she could, in her own tongue; and Twig, who did what he suggested most of the time without thinking, had obeyed.

But along with the human knowledge she had picked up through the Grandfather's prodding, she had also picked up a great deal of other, wordless wisdom and many skills belonging more to the Grandfather's environment than to her own. Also, the human knowledge she acquired through the Grandfather had been affected in transmission by the fact that the Grandfather was not human and did not think in human terms.

For example, while other humans wore clothes and the Grandfather knew it, such coverings were an alien concept to him; and in any case he forced nothing and no one. When Twig did not want to wear clothes, he taught her how to control her skin temperatures for comfort; then he let the matter go. And there were other ways in which he let Twig be herself, and different from her own kind.

So when Twig and Hacker met at last, it was something like an encounter between two aliens having an only limited amount of language and experience in common. They found each other fascinating in their differences; and from that first meeting their partnership began.

"You wear clothes now," said John Stone at this point in Twig's story, glancing at the soft bark bound about her body.

"That was Hacker's idea. He's right, of course," said Twig. "I don't mind the bark. It was living once, and real. It rubbed a little at first when I wore it, but I taught my body not to be bothered where it touched me."

"Yes," said John Stone, nodding his great head with the wavy, light-colored hair glinting in the firelight. "But how did Hacker get involved in the planetary government here, so that he could arrange to have me called? And why are his own constituents out to murder him now?"

"Hacker got a teaching machine and taught me a lot of things," said Twig. "But he learned a lot too. About the Grandfather and everything. He can't talk to the Grandfather, but Hacker knows he's there, now."

"Downcountry, your people seem to think the Plant-Grandfather is a superstition," said John.

"The Grandfather never paid much attention to them downcountry," said Twig. "But the other croppers up here know about him. That's why they want to find and kill him, just like they want to kill Hacker."

"Why?" asked John patiently.

"Hacker ran for the Legislature two years ago," said Twig. "And at first the other croppers thought it was a great thing, one of their own people trying for the delegate-at-large post. So they all voted for him. But then he stood up in the Legislature-House and talked about the Grandfather and why the woods-burning should be stopped. Then the other croppers hated him because the downcountry people laughed and because they didn't want to give up cropping and burning. But as long as he was a delegate, the eye of downcountry law was on him to protect him. But his two-year term ran out yesterday; and now they think no one cares."

"Easy. Be easy . . ." said John, for Twig was becoming frightened and unhappy again. "There are people on other worlds who care—for all Hackers, and for all beings like your Plant-Grandfather. I care. Nothing's going to happen to either of them. I promise you."

But Twig sat rocking on her heels, now that she had remembered, refusing to let herself be comforted for fear that in some strange way to do so would bring down disaster.

In the dark morning, after they both had slept for some four hours, they rose and John packed his things, then mounted his horse. With Twig leading the animal through the woods, they started off for Rusty Springs.

Dawn began to join them before they were more than halfway there. As they rode into the growing sunlight, the horse could see where to place his large hooves and they began to pick up speed. But by this time, Twig hardly noticed—though she had fretted at the slowness of their going earlier—because she was becoming more and more fascinated with John Stone. Just as he was big in body, he was big in mind as well—so big that Twig walked around and around the way he thought with questions. But in spite of the fact that he answered willingly enough, she could not seem to see all at one time what he was by his answers.

"What are you?" she kept asking.

"An ecologist," said John.

"But what are you really?"

"Something like an advisor," said John. "An advisor to the social authorities on new worlds."

"Hacker said you were something like a policeman."

"That, too, I suppose," said John.

"But I still don't know what you *are*!"

"What are you?" asked John.

She was surprised.

"I'm Twig," she said. "A small runner." Then she thought and added, "A human . . . a girl . . ." She fell silent.

"There; you see?" said John Stone. "Every one is many things. That is why we have to go cautiously about the universe, not moving and changing things until we know for sure what moving or changing will do to the universe as a result, and eventually, therefore, to ourselves."

"You sound like the Plant-Grandfather," Twig said. "Only he won't even fight back when things are done to him and his children, like the woods-burning of the croppers."

"Perhaps he's wise."

"Of course he's wise!" said Twig. "But he's wrong!"

John Stone looked from his big horse down at her where she ran alongside them. He was riding with his head a little cocked on one side to catch the faint sound of her whispered words.

"Are you sure?" asked John.

Twig opened her mouth and then closed it again. She ran along, looking straight ahead, saying nothing.

"All things that do not die, grow," said John. "All who grow, change. Your Plant-Grandfather is growing and changing—and so are you, Twig."

She tried to shut the sound of his voice out of her ears, telling herself he had nothing to say that she needed to hear.

They came to Rusty Springs just before noon. The place was named for a small waterfall that came directly out of a small cliff about a quarter of the way down from its top. The stream fell into a wide, shallow basin of rock streaked with reddish color, and the water had a strong taste of iron. When they got there, Hacker was sitting waiting for them on a boulder beside the pool.

"You just made it," he greeted them as they came up. "Another couple of minutes and I'd have had to move on without waiting for you any longer. Hear up a ways, there?"

He tiled his head toward the woods at the opposite side of the basin of spring water. Twig did not have to reach out to one of the Grandfather's children for information this time. Like the others, in fact much more clearly than the two men with her, she could hear the distant smashing of undergrowth as a body of people moved toward them.

"Hacker!" whispered Twig. "Run!"

"No," said Hacker.

"No," said John Stone from high on his horse. "We'll wait here and have a word with them."

They stood together, silent and waiting, while the noise increased; and after a while it came right into the clearing along with the ten men and three women of the posse. They emerged from the woods, but stopped when they saw Hacker and Twig together with John Stone on his big horse.

"Looking for somebody?" said Hacker derisively.

"You know damn well we are," said Berg. He had gotten himself another ion drill, and he pulled it from his belt as he started toward Hacker. "We're going to take care of you now, Hacker—you and that kid and that friend of yours, whoever he is."

The other members of the posse started to move behind him, and they all flowed forward toward the three.

"No," said John Stone. His deep voice made them all look up at him. "No."

Slowly, he dismounted and stood on the ground beside his horse. There was something unstoppable in the way he first stood up in his stirrups, then swung one long leg over the hind-quarters of the beast and finally stepped down to the ground. The posse halted again; and John spoke to the people.

"I'm a Paraplanetary Government ecologist," he said, "assigned to this planet to investigate a possibly dangerous misuse of natural resources. As such, I've got certain areas of authority; and one of them is to subpoena individuals for my official hearing on the situation."

He lifted his left wrist to his lips, and something on that wrist glinted into the sunlight. He spoke to it.

"Hacker Illions, I charge you to appear as a witness at my hearing, when called. Twig, I charge you to appear as a witness at my hearing when called," he said. "The expenses of your appearance will be borne by my authority; and your duty to appearance takes precedence over any other duty, obligation or restraint laid upon you by any other local law, source or individual."

John dropped his wrist gently onto the curved neck of the horse beside him; and it looked like nothing more than some large dog that he petted.

"These witnesses," he said to the posse, "must not be interfered with in any way. You understand?"

"Oh, we understand, all right," said the thick-bodied woman in the white raincoat.

"Understand? What do you mean, understand?" raged Berg. "He's not armed, this ecologist. There's only one of him. Are we going to let him stop us?"

Berg started forward toward John, who stood still. But as Berg got closer he began to look smaller, until at a few steps from John, who had not moved, it became plain that his head would not reach to John's shoulder and he was like a half-grown boy facing a full-grown man. He stopped and looked back, then, and saw none of the others in the posse had moved to follow him.

As his head turned around to look, the woman in the white raincoat burst into a jeering laugh.

"You, Berg!" she crowed. "Your guts always were in your muscles!"

She came forward herself, elbowing Berg aside, stepping in front of him and staring fiercely at John.

"You don't scare me, Mr. Ecologist!" she said. "I been looking up at people all my life. You don't scare me, your supraplanetary government doesn't scare me, nothing scares me! You want to know why we don't take and hang Hacker right now and carry this kid home to grow up decently, right now? It's not because of you—it's because we don't need to. Hacker isn't the only one who's got connections down at Capital City. It happens we heard on our belt phones just two hours ago you were on your way up here."

John nodded.

"I'm not surprised," he said. "But that doesn't change anything."

"Doesn't it?" The tone of her voice hit a high note of triumph. "All we wanted Hacker and the girl for was to find out where that plant-devil lives. Hacker sent for you, but we sent for equipment to help us find it. Two days ago, we put that equipment in an aircraft and began mapping the root systems in this area. We figured it was probably in this area because here was where it brought up the girl—''

"That's got nothing to do with it!" cried Twig in her loudest whisper. "The Grandfather reaches everywhere. All over the continent. All over the world.''

But the woman did not hear her and probably would have paid no attention if she had.

"Yesterday, we found it. Protect Hacker and the girl all you want to, Mr. Ecologist. How're you going to stop us from digging in our own earth, and setting fire to what we find there?''

"Intelligent life, wantonly destroyed—'' began John, but she cut him short.

"What life? How do you know it's intelligent until you find it? And if you find it, what can you do—subpoena some roots?''

She laughed.

"Hey," said Berg, turning to her. She went on laughing. "Hey," he said, "what's all this? Why didn't you tell me about it?''

"Tell you?" She leaned toward him as if she would spit into his black beard. "Tell you? Trust you? *You?*''

"I got the same rights—''

But she walked around him, leaving him with the protest half-made, and went back to the rest of the posse.

"Come on," she said. "Let's get out of here. We can pick up these two after that hearing's over. They won't be going anyplace we can't find them.''

The rest of the posse stirred like an animal awakening and put itself in motion. She led them past the basin and forward, right past Twig, Hacker and John Stone with his horse. She passed so close by Twig that she was able to lean out and pat the back of Twig's right shoulder in passing—or, rather, where Twig's right shoulder would have been, except for the covering bark that protected it. Twig shrank from the touch; but Lucy Arodet only grinned at her and went on, leading her posse off into the woods, headed back the way John Stone and Twig had just come. Berg ran after them; and in a few moments the sound of their going was silenced by distance.

"Is that right?" Hacker asked John into the new quiet. "Is there equipment that can find a root mass like the Grandfather's?"

John's blue eyes in his massive face were narrowed by a frown.

"Yes," he said. "It's a variety of heat-seeking equipment—capable of very delicate distinctions, because all it has to go on is the minimal heat changes from liquid flow in the root. I didn't think anyone out here on your planet would know about it, much less—" He broke off. "And I can't believe anything like that could be sent here by anyone without my hearing of it. But in the commercial area there are always some who'll take chances."

"Arrest them!" whispered Twig. "Make it illegal for them to use it!"

John shook his head.

"I've no sure evidence yet that your Grandfather is a sentient being," he said. "Until I do, I've got no legal power to protect him."

"You don't believe us?" Hacker's lean face was all bones under the beard stubble.

"Yes. I believe, personally," said John. "Before man even left the world he started on, it was discovered that if you thought of cutting or burning a plant it would show a reaction on a picoammeter. Mental reactions of and by plants has been established for a long time. A community intelligence evolving from this, like the Grandfather you talk about, is only logical. But I have to contact it myself to know, or have some hard evidence of its existence."

"In another day or two, according to what that Lucy Arodet said just now," Hacker added, "perhaps there will not be anything to contact."

"Yes," said John. He turned to Twig. "Do you know where the Grandfather-Plant is?"

"He's everywhere," said Twig.

"Twig, you know what he means," said Hacker. "Yes, Stone, she knows."

Twig glared at the stubble-faced man.

"You must tell me," said John Stone. "The sooner I can get to the Grandfather, the sooner I'll be able to protect him."

"No!" whispered Twig.

"Honey, be sensible!" said Hacker. "You heard Lucy

Arodet say they'd found the Grandfather. If they know, why keep it a secret from John Stone, here?"

"I don't believe it!" said Twig. "She was lying. She doesn't know!"

"If she does," said John, "you're taking a very long chance. If they can dig down to your Grandfather-Plant and destroy him before I can get to him, won't you have lost what you most want to save?"

"None of the Grandfather's children would tell where he is, even if they could," Twig whispered, "and I won't."

"Don't tell me then," said John. "Just take me to him."

Twig shook her head.

"Twig," said Hacker, and she looked at him. "Twig, listen. You've got to do what Stone says."

She shook her head again.

"Then ask the Grandfather himself," Hacker said. "Let him decide."

She started to shake her head a third time, then went over to a tree and put her arms around it; not because she needed the tree to help her talk with the Grandfather, but to be able to hide her face from the two men.

"Grandfather!" she thought. "Grandfather, have you been listening? What should I do?"

There was no answer.

"Grandfather!" she called with her mind.

Still no answer. For one panic-filled moment she thought that she could not feel him there at all, that he had either been killed or gone to sleep. Then, reaching out as far as she could, she felt him, still there but not noticing her call.

"*Grandfather!*"

But it was no use. It was as if with her whisper-limited voice she tried to shout to someone far off on the top of a high mountain. The Grandfather had gone back into his own thoughts. She could not reach him. She fought down the surge of fear and hurt that leaped inside her. Once, the Grandfather had always been there. Only in these last couple of years, since the burnings by the croppers had been so widespread, had he started to draw into himself and talk of going to sleep.

Slowly, she let go of the tree and turned back to face the other two humans.

"He won't answer," she said.

There was a moment's silence.

"Then it's up to you to decide, isn't it?" Hacker said gently.

She nodded, feeling all torn apart inside. Then an idea came to her.

"I won't take you to him," she said, raising her eyes to John Stone's face. "But I'll go by myself and see if it's true, if the croppers have found him. You wait here."

"No," said John. "I came up here to see some of the burned-over areas for myself; and I should look at those now while I have time. If I have to make it a court matter without waiting to protect your Plant-Grandfather, I need as much evidence as possible."

"I'll show you places," said Hacker to him.

"No," John said again. "You go straight south to the first town or village you can get to and report yourself to the authorities there as being under my subpoena. That will make your protection under law a matter of public record. Can you go straight there without that gang that just left here catching you?"

Hacker snorted in disgust.

"All right," said John. "I had to ask to make sure. You go to the closest community center, then—what's its name?"

"Fireville," said Hacker. "About twelve klicks southwest."

"Fireville. I'll meet you there after I've seen a couple of burned-over areas. I've got a map with a number of them marked. And Twig," John turned toward her, "you'll go check on the Plant-Grandfather to see if there's any sign he's been located. Then you better find me again as soon as you can. Do you think you can do that?"

"Of course," said Twig contemptuously. "The plant brothers and sisters will always tell me where you are."

But instead of turning to leave, she hesitated, looking at Hacker with the sharp teeth of worry nibbling at her.

"Don't you drink, now," she said. "If you get drunk, they might find some way to do something to you."

"Not a drop," said Hacker. "I promise."

Still she hesitated, until it came to her that if she stood here much longer she would not go at all; so she turned and ran, the forest opening before her and the other two left swallowed up from sight behind.

She went swiftly. She was not about to lose herself in the pleasure of her running now; for worry, like an invisible posse, followed right at her heels. From time to time she called to the Grandfather with her mind; but he did not answer and she settled down to getting to his root-mass as soon as possible.

In the woods, growing and changing every day, she had never had any means of measuring how fast she could go when the need was really upon her. She was only human, after all; so probably her top speed was not really much faster than that of a winning marathon runner back in the years when man was just beginning to go forth into space, before the Earth had died. But the difference was that she could run at that speed—or at very nearly that speed—all day long if she had to. Now, she did not know her speed; but she went fast, fast, her legs flashing in and out of the early afternoon sunlight and shadow as she raced down the corridor among the trees and bushes that opened before her as she went.

It was midafternoon before she came to the edge of the place where the great root-mass belonging to the Grandfather lay fifteen to forty meters below the ground and the forest above it. All the way here, the plant sisters and brothers of this area had showed her an empty woods with no sign of croppers anywhere about. But none of them could tell her about an earlier moment until she could actually reach and touch them. Now, arrived, she put her arms around one tall tree-sister and held her, forcing the slow-thinking leaves to remember daylight and dark, dark and daylight, through the past week.

But, other than the wind, the leaves remembered only silence. No humans had passed by them, even at a distance. No mechanical sounds had sounded near them. In the sky over them, only the clouds and an occasional spurt of rain had mingled with the regular march of sun and moon and stars.

The woman Lucy Arodet had lied. The croppers either had no special equipment as claimed, or if they had it, they had not used it here where they could find the Grandfather. Sighing with relief, Twig fell face down on the ground, spreading out her arms amongst the littlest brothers to hug and hold her world.

The Grandfather was safe—still safe. For a little while Twig simply closed her eyes to let herself ride off on the wave of her relief. And so sleep took her without warning, for in fact she had done a great deal of running and worrying in past hours.

When she woke, it was night. The moon was already high in

the sky and the Grandfather was thinking—not at her, but around her, as if he mused over her, under the impression she did not hear.

". . . I have never reached beyond the atmosphere that envelops this one world," he was thinking. "But now, my little runner will run to the ends of the universe. Beyond are the stars, and beyond them more stars, and beyond and beyond . . . to depths beyond depths, where the great galaxies float like clouds or scatter like a whole crowd of little runners, pushing against each other, scattering out from one common point to the ultimate edges of time and distance. And in all that distance there are many lives. My little runner will come to know them, and the beginning and the end, and all that goes between. She will know them in their birth and their growing and whether it is chance or purpose that makes a path for all life in all time and space. So out of destruction will have come creation, out of sleep an awakening, and out of defeat a conquest, just as even at the poles of this world warm summer succeeds the harsh winter. All they have done to destroy me will only bring about the birth of my little runner into a Great Runner between the stars—"

"Grandfather!" called Twig; and the thoughts flowing about her broke off suddenly.

"Are you awake, little sister?" asked the Grandfather. "If you are, it's time for you to go now."

"Go?" demanded Twig, still stupid with sleep. "Go . . . why? Where? What for?"

"Your old friend Hacker is dying now, and your friend-to-be John Stone rides toward him," said the thought of the Plant-Grandfather. "Those who wished to destroy him and me have tricked Hacker to death, and soon they will be here to kill me also. It is time for you to go."

Twig was awake and on her feet in one reflexive movement.

"What happened?" she demanded. "Where is Hacker?"

"In a gully north of Fireville, where he has been pushed to fall and die, as if he had drunkenly wandered there and slipped. Those who are our enemies made him drunk and brought him there to fall, and he has fallen."

"Why didn't you wake me and tell me before?" Twig cried.

"It would have made no difference," said the Grandfather. "Hacker's death was beyond the stopping, even as those who come now to destroy me are beyond stopping."

"Come?" raged Twig. "How can anyone be coming? They don't even know where you are!"

"They do now," said the Grandfather. "When you came to me this time, you carried pinned to the bark behind your shoulder something placed there by the woman called Lucy Arodet. A small thing which cried out in a voice only another such thing could hear to tell her where you were at any moment. When you reached me and stopped traveling in this place, they knew you had found me and they knew where I was."

Twig threw a hand around to feel behind her shoulder. Her fingers closed on something small, round and hard. She pulled it loose from the bark and brought it around where she could see it. In the moonlight, it looked like a dulled pearl with small, sharp points on its underside where it had clung to the bark of her clothing.

"I'll take it away!" she said. "I'll take it someplace else—"

"That would make no difference either," said the Grandfather. "Do not suffer. Before they come I will have gone to sleep in a sleep without waking, and they can only destroy roots that mean nothing."

"No!" said Twig. "Wait . . . no! I'll run and find John Stone. He can get here before they can do your roots much damage. Then you won't have to sleep—"

"Little runner, little runner," said the Grandfather. "Even if your John Stone could save me this coming day, he would only put off the inevitable for a little while. From the day your people set foot on this world, it was certain that sooner or later I would have to sleep forever. If you understand that I go now to sleep gladly, you would not mourn as you do. What is of value in me goes forward in you, and goes where I could not, further and deeper, beyond all distance and imagination."

"No!" cried Twig. "I won't let you die. I'll run to where Hacker is and meet John Stone. He'll come and save you. Wait for me, Grandfather! Wait . . ."

Even as she continued talking with her mind to the Grandfather, she had spun about and begun to run toward Fireville. The little brothers opened a path before her, marking the way, and the bushes and trees leaned aside. But she was scarcely conscious that they did so. All her mind was on the fact that the Grandfather must not die . . . must not die . . .

She ran faster than she had ever run before. But still it was

nearly dawn when she came near to Fireville, to the dark gully
where the path of the little brothers led her. On the far side of
the gully, silhouetted blackly against the paling sky between
the trees, was the figure of a gigantic man on a gigantic horse.
But down in the blackness of the gully itself was a little patch
of something light that was Hacker. At the sight of that patch
even the Grandfather went out of Twig's mind for a moment.
She plunged recklessly down the side of the gully. Anyone else
would have tripped and fallen a dozen times, but she felt the
uneven ground and the presence of bush and sapling with her
mind and kept her feet. She reached the shape of Hacker and
dropped on her knees beside it.

"Hacker!" she cried. The tears ran down her face.

There was a great noise of tearing and plunging—the de-
scent of a heavy body down the far side of the gully—and
then John Stone, on foot, appeared on the far side of Hacker.
He squatted and reached out to touch his fingers gently to
Hacker's throat, under the sharp, bony line of Hacker's jaw.

"He's gone, Twig," John said, looking from Hacker to her.

Grief burst inside her like a world exploding. She lifted
Hacker's head to her lap and rocked with it, weeping.

"I told you not to drink, Hacker!" she choked. "You
promised me! You promised you wouldn't drink . . ."

She was aware that John Stone had moved around to squat
beside her. He loomed over her like some huge cliff in the
darkness. He put a hand on her back and shoulder, and the
hand was so big that it was like an arch around her.

"It had to happen, Twig," the deep voice rumbled and
rolled in her ear. "Some things have to happen . . ."

It was so like what the Grandfather had said that she was
suddenly reminded of him. She lifted her head sharply, listening, but there was nothing.

"*Grandfather!*" she cried, and for the first time in her life,
it was not only her mind that called. Her voice rang clear and
wild under the brightening sky.

But there was no answer. For the first time not even the
echo came back that said the Grandfather was there but not
listening. The unimaginable network of the plant-children still
stood connected, listening, waiting, carrying her call to the
farthest limits of the world. But there was no response. The
voice of the planet had fallen silent.

"He's gone!" she cried. And the words flew among the

leaves and the branches, from grass-blade to grass-blade and along the roots under hill and valley and plain and mountain. "Gone . . ."

She slumped where she sat, even the head of Hacker forgotten on her knees.

"The Plant-Grandfather?" Stone asked her. She nodded numbly.

"It's over," she said, aloud, her new voice dead and dull. "He's gone . . . gone. It's all finished, forever."

"No," said the deep voice of John Stone. "It's never finished."

He stood up beside her, looking at her.

"Twig," he said again, gently but insistently, "it's never finished."

"Yes it is. Listen . . ." she said, forgetting that he, like all the others, had never been able to hear the Grandfather. "The world's dead now. There is no one else."

"Yes, there is," said John Stone. "There's you. And for you, there's everything. Not only what's on this world but on many others that never knew a Plant-Grandfather. They're out there, waiting for you to speak to them."

"I can't speak to anyone," she said, still kneeling, slumped by the dead body of Hacker. "It's all over, I tell you. All over."

John Stone reached down and picked her up. Holding her, he walked up the dark side of the gully to his horse and mounted it. She struggled for a second, then gave up. His strength overpowered hers easily.

"Time moves," he said. She hid her face against the darkness of his broad chest and heard his voice rumbling through the wall of bone and flesh. "Things change, and there's no stopping them. Even if the Grandfather and Hacker had stayed alive here, even if Jinson's Planet had stayed just as it was—still you, by yourself, would have grown and changed. What doesn't die has to grow. What grows, changes. Our decisions get bigger and bigger, whether we want them to or not— our jobs get larger and larger, whether we plan them to or not —and in the end the choice has to be to love all or to love none. There may be others like Hacker on other worlds, and perhaps somewhere there may be another Jinson's world. But there's never been another Plant-Grandfather that we've been able to find, and not another Twig. That means you're going to have to love all the worlds and all the growing things on them as the Grandfather would have, if he could have gone to them the way you're going to be able to. That's your job, Twig.''

She neither spoke nor stirred.

"Try," he said. "The Grandfather's left it all to you. Take up the duty he left to you. Speak to the growing things on Jinson's Planet and tell them that losing the Grandfather wasn't the end.''

She shook her head slightly against his chest.

"I can't," she said. "It's no use. I can't."

"Speak to them," he said. "Don't leave them alone. Tell them they've got you now. Wasn't that what the Grandfather wanted?''

Again she shook her head.

"I can't . . .," she whimpered. "If I speak to them, then he *will* be gone, really gone, forever. I can't do that. I can't put him away forever. I can't!"

"Then everything the Grandfather counted on is lost," said John Stone. "Everything Hacker did is wasted. What about Hacker?''

She thought of Hacker then, what was left of Hacker, being left farther behind them with every stride of the horse's long legs. Hacker, going down now into forgottenness too.

"I can't, Hacker!" she said to the memory of him in her mind.

"Can't . . . ?" The image of Hacker looked back at her, cocked one eyebrow at her and began to sing:

> *"As game as Ned Kelly," the people would say.*
> *"As game as Ned Kelly," they say it today . . .*

The familiar words in his cracked, hoarse voice went through her like a sword-sharp shaft of sunlight, and through the dark, hard wall of grief that had swelled up within her at the loss of the Grandfather. All at once, she remembered all the flowers that also were alone now, left voiceless and in darkness of silence; and contrition overflowed within her. From now on, she would be gone, too!

"It's all right!" she called out to them, with her voice and her mind together. "It's all right, *I'm* still here. Me, Twig. You'll never be alone, I promise! Even if I have to go someplace else, I'll always reach out and touch you from wherever I am . . .''

And from valley and hill, from plain and forest, from all over, the words of her mind were picked up and passed along, tossing joyously from smallest brother to largest sister, on and on to the ends of the world.

Twig closed her eyes and let herself lie at last against the wide chest of John Stone. Where he was taking her, she did not know. No doubt it would be very far away from Jinson's world. But no world was too far, she knew that now; and also, out there in the great distances of which the Grandfather had dreamed and to which he could never go, there were other brothers and sisters, waiting for the sound of a voice, waiting for her.

Grandfather was gone beyond returning, and so was Hacker. But maybe it was not the end of things, after all; maybe it was only a beginning. Maybe . . . at least she had spoken to all the others who had lived through the Grandfather, and they now knew they would never be alone again. Letting go of her grief a little, just a little, Twig rocked off to sleep on the steady rhythm of the pacing horse.

_____ GOD BLESS THEM _____

"Nobody in Congress or the federal government or the public has put forward a case for a U.S. manned Mars Mission," Press said in an interview. *"And if the Soviets decide to spend $70 billion to land men on Mars in five years, we say: God bless them."*

—Los Angeles *Times*, reprinted in the Minneapolis *Star*, Thursday, October 12, 1978. (From an interview with Frank Press, science adviser to U.S. President Jimmy Carter and chairman of the presidential review committee whose four-month study formed the basis for Carter's policy statement on the space effort.)

There was no mail at the Main Minneapolis Post Office for Merlin Swenson. Almost no one got any mail at General Delivery on Mondays now. But people went there, anyway, although lately the air conditioning was always off.

Merlin left the post office and walked slowly the twenty-seven blocks to the slave market. It was a blue-bright July morning, already turning hot, and he could feel the heat of the sidewalk through the thin soles of his shoes. At Twelfth Avenue and Third Street, he stepped on something hard and stopped in a panic to check the sole of the right shoe. But whatever it was, he discovered, standing on one foot, had not gone through—although the sole was now like soft cardboard and gave at a touch.

He started walking again. The shoes would be too expensive for him to replace, these days, and there was no hope of getting any worthwhile work without them. When the soles finally wore through there would be several things he could do to patch them, temporarily, but it would be the beginning of the end. And it was inevitable that they would wear through. Any day now.

In the narrow waiting room of the slave market, the hard, upright chairs along the walls were all filled. The air conditioning, roaring from the ventilator grills, barely removed the stink of unwashed bodies. Merlin, himself, was clean this morning. It had cost him, but this was a special day.

"You planning to work dressed like that?" asked the hiring clerk behind the desk. His narrow, white face, under an upright shock of brown hair, was pinched by an expression of habitual annoyance.

"I am if you can get me something clean for half a day," Merlin said. In the mirror tile behind the clerk's desk he saw his own face, square, large-boned, trained now to show no expression at all. "I've got an engineering job interview this afternoon."

"Oh?" said the clerk, staring at his computer screen. He punched the keys of the terminal. "All right. You're on the half-day list. I can tell you right now there's not much chance."

"I could manage another ten percent," Merlin said.

The clerk's shrug told the true story. It was too much to expect a clean job somewhere for just half a day. Still, the chance could not be passed up. Money was everything.

Merlin waited for a chair; then, sitting, he tried to rest with his eyes open. You could lose your connection with a place like this if they caught you dropping off—that explained the hard chairs and the icy air conditioning. Everybody wanted a safe place to sleep. But this was the best of the slave markets. They were honest and made a specialty of hiring people who had degrees. *The Qualified Laborer Is a Conscientious Laborer* was their slogan. Merlin drifted into a mindless period hearing nothing until the man next to him began reading aloud from a morning newspaper.

"All hope of possible U.N. assistance for the U.S. economy

seemed doomed today in light of comment by the Soviet Representative, Anatoly Pirapich, that this country had historically refused to fund its space program adequately and that aid now to U.S. orbital industries, in particular, would be an open invitation to impoverished nations to rely on other countries for large investment capital.

"Pirapich read aloud in session a 1978 quote from the Los Angeles *Times*, reprinted in the Minneapolis *Star* on October twelfth of that year:

" '*The White House statement says America's civil space policy centers on these tenets: that activities will reflect a balanced strategy of application, science and technology development . . . it is neither feasible nor necessary at this time to commit the U.S. to a high-challenge space engineering initiative comparable to Apollo . . .*' "

The man stopped reading, folded his paper and turned to Merlin.

"Can you imagine that?" he said. "Just fifteen years ago, a White House statement says that. What were they using for brains?"

"What good does it do to keep rereading that sort of thing?" Merlin said dully. "It doesn't change anything."

"But how could anyone be so blind?"

It was a trite question. Merlin felt no urge to answer, but he was not surprised to hear it asked. Although probably his own age, the other man had the kind of appearance that made him seem barely out of adolescence. Curly black hair, slight body, pale face—an innocent in a time when innocents got eaten for breakfast. Merlin had never seen him before.

"Does it matter now?" Merlin finally said.

"There'd still be a chance for this country if . . ." The other broke off. "Oh, my name's Sam Church. My degree's in electronics. How about you?"

"Flow mechanics, gravityless."

"Gravityless? You must really have thought you'd make it with an off-world job. But don't you know you shouldn't wear good clothes for this kind of place? No telling what kind of work they'll offer you."

The assumption of experience by someone obviously new here irritated Merlin enough to rouse him from the chronic fatigue he shared with most adults nowadays.

"I'm dressed like this because I've got a job interview this afternoon," he said. "In my own field."

He was sorry he had mentioned it, the moment the words were out of his mouth. Sam Church's pale face was suddenly wiped naked of pretension; it was now desperate with longing.

"Oh, God!" Church breathed. "You really have an interview?"

"I've been waiting nine months," Merlin said gruffly. He was sorry now he had talked to this man at all. Luckily, Church seemed to be the only one who had heard his mention of a professional job interview. They were all in the same straits. Church lowered his voice.

"Where? Who with?"

"International Positions," Merlin said. "One o'clock."

"God!" said Church again. He sniffed the air. "You took a shower, too."

Merlin's small, bitter laugh caught in his throat.

"Not damn likely!" he said. "I used the washbasin on my crash floor, and it cost me three hundred for five minutes. My own soap and towel, and a hundred to hire somebody to stand guard."

Church's attitude had changed. He was now utterly the awe-struck neophyte looking at an old hand.

"You're office-crashing?" he said. "How dangerous is it?"

"If you know what you're doing, it's workable," Merlin said.

"You carry a knife?"

"Of course." Merlin felt trapped by the conversation but unable to think of a way to change the subject. "That doesn't mean much. There's always someone around who's better with a knife. The real trick is knowing who's sharing the office with you, and all of you take turns on watch. You've got to know how to wheel and deal with the hall-patrol guards, too."

Church breathed out softly. He looked enviously at Merlin's large frame.

"I couldn't do it," he said.

Merlin looked at him. He was quite ready to believe that the other could not do it, would not be able to survive in one of the empty office buildings that had been converted to dormitories. Only the fittest survived very long.

"Where do you live?" he asked, to change the subject.

"I've only been married five months. My wife and I, we've got a room with my in-laws."

"Wife . . ." Merlin caught himself just in time. He had had a sudden, unbearably poignant, vision of someone to go home to, only one other person and a room where you could be alone, just the two of you.

"You're married too?" Church asked.

"Yes. She's on the west coast."

"Oh."

Church did not make the mistake of asking more than that —there were limits even to his innocence, apparently. Many families had been split by the galloping inflation and the lack of jobs.

"Do you hear from her much?" Church asked.

"No."

The monosyllable finally stopped Church's questioning. They sat a while longer in silence; then, glancing at the clock, Merlin saw that it was almost noon. His mindless period had lasted longer than it seemed. He stood up, went over to the desk and told the clerk he was checking out.

"Right." The clerk punched keys on his computer terminal, not looking up. As he turned away from the desk, Merlin bumped into Church, also on his feet.

"I haven't gotten anything all morning here, either," said Church. "Do you mind if I walk along with you?"

"Yes," said Merlin.

Church blinked. "Yes? You do mind?"

"That's right. No company."

"Oh." Church fell back. Merlin turned and went past him and out the door into midday heat that was now like radiation from the hearth of a blast furnace.

He walked back the way he had come, downtown toward the International Trade Center. On the way he stopped at a discount market and bought a quarter-liter foil package of uncooked Quaker Oats for eighteen dollars. A small detour took him to Almsbury Park, where he ripped open the package and ate the dry oats by the handful, washing them down with water from a public fountain. The oat flakes, under their dustiness, had an almost rutty taste. They were the most food available for the money, and he felt better with something in his stomach. "Courage is food; food is courage." Someone had told him that when he was young.

It was nearly one o'clock. He went on to the International Trade Center, to the office of International Positions, and gave his name to the receptionist.

"Oh, yes." She checked her computer screen. "Mr. Ghosh will see you. Just a few minutes . . . if you'll sit down."

It was, of course, more than just a few minutes. His mouth began to feel dry from the oat flakes, and he got to his feet.

"Would I have time to find a drinking fountain?" he asked.

"I'm sure you will." She smiled at him. She was thin, in her forties, and in spite of having a steady job, she seemed prey to inner anxiety. "There's one just outside, to your left."

He went out through the glass door and found the fountain. After drinking, as he straightened up, he heard a throat cleared behind him. He turned to see Church standing there.

"I hope you don't mind," Church said. "I just wanted to see how you'd come out . . ."

Under his immediate irritation, something he thought he had long since repressed, something dangerous—sympathy for another human being—stirred in Merlin. Church was so helpless, so inoffensive, it was impossible not to feel sorry for him.

"All right," said Merlin. "But don't hang around here. Wait for me outside and I'll tell you about it when I leave."

"Thanks," said Church, looking up at him. "Really, I mean thanks!"

"I'm not doing anything special for you," said Merlin. He went back into the office.

"Oh, good. There you are," said the receptionist as he stepped through the door. "Hurry! Mr. Ghosh is waiting for you. Straight ahead and to your right!"

Merlin hurried into the corridor beyond her desk and found his way to the open doorway of a wide room, brightly lit by a wall-wide window. The room was pleasant with air conditioning and the green of potted plants. Behind a wood-and-chrome desk sat a dark-skinned man in his forties, wearing a chalk-striped blue suit—the value of which would have given Merlin financial security for a year. *Ram Ghosh* said the nameplate on his desk. But his eyes were not unkind, and he did not exhibit the condescension, the air of veiled exasperation and impatience with Americans, that so many foreigners showed these days.

"Mr. Swenson? Sit down, please." Ram Ghosh's English was almost accentless, with only a slight prolongation of the vowels. Merlin took a chair. Ghosh tapped the papers on his desk with the nail of an index finger.

"Six months," he said. "You've waited a long time for a job offer from us."

"Lots of people wait longer," Merlin said.

Ghosh smiled at him, a little sadly.

"Yes . . ." he said. He became more brisk. "Well, the matter at hand is that you now have an offer. Your education was in null-gravity flow mechanics, I see. But no experience?"

"They aren't hiring many U.S. citizens to work outside the atmosphere these days." Merlin knew his bitterness was showing. He felt a twinge of fear at the thought that he might already have prejudiced the interview, but the words had come by themselves before he could stop them. Ghosh, however, did not seem offended.

"Very true," he said, nodding. "But you can't blame off-Earth installations and factories for giving first chance to their own nationals. Many people, you know, want to work in space these days."

As many, thought Merlin, as want to enter heaven.

"No experience," Ghosh went on. "Well, we could wish you had. But, in this case, the fact you don't isn't a complete barrier. I can offer you a job in your specialty. But I warn you to treat this offer, and all information concerned with it, as a matter of secrecy, whether you accept the job or not."

Merlin felt an icy shock that gave way to a glow of hope so powerful that he feared it showed on his face.

"Of course," he said, slowly and clumsily. "Professional confidentiality . . . I understand."

"Good," said Ghosh, smiling again. "All right. The job will be in the metals-forming group of an electronics research unit to be placed in high orbit in the next two years. Your work would be classified and would have to be explained to you later if you accept the job. But it's within your ability and education, and you'd be paid at going rates for a space-qualified engineer of your specialty and experience . . ."

Merlin's mind reeled. The pay rate Ghosh was talking about would make him comfortably well off in any other society in the world. Here in the U.S., it would make him wealthy, by comparison with those at the income level at which he had been living for the last five years.

"I should say, that's what your pay rate would be once you

were in orbit and on the job,'' Ghosh continued. ''During your training period, here on the surface, you'd be paid at a standby rate of half your space-borne pay. Should you accept . . .''

In a euphoric daze, Merlin found himself signing papers, shaking Ghosh's hand and receiving congratulations as a new employee of something called Trans-Space Electronics.

''You'll report to the training center in Huntsville, Utah,'' Ghosh said. ''The receptionist outside has all the necessary information, transportation vouchers and the rest . . .'' He coughed. ''If you could use an advance on your first month's wages . . .''

''I . . . yes,'' Merlin said. He had been so overwhelmed by good fortune that he had completely forgotten he would need decent clothes, luggage, a dozen other things he had once taken for granted but no longer owned.

''My secretary can give you a check for up to a third of your first pay period's wages.''

''Thank you,'' said Merlin. ''I don't know how to thank you.''

''Not at all.'' Ghosh smiled. ''I must admit I like this job. I've had less happy ones. If you know of anyone else whom you think might work out for us . . .''

''I'm afraid not,'' Merlin said quickly. The hard years had taught him not to recommend anyone. There was too much risk; the other person's actions might recoil against one's own record. Life had become too brutal for casual favors.

They shook hands and Merlin went out. With the advance check and other materials in hand, he stepped back out into the lobby of the Trade Building. For a moment he hesitated, his mind whirling, unable to think of what to do first.

He turned toward the drinking fountain. The cold water tasted like expensive wine. Then he saw Church.

''I got the job,'' said Merlin.

''God!'' said Church.

''Engineering, in my specialty,'' said Merlin. ''Half-pay at the trainee level until I go into space, then full pay.''

Church said nothing, but there was a look on his face—one of incredulity and envy and disbelief, all mixed.

And it was a look that touched Merlin's inner core. In this moment of incredible happiness, he saw himself standing where Church was, hearing of someone else's good fortune.

He knew too well what the other must be feeling. Impulsively, he spoke.

"You've got an electronics degree, you said?"

Church nodded, his face suddenly wary.

"Go in there right now," said Merlin. "You may be able to get hired yourself. Tell the secretary you heard about it at the post office—anything. Just don't tell them I sent you. The name of the outfit is Trans-Space Electronics. Remember, you didn't hear about it from me."

Church stared as if he had just heard some unknown language. Then his eyes opened wide. He spun on his heel, ran to the entrance of the offices and let himself in.

Merlin departed, clutching his check and the other papers.

His transportation vouchers got him on the evening flight to Salt Lake City. He boarded carrying a new suitcase with nothing but his old clothes and shoes in it. After being so poor for so long, he found he could not bring himself to throw things away.

It was only the first of his conflicts with the unconscious habits of near-starvation. When he got to the training camp at Huntsville, he found the Reception Center closed for the day and only the thought of the consequences to his employment record, if he should be picked up for vagrancy, drove him to a hotel. There, in the palatial privacy of his single room, in the luxury of his mattressed bed, he finally fell asleep.

In the morning he reported to the Reception Center. He was put through processing, presented with a schedule of refresher and training classes and assigned to a barracks with other new employees. The barracks were two-story wood frame buildings, with a large dormitory room upstairs and a day room and a latrine downstairs. White partitions surrounded the individual beds in the dormitories, giving each employee the privacy of a tiny cubicle.

There were no women in the barracks. He was told that new employees were segregated by sex, even those husband-and-wife pairs who had signed their five-year employment contracts together.

In the latrine he found showers in which hot water was available day and night. Soap and towels were provided. Although he understood that this must be characteristic of newcomers like himself, he was unable to resist the luxury of immediately soaking himself in the shower.

He was stepping out of the shower when he saw a familiar-looking man standing at one of the washbasins. He circled to get a glimpse of the other's face, reflected in the long mirror above the washstands. It was Church.

"You made it!" he said.

Church turned around.

"Yes. I made it!" he said. They shook hands solemnly.

"I didn't see you at any of the processing sessions," Merlin said, wrapping a towel around his waist.

"I had some special interviews," said Church. "I'm to be considered for cadre. It could mean a move to better quarters."

"Cadre?" Merlin stared at him. "I thought all cadre would be previous employees."

"I think they'd rather have it that way. But this project's expanding so fast . . ."

"But how did you get picked for that?"

"Well . . ." Church looked at the open door to the latrine. He stepped over so he could see through it, then stepped back again. "I think they picked me because I told them I'd had experience. Didn't you?"

"How could I? I haven't ever been in space."

"Well, neither have I, of course. But it doesn't hurt to fib a little. By the time they check, they'll have already tried you out in a position. If they like what you've done, then it doesn't matter, and if they're displeased, then you just tell them you didn't understand the original question or blame it on computer error. They're not going to go to the trouble of checking personally with whoever it was that hired you."

"It could still catch up with you," Merlin said.

"Oh, I don't think so." Church's manner was almost airy. "Well, I've got to run. One of the advantages of being considered like this is that I can phone from the offices, instead of standing in line like the rest of you. I told my wife I'd call."

"Yes, see you later," said Merlin.

He watched the other man go. Later, dressed and standing in line himself at the phone booths in the communications building, he felt his first touch of envy. Even if Church's lie caught up with him, it was almost worth it not to have to wait here like this. The camp had a direct satellite hookup. Long-distance phone charges could be put against your first six-months' salary. Everyone just hired was desperate to talk with someone, with the mail as unreliable as it was and the cost of ordinary phoning astronomically out of reach.

He got to a phone at last and called everyone he could think of on the west coast who might know where his wife could be reached. But, as he had half-expected, he learned nothing. With his last call he hired a detective agency in San Francisco —another indulgence that would have been impossible two days before, but his only real chance of finding her. Ona had no engineering degree, but there might be other work openings on this space factory. Even if that did not pan out, his own salary would be enough to make life secure for her, and once a year he would be getting furloughs to come back and see her.

He returned to the barracks, looked for Church's cubicle and found him sitting on his bed, talking with two of the other trainees.

"Oh, hello, Merlin," Church said, looking up. "Come in and shut the door. We're just comparing notes on the situation here."

He introduced Merlin to the other two: a middle-aged, slightly overweight man named Stoller Fread, with the patient face of a basset hound, and a blond young man named Bill Sumash, who looked as if he was just out of school. The comparing of notes Church referred to was clearly a gossip and rumor session. Merlin sat on a corner of Church's bed and listened.

"Oh, it's a scam," Church was saying. "The idea's not so much to set up a factory station in orbit as to get their share of U.N. development funds for nations with low GNP like ours."

"But," said Stoller, "the U.N. doesn't fund private corporations."

"This isn't a private corporation," said Church. "It's a consortium of corporations with federal backing. As that, of course, it still can't get U.N. funds directly, but the federal government can, and then make funds of its own available to the consortium."

"But that's a great thing, isn't it?" said Sumash. "It could be the beginning of a national space-based industry, after all."

"Don't be a dupe," Church said. "This country's too impoverished to maintain a space-based industry. If we'd already had one—if the government had pushed one when they should've, twenty years ago—we could be in a position to compete nowadays. But we're not."

"We dropped out," said Sumash. "Now we don't have the chips to get back into the game."

"The point is that the U.S. lost the original virtues that made it what it was," Church said. "And like an old, fat-bellied ex-athlete, it wouldn't exert itself while a bad situation ran downhill and got to be a situation nobody could get out of. You're right, you know, we don't have the chips to get back into the space game—and we never will. Our golden age is gone."

Merlin got up. He had heard all this too often. It was all true, but life had no room for such large concerns now. Life was lying in the blessed privacy of his cubicle and a dream about Ona being found by the detective agency, and of their being together again.

"Sorry," he said to Church, "I can't keep my eyes open. Next time . . ."

He nodded to the other two as he stepped to the door of Church's cubicle.

"Glad to have met you," he said, and a moment later he was out on the barracks floor, headed for his own cubicle and peace.

The next few weeks were filled with classes and training. He found himself going to bed exhausted every night. He did not miss Church, so it was something of a shock, when he was next in the central administration building, to see him there, dressed in a regular civilian office suit. Merlin had come in to get approval for a draw against his wages to pay the detective agency.

"Church!" he said, as the other walked hastily by him in the corridor. "Sam Church!"

Church looked around and saw him. He came over to shake hands.

"Merlin!" he said. "How're you doing? I meant to get down to the barracks and look you up, but they've got us all so busy here on planning . . ."

"You did make cadre, then!" said Merlin. "Good for you!"

"Thanks," said Church. He lowered his voice and looked around, but the corridor was momentarily deserted. "I really was going to get in touch with you, in fact. Working in this place, I hear about things ahead of time. They've got wind of some agitators in the trainee corps. They're going to begin making inquiries tomorrow. I wanted to warn you."

"Me?" Merlin laughed. "I don't know any agitators."

"Of course not. I don't think there actually are any. That's why I was going to warn you. Investigations like this are under pressure. They've got to produce results to justify whoever authorized them. That means they're going to be picking up on anything at all that can be made to seem socially destructive. You remember how you sat in on some of those sessions in my cubicle . . ."

"Once," said Merlin.

"Only once? Well," said Church, "at any rate, you know how harmless they were. I've already told the investigation team all about them and no one's worried. But just the same, you might want to say you didn't know anything about them . . ."

Merlin stared at Church. He had not thought of the other man in the role of protector, and he felt embarrassed at not giving Church more credit. In a way this warning repaid the favor Merlin had done him by putting him on the track toward getting his job. It testified to an awareness of obligation in Church that Merlin had not expected.

He got the contingency payment approved and stood in line at the phones to tell the detective agency.

"Fine, fine!" the voice of the woman at the agency crackled in his ear. "I think we've just about located your wife, Mr. Swenson. With this payment against expenses we should find her this week."

"Splendid," said Merlin. "You'll call me?"

"As soon as we've got something to report. Now, Mr. Swenson, it *was* explained to you that your payment in full would have to be in our hands before we released any hard information?"

"Of course," said Merlin. "I've already talked to my employers here, and there'll be no problem getting an advance for the rest. They just want to be sure I've really found her, and they won't have to turn around and give me another advance next week."

"Good. We'll be calling you this week, Mr. Swenson."

He went back to the barracks, his mind full of Ona and her happiness when she would learn what had happened to him.

He had completely forgotten about Church's warning, when, two days later, he was called out of class with orders to report to Conference Suite 460 in the Headquarters Building. Suite 460 turned out to be a spacious room with a long table capable of seating perhaps sixteen people. But when Merlin stepped in, the only ones there were a fiftyish, tired-looking man and a woman of about the same age, raw-boned and with graying red hair. They were seated side by side at the far end of the table.

"Come sit here, Mr. Swenson," said the woman. She pointed to the first chair on the long side of the table, at her right. He obeyed.

"Now," said the woman, glancing at a printout sheet before her. "Of those trainees presently in your barracks, Mr. Swenson, were there any you knew before you came here?"

"No," said Merlin. He did not have to stop and think in order to answer. "No," came automatically to everyone's lips these days. It was a "yes" answer that called for thought and hesitation.

The woman looked again at her printout. So far the man had said nothing. It occurred to Merlin that the psychological profile they had worked up on him might have indicated that he was more likely to trust a woman.

"Do you know a Stoller Fread or a Bill Sumash, Mr. Swenson?"

"I think they're in the barracks."

"This Fread and Sumash," the woman said, "have you ever noticed them talking together, or attempting to gather others in the barracks to talk?"

"No," said Merlin.

"Have either of them ever tried to talk to you privately, Mr. Swenson?"

"No," said Merlin. "Not that I can remember, anyway."

"Do you know anyone here whom you might have cause to suspect as an activist or subversive?"

"I'm afraid," said Merlin, "I've been so busy with the training courses, I haven't really had a chance to talk with the others much."

"Yes or no to the question I asked, Mr. Swenson?"

"Definitely no," said Merlin. "I haven't met anyone like that."

"But you'd tell us if you did, wouldn't you, Mr. Swenson?"

I'd tell you anything I needed to, true or false, thought Merlin grimly. *I'd cry, dance, or crawl on the floor to keep this job, now that Ona's almost found.*

"I surely would," he said aloud.

"Thank you," she said. The man continued to sit. With eyes pouched in finely wrinkled flesh, he silently studied Merlin.

Merlin was released, finally, and the next few days went by swiftly. He struggled with his training courses and impatiently wondered when the detective agency would phone with word of Ona's whereabouts.

But no call came. On the Thursday after his security interview, he discovered a memo in his message box that asked him to report to the Payroll Center at nine o'clock the next morning.

He assumed it must have something to do with the last advance against his wages. Annoyed that he would be late for his second class of the morning, he hurried to the Center, hoping that whatever it was would not take too long.

At the Center he was directed to the Pay-Outs Cashier. Only one window was open, with two security guards standing nearby. Merlin stood in line behind three men, two of whom were cadre. From their conversation, he assumed they were here to get an advance on wages. The third man merely signed a form and left. Now Merlin was facing the clerk behind the window.

"Merlin Swenson?" asked the clerk. He searched below the counter level on his side and came up with two pieces of paper.

"Sign this," he said, pushing one ahead of the other at Merlin. "The second one you keep."

With his pen poised in his hand, Merlin read the first paper.

"I, Merlin James Swenson, acknowledge the following indebtedness to Trans-Space Electronics Corporation, Limited:

Advances:	$43,432.54
Per diem:	22,806.00
Equipment issued:	28,099.10
Miscellaneous:	9,847.78
Subtotal:	$104,185.42
Less trainee wages to date:	60,765.70
Total:	$43,419.72

Signed. . . . .

"What's this?" Merlin asked.

"Just your account to date. We need a signature."

"All right," said Merlin.

He signed. The clerk took back the form and separated a top copy from a bottom one. He pushed the bottom copy to Merlin, along with the other paper.

He took both sheets and started to turn away, glancing at the second paper. Suddenly, he stopped and turned back.

"What's this?"

"I just hand it to you, that's all," said the clerk. He turned and walked out of sight inside the cage.

Merlin stared at the second paper.

Termination Notice

As of the present date . . . the lines blurred in Merlin's vision, then came back into focus. . . . *services no longer required. After advances and expenses of the Corporation, it has been determined that the balance of your employee account with Trans-Space Electronics shows an indebtedness of $43,419.72. Payment should be made within three months, or arrangements must be made at the end of that time to repay any amount still outstanding. . .*

"*Come back here!*" Merlin shouted through the window —and found himself seized from behind, his elbows pulled toward the small of his back and his whole body wrenched away from the window.

He was facing one of the gray-uniformed security guards. The other guard was holding Merlin's arms in a painful backlock. A dull throbbing had already begun in the socket of each shoulder.

"You subverts are all alike," said the security guard facing Merlin. "The minute things stop going your way, you start yelling and pretending you're being picked on. Well, you're fired and you're leaving. How do you want to go? It's up to you."

Merlin choked back the bubble of fury in his chest.

"I'll go easy," he said.

"Good," said the guard. He nodded, and the other guard released Merlin's arms. "Let's go."

They marched Merlin to the door of the building, put him in

a gleaming white car bearing the Trans-Space emblem on its front doors and rode with him to the compound by the entrance gate where personnel on pass waited for the hover-bus into Ogden.

"Who've you got there, Gus?" called the guard at the gate.

"Another of them," Gus called back. He and his cohort walked a small distance off and stood together, talking and glancing at Merlin from time to time.

Merlin turned his back and stared out through the heavy wire mesh that fenced the compound. Beyond, he could see the warehouse buildings of the supply area, gray silhouettes in the morning sunlight.

"Merlin!"

He looked around, but saw no one.

"Merlin, over here!"

He looked down along the fence to his left. About ten meters away was a gate, now padlocked. Merlin glanced at the guards, but they seemed indifferent to the situation. He walked along the fence until he saw Sam Church's face looking between the vertical iron pipes that supported the gate-door.

"Merlin . . ." he said. "I got here as soon as I could . . ."

"I don't know what's happened. They're kicking me out without a chance to talk to anyone!" Merlin clung to the bars. "It has to be a computer error, or something like that. But how do I do anything about it when they're running me out like this, without a chance to talk to anyone?"

"You can't, of course . . ." Church began.

"Sam, listen! Try and get to someone! You're cadre. You can find out what went wrong and fix it, can't you? Sam . . . can't you?"

"Well . . ." said Church.

"You've got to! Don't you know what this means? It's not just this job. What outfit, anywhere, is going to hire me for anything but slave labor as long as the records here say I was a subvert? I've got to get it straightened out! What's the matter with you, Sam? Won't you even try?"

"Oh, I'll try," said Church.

"And something else—something else you can do for me right away, Sam, and it won't be hard. Not for you. You know that detective agency I had hunting my wife? They called, just Monday, and said they'd almost found her, that they'd be calling this week to tell me where she is. Sam . . ."

He fumbled in his shirt pocket and came up with a pen and a piece of paper. He scribbled on the paper and passed it between the vertical pipes into Church's hands.

"It's easy for you to phone out. Call them, Sam. Don't tell them what's happened to me, but tell them they can reach me at—they can leave a message at . . ."

He stopped and searched his mind desperately.

"I know!" he burst out. "You remember that slave market in Minneapolis, where you first met me? The Availables, Fifth and First Avenue North? Tell them they can leave a message for me there. I'll be back Monday. I can pay off that dayclerk, and he'll go along with it."

"All right." Sam Church looked at him strangely.

"And another thing you can do for me . . ."

He was interrupted by the roar of blowers as the bus turned a corner into the compound.

"All right, Swenson!" shouted one of the guards. "Get over here!"

"Sam, listen, if you have a chance . . ."

"There's no more time, Merlin." Church was thrusting a white envelope at him between the pipes. "It's not much, but it's all I could raise in a hurry."

Merlin took it automatically. The guards were coming for him. There was not even time to take Church's hand.

"I'm sorry, Merlin," said Church. "I'm really very sorry. I couldn't help it. I have my own wife to think of."

The guards grabbed Merlin, whirled him around and marched him toward the bus. Dazedly, he found himself aboard.

"Company billing, Jake," said one of the guards. "This one to Denver Central. If he gives you any trouble, let us know."

They stood back. There were no other passengers boarding. The doors of the bus closed with a pneumatic hiss. The driver lifted the vehicle on the downward thrust of its underjets until it floated free. He turned it in its own length and headed toward the highway.

Merlin, catching at seatbacks to keep his balance in the turning bus, stumbled to the mid-section of the vehicle and sat down. Only then he realized he was still clutching the envelope that Church had given him. Numbly, he opened it. Inside were twenty hundred-dollar bills.

He laughed bitterly. This, together with the twenty-five hundred or so he had in his wallet, might be just enough to buy a bus ticket back to Minneapolis. He would have to take a bus to get there by next Monday. If you were caught hitchhiking, the police either beat you up so badly that you ran the chance of being crippled, or shot you on some pretext or other to save themselves the trouble of beating you up.

He tucked the envelope into an inside pocket. His old work clothes and everything else he owned were getting farther behind him by the minute. Once back in Minneapolis he would have to work in what he was wearing now—for as long as it stood up. Ironically, he had been saving his good new shoes lately by wearing his old ones with the paper-thin soles; he had found out that the instructors did not care. Shoes would be a critical matter once he went back to day work. The money that would buy his bus ticket could be used to purchase a pair of heavy work boots instead. With those, at slave markets in Denver, he could last indefinitely. Given enough time, anything could happen. He could be reinstated with Trans-Space, if Church could get to the right person—

His thoughts broke off suddenly as he remembered Church's parting words. What had he meant by saying he couldn't help it—that he had his own wife to think of?

Understanding exploded in Merlin.

"*The bastard!*" he screamed.

He woke to the fact that he had half-risen out of his seat. Remembering where he was, he sank back down again. The few other passengers on the bus and the driver, in his rear-view mirror, were all staring at him.

Merlin sat stunned, the whole pattern taking shape before him like a puzzle picture that suddenly becomes comprehensible. He remembered how Church had lied about having space experience in order to qualify for the cadre. He remembered Church wanting to walk downtown with him to his interview, Church meeting him there after all—which he could only have done if he had followed Merlin—and wanting to hang around and see how this perfect stranger made out in an interview. Merlin remembered the look of terrible longing on Church's face when Merlin told of his own good fortune. How many times, he wondered now, sickened, must Church have used that look on other people?

He should have been on his guard when Church warned him to deny having been at any of the obviously subvert talk sessions in Church's cubicle. The meaning of Church's last words were clear. He had insured his own job security by throwing the corporate people a substitute victim and telling them that victim would deny everything when questioned. Then he made sure by advising Merlin to do just that.

A deep wave of rage erupted in Merlin. It rose, crested, and broke. But fury was useless. Church was out of reach—and he had always been just what he was. The way life was now, it had been up to Merlin to protect himself—and he had failed to do so. He remembered, in The Availables' slave market, how he had taken Church for an innocent. Not Church. He, himself, had been the innocent.

Fifty-six hours later, at midnight, he stumbled off the Greyhound bus at the Minneapolis terminal. He had enough money left for a week's crash space in one of the office buildings —but this late at night, he would be taking unreasonable chances. His roommates might be relatively honest, but any stranger was fair game for the pack. Better to take his chances on the streets than pay to lie awake all night with his eyes open.

He headed east toward the University area, where people would be on the streets all night. The time had been when someone like himself could ease his way into a party of students, go back with them to whatever apartment, room or warehouse they were headed to, and pick up free crash space by pretending to pass out in a corner. But those easy days were gone. The best to hope for was to stay on the streets without attracting the attention of the police.

But this night the University district was swarming. He had the incredible luck to catch on with a student party that ended up down in the park along the Mississippi riverbank. Anyone but students would have been rousted out of there by the police. But they were left alone; and so he made it through until Monday, and was waiting first in line outside the door when the slave market opened at six o'clock that morning.

The clerk came up the street to the door, recognized him as a familiar face and grunted at him sleepily before unlocking the door and letting them all inside. He took his time, yawning as he set up for the day. Finally, he was ready, seated behind his computer screen and keys.

"Name?" he said ritually, not glancing up.

"Merlin. Merlin Swenson. Did a long-distance phone call come here for me? Now look," said Merlin, swiftly, "I know this isn't the sort of thing you do, but I can reimburse you for your trouble. Did a long-distance call come in here for me, Thursday afternoon or Friday?"

"Maybe," said the clerk and looked sour. "It was collect. I had to pay two hundred and eighty to accept it for you."

"Two hundred and—"

"Look, man!" said the clerk loudly. "You want to stiff me on money I've already paid out for you, that's all right. I'll live. But don't come around here again asking me to put you on somebody's payroll. Deadbeats like you don't deserve jobs."

"All right!" said Merlin, low-voiced. "I'll pay! What's the message—and tell me privately or it's no deal!"

"You come into the office with me," said the clerk, still loudly.

He stood up from behind his desk and opened the half-door in the barricade that joined his desk to the wall on either side of it to create a small privacy space. Merlin walked in and followed him through a door in the back wall to a tiny office.

"Here you are," the clerk said. His tone was cheerful and friendly once the office door had been closed behind them. He pulled down a sheet of paper that was thumbtacked to a cork bulletin board. "I didn't understand a word of it, but I figured someone like you would be along asking for it. That'll be two hundred and eighty."

He kept his grip on the paper until Merlin had counted over the money. Then he held it out in his fingertips. Merlin snatched it.

"This is no message!" said Merlin. "It's only a telephone number!"

"You expected more?" The clerk was curious. "That's all they gave me."

"But now I've got to call them long distance!" said Merlin. "And you cleaned me out. I don't have any money left!"

"Call them collect," advised the clerk.

"I can't call collect to a detective agency," said Merlin desperately. "And I've got to reach them. It's a west coast outfit that's been locating my wife, and they were to phone like this when they found her."

"Sure, you can call collect," said the clerk. "For another two hundred, I'll show you how."

"Don't you understand?" said Merlin desperately. "You cleaned me out. I'm broke! Do you think I'd be standing in line here if I had more than what I gave you already?"

"Oh, what the hell!" the clerk said. He left the table, sat down before the phone terminal at the desk, and punched buttons. The screen lit up with the face of a young man.

"Yes?" he said, "who's calling collect, please?"

"Merlin Swenson, The Availables," said the clerk.

"I'm sorry. I don't have any Availables or Merlin Swenson on my list to accept."

"Well then, just forget it, man. Forget it!" barked the clerk. "You people called here. If you don't want to talk to us, we sure don't want to talk to you!"

"Are you Merlin Swenson?" asked the young face. "If you're Merlin . . ."

"Me? Merlin Swenson? You people must think a lot of yourselves. Merlin Swenson doesn't answer any outfit that calls and leaves word for him to call back. Let me talk to whoever called him, and I'll decide whether it's something to bother Merlin Swenson about."

"Just a minute," said the face, "let me check with . . ."

"Never mind. Forget it!" shouted the clerk, and warded off Merlin with one hand. "I've wasted enough time with you already, and all you've done is stall . . ."

"Wait. Wait just a minute," said the other. "I think it was Maria Balsom who wanted to talk to Merlin Swenson. Just a minute . . ."

The screen went blank for a moment, then the face of the woman Merlin had spoken with before at the agency came on the screen.

"Hello? Mr. Swenson?" Her face was puzzled.

"One moment," said the clerk. He slid out of the seat and Merlin replaced him.

"I don't understand, Mr. Swenson," said Maria Balsom, "we don't accept collect calls from clients who owe us money . . ."

"Have you found her?" The words burst from Merlin.

"Of course. That's what we called you about. Then we had

a message to find you at this number, so we called and left word for you to call us. But you were not being invited to call us collect. As I say, we don't accept calls from . . ."

"Where is she?"

"Really, Mr. Swenson. You don't expect this agency to furnish information before it's paid? You've got a balance outstanding of fifteen thousand, four hundred and eighteen dollars and twelve cents. If you'll make your payment to us in that amount . . ."

"But that's why I had to talk to you," Merlin said quickly. "You see, just for the next week or so, there's been a little hitch. There was a crazy mix-up in my computer records, and until it's cleared up, they're holding up my ability to get advances of the kind I've been paying with. It's just a temporary thing because they're understaffed in the records section, but it'll hold things up for a couple of weeks. But I have to make a decision about housing my wife while I'm in orbit, and I need to talk to her about this right away. So I thought if you could just let me know what you've turned up so far—after all, I have paid you over thirty thousand dollars already . . ."

"Mr. Swenson . . ." Maria Balsom's voice had stepped far back from him. "Are you telling me that you're not connected with Trans-Space any longer?"

"Yes and no. The point is, I can't pay your bill right now, but if you'll wait . . ."

"Of course." Maria Balsom's voice came now from a different world. "When you've got what you owe us, Mr. Swenson, send us a credit voucher, and we'll be glad to give you the full results of our investigations."

"Don't you understand . . ." Merlin began.

"I understand perfectly, Mr. Swenson. Do you?" said the woman grimly. "Like everyone else in this business I live on my commissions from accounts *collected!*"

She broke the connection.

"Well, there you are," said the clerk. He slapped Merlin on the shoulder. "Come on out and I'll find you a job with some overtime."

Merlin shook him off. He stalked out of the office, out through the half-door, past the other day-laborers still lined up at the counter, staring at him, and out of the building.

The heat of the day was stifling as he hurried away from The Availables office. He paid no attention to where he was going until he felt grass beneath his feet and looked around at Almsbury Park.

He stared about like someone just awakened from a heavy sleep. At this hour of the day, the park was only sparsely occupied. The nearest bench to him, half in sunlight, half in shadow, had only one person on it, a very old man, apparently asleep on the end in sunlight that was growing hotter by the minute.

It was a consolation prize of fate. The shady ends of the bolted-down benches were normally occupied on a hot summer day like this. Merlin gratefully sat down in the shade.

An empty hour passed. But then, slowly, little by little, the desire to live crept back into him like a dull ache. Life was still with him. Everything was lost, but his heart still beat. His chest still pumped. In a few hours—whatever else might happen—he would be hungry again. And soon after that, he would once more need to sleep.

The heat of the advancing sunlight against the thin sole of his right shoe roused him from his thoughts. Any day now, he thought, the sole would wear through and there would be no replacing it. The day was heating fast, and the shadow in which he sat had retreated until it could not much longer protect him. He felt chilled in the midst of heat, naked and lonely.

He squinted along the bench at the old man, still sitting squarely in the sunlight. The other looked very old and weary. A lifetime of outdoor living had once darkened his skin to the color of old leather, but age and general debility had paled and faded the leather tone to a gray shade. The bones of his face seemed unnaturally large under the thin mask of old skin. A white stubble blurred the outlines of his lower jaw and his wrinkled eyelids rested on his cheeks. He did not move, but his chest stirred slowly under his heavy checked shirt, its colors —like his—grayed by time.

Merlin leaned toward the man, at which the smell of death came faintly into his nostrils. A wisp of feeling he thought he had lost stirred within him.

"Why don't you move this way?" he said to the old man. "There's still shade enough for both of us at this end."

There was no answer. He said it again.

"Leave me be," said the other, without opening his eyes.

"The sun'll kill you."

"It feels good."

They sat together. It was not much, but Merlin's racking loneliness had eased slightly with the exchange of those few words with the weary figure beside him.

"I'm at the end of my rope," Merlin said. "You know how it is?"

"I know," said the old man, after a long pause. It was as if he were so far off that the sound of Merlin's voice took some time to reach him.

"I'll never find my wife now," said Merlin. "I'll never get a job now. It's all gone. That's the worst part, knowing there's no use. Once, I had hope, but now . . ."

He found himself telling the old man all about it. There was no one else to tell, and he had to tell someone. The old man sat in the sun, smelling faintly of death. He said nothing. As Merlin talked, a fly circled and landed on the pocket of the old man's checked shirt. It stayed there, resting with the old man in the sun.

"You see," Merlin went on, "there's nothing to be done. Nowhere to go."

He stopped talking, but the old man still said nothing. Merlin leaned into the sun and put his lips close to the gray ear nearest him.

"I say," he said loudly, "there's no place to go, is there? Where can you go?"

The eyelids twitched slightly. The dry lips parted.

"Get off the Earth," said the old man. "If you can't scratch a living down here, you got to get off the Earth."

Merlin sat back. The advancing sun had found the thin sole of his left shoe again. The heat was burning his foot now, but he could not summon up the will to pull it back into the shade. He sat.

It was locked—from the outside.

Not only that, but the mechanical latch handle that would override the button lock on the tiny tourist cabin aboard the *Star of the North* was hidden by the very bed on which Cully When sat cross-legged, like some sinewy mountain man out of Cully's own pioneering ancestry. Cully grinned at the image in the mirror which went with the washstand now hidden by the bed beneath him. He would not have risked such an expression as that grin if there had been anyone around to see him. The grin, he knew, gave too much of him away to viewers. It was the hard, unconquerable humor of a man dealing for high stakes.

Here, in the privacy of this locked cabin, it was also a tribute to the skill of the steward who had imprisoned him. A dour and cautious individual with a long Scottish face, and no doubt the greater part of his back wages reinvested in the very spaceship line he worked for. Or had Cully done something to give himself away? No. Cully shook his head. If that had been the case, the steward would have done more than just lock the cabin. It occurred to Cully that his face, at last, might be becoming known.

"I'm sorry, sir," the steward had said, as he opened the

cabin's sliding door and saw the unmade bed. "Off-watch steward's missed making it up." He clucked reprovingly. "I'll fix it for you, sir."

"No hurry," said Cully. "I just want to hang my clothes; and I can do that later."

"Oh, no, sir." The lean, dour face of the other—as primitive in a different way as Cully's own—looked shocked. "Regulations. Passengers' gear to be stowed and bunk made up before overdrive."

"Well, I can't just stand here in the corridor," said Cully. "I want to get rid of the stuff and get a drink." And indeed the corridor was so narrow, they were like two vehicles on a mountain road. One would have to back up to some wider spot to let the other past.

"Have the sheets in a moment, sir," said the steward. "Just a moment, sir. If you wouldn't mind sitting up on the bed, sir?"

"All right," said Cully. "But hurry. I want to step up for a drink in the lounge."

He hopped up onto the bed, which filled the little cabin in its down position; and drew his legs up tailor-fashion to clear them out of the corridor.

"Excuse me, sir," said the steward, closed the door, and went off. As soon as he heard the button lock latch, Cully had realized what the man was up to. But an unsuspecting man would have waited at least several minutes before hammering on the locked door and calling for someone to let him out. Cully had been forced to sit digesting the matter in silence.

At the thought of it now, however, he grinned again. That steward was a regular prize package. Cully must remember to think up something appropriate for him, afterward. At the moment, there were more pressing things to think of.

Cully looked in the mirror again and was relieved at the sight of himself without the betraying grin. The face that looked back at him at the moment was lean and angular. A little peroxide solution on his thick, straight brows had taken the sharp appearance off his high cheekbones and given his pale blue eyes a faintly innocent expression. When he really wanted to fail to impress sharply discerning eyes, he also made it a point to chew gum.

The present situation, he considered now, did not call for that extra touch. If the steward was already even vaguely suspicious of him, he could not wait around for an ideal opportunity. He would have to get busy now, while they were still working the spaceship out of the solar system to a safe distance where the overdrive could be engaged without risking a mass-proximity explosion.

And this, since he was imprisoned so neatly in his own shoebox of a cabin, promised to be a problem right from the start.

He looked around the cabin. Unlike the salon cabins on the level overhead, where it was possible to pull down the bed and still have a tiny space to stand upright in—either beside the bed, in the case of single-bed cabins, or between them, in the case of doubles—in the tourist cabins once the bed was down, the room was completely divided into two spaces—the space above the bed and the space below. In the space above, with him, were the light and temperature and ventilation controls, controls to provide him with soft music or the latest adventure tape, food and drink dispensers and a host of other minor comforts.

There were also a phone and a signal button, both connected with the steward's office. Thoughtfully he tried both. There was, of course, no answer.

At that moment a red light flashed on the wall opposite him; and a voice came out of the grille that usually provided the soft music.

"We are about to maneuver. This is the Captain's Section speaking. We are about to maneuver. Will all lounge passengers return to their cabins? Will all passengers remain in their cabins, and fasten seat belts. We are about to maneuver. This is the Captain's Section—"

Cully stopped listening. The steward would have known this announcement was coming. It meant that everybody but crew members would be in their cabins, and crew members would be up top in control level at maneuver posts. And that meant nobody was likely to happen along to let Cully out. If Cully could get out of this cabin, however, those abandoned corridors could be a break for him.

However, as he looked about him now, Cully was rapidly revising downward his first cheerful assumption that he—who had gotten out of so many much more intentional prisons—would find this a relatively easy task. On the same principle that a pit with unclimbable walls and too deep to jump up from and catch an edge is one of the most perfect traps designable—the tourist room held Cully. He was on top of the bed; and he needed to be below it to operate the latch handle.

First question: How impenetrable was the bed itself? Cully dug down through the covers, pried up the mattress, peered through the springs, and saw a blank panel of metal. Well, he had not really expected much in that direction. He put the mattress and covers back and examined what he had to work with above-bed.

There were all the control switches and buttons on the wall, but nothing among them promised him any aid. The walls were the same metal paneling as the base of the bed. Cully began to turn out his pockets in the hope of finding something in them that would inspire him. And he did indeed turn out a number of interesting items, including a folded piece of notepaper which he looked at rather soberly before laying it aside, with a boy scout type of knife that just happened to have a set of lock picks among its other tools. The note would only take up valuable time at the moment, and—the lock being out of reach in the door—the lock picks were no good either.

There was nothing in what he produced to inspire him, however. Whistling a little mournfully, he began to make the next best use of his pile of property. He unscrewed the nib and cap of his long, gold fountain pen, took out the ink cartridge, and laid the tube remaining aside. He removed his belt, and the buckle from the belt. The buckle, it appeared, clipped on to the fountain pen tube in somewhat the manner of a pistol grip. He reached in his mouth, removed a bridge covering from the second premolar to the second molar, and combined this with a small metal throwaway dispenser of the sort designed to contain antacid tablets. The two together had a remarkable resemblance to the magazine and miniaturized trigger assembly of a small handgun; and when he attached them to the buckle-fountain-pen-tube combination the resemblance became so marked as to be practically inarguable.

Cully made a few adjustments in this and looked around himself again. For the second time, his eye came to rest on the folded note, and, frowning at himself in the mirror, he did pick it up and unfold it. Inside it read: "O wae the pow'r the Giftie gie us" Love, Lucy. Well, thought Cully, that was about what you could expect from a starry-eyed girl with Scottish ancestors, and romantic notions about present-day conditions on Alderbaran IV and the other new worlds.

". . . But if you have all that land on Asterope IV, why aren't you back there developing it?" she had asked him.

"The New Worlds are stifling to death," he had answered. But he saw then she did not believe him. To her, the New Worlds were still the romantic Frontier, as the Old Worlds Confederation newspapers capitalized it. She thought he had given up from lack of vision.

"You should try again . . ." she murmured. He gave up trying to make her understand. And then, when the cruise was over and their shipboard acquaintance—that was all it was, really—ended on the Miami dock, he had felt her slip something in his pocket so lightly only someone as self-trained as he would have noticed it. Later he had found it to be this note— which he had kept now for too long.

He started to throw it away, changed his mind for the sixtieth time and put it back in his pocket. He turned back to the problem of getting out of the cabin. He looked it over, pulled a sheet from the bed, and used its length to measure a few distances.

The bunk was pivoted near the point where the head of it entered the recess in the wall that concealed it in Up position. Up, the bunk was designed to fit with its foot next to the ceiling. Consequently, coming up, the foot would describe an arc—

About a second and a half later he had discovered that the arc of the foot, ascending, would leave just enough space in the opposite top angle between wall and ceiling so that if he could just manage to hang there, while releasing the safety latch at the foot of the bed, he might be able to get the bed up past him into the wall recess.

It was something which required the muscle and skill normally called for by so-called "chimney ascents" in mountain climbing—where the climber wedges himself between two opposing walls of rock. A rather wide chimney—since the room was a little more than four feet in width. But Cully had had some little experience in that line.

He tried it. A few seconds later, pressed against walls and ceiling, he reached down, managed to get the bed released, and had the satisfaction of seeing it fold up by him. Half a breath later he was free, out in the corridor of the Tourist Section.

The corridor was deserted and silent. All doors were closed. Cully closed his own thoughtfully behind him and went along the corridor to the more open space in the center of the ship. He looked up a steel ladder to the entrance of the Salon Section, where there would be another ladder to the Crew Section, and from there eventually to his objective—the Control level and the Captain's Section. Had the way up those ladders been open, it would have been simple. But level with the top of the ladder he saw the way to the Salon Section was closed off by a metal cover capable of withstanding fifteen pounds per square inch of pressure.

It had been closed, of course, as the other covers would have been, at the beginning of the maneuver period.

Cully considered it thoughtfully, his fingers caressing the pistol grip of the little handgun he had just put together. He would have preferred, naturally, that the covers be open and the way available to him without the need for fuss or muss. But the steward had effectively ruled out that possibility by reacting as and when he had. Cully turned away from the staircase and frowned, picturing the layout of the ship, as he had committed it to memory five days ago.

There was an emergency hatch leading through the ceiling of the end tourist cabin to the end salon cabin overhead, at both extremes of the corridor. He turned and went down to the end cabin nearest him, and laid his finger quietly on the outside latch handle.

There was no sound from inside. He drew his put-together handgun from his belt and, holding it in his left hand, calmly and without hesitation, opened the door and stepped inside.

He stopped abruptly. The bed in here was, of course, up in the wall, or he could never have entered. But the cabin's single occupant was asleep on the right-hand seat of the two seats than an upraised bed left exposed. The occupant was a small girl about eight years old.

The slim golden barrel of the handgun had swung immediately to aim at the child's temple. For an automatic second, it hung poised there, Cully's finger half-pressing the trigger. But the little girl never stirred. In the silence, Cully heard the surge of his own blood in his ears and the faint crackle of the note in his shirt pocket. He lowered the gun and fumbled in the waistband of his pants, coming up with a child-sized anesthetic pellet. He slipped this into his gun above the regular load, aimed the gun, and fired. The child made a little uneasy movement all at once and then lay still. Cully bent over her for a second, and heard the soft sound of her breathing. He straightened up. The pellet worked not through the blood stream, but immediately through a reaction of the nerves. In fifteen minutes the effect would be worn off, and the girl's sleep would be natural slumber again.

He turned away, stepped up on the opposite seat, and laid his free hand on the latch handle of the emergency hatch overhead. A murmur of voices from above made him hesitate. He unscrewed the barrel of the handgun and put it in his ear with the other hollow end resting against the ceiling which was also the floor overhead. The voices came, faint and distorted, but understandable to his listening.

". . . hilifter," a female voice was saying.

"Oh, Patty!" another female voice answered. "He was just trying to scare you. You believe everything."

"How about that ship that got hilifted just six months ago? That ship going to one of the Pleiades, just like this one? The *Queen of Argyle*—"

"*Princess of Argyle*."

"Well, you know what I mean. Ships do get hilifted. Just as long as there're governments on the pioneer worlds that'll license them and no questions asked. And it could just as well happen to this ship. But you don't worry about it a bit."

"No, I don't."

"When hilifters take over a ship, they kill off everyone who can testify against them. None of the passengers or ship's officers from the *Princess of Argyle* was ever heard of again."

"Says who?"

"Oh, everybody knows that!"

Cully took the barrel from his ear and screwed it back onto his weapon. He glanced at the anesthetized child and thought of trying the other cabin with an emergency hatch. But the maneuver period would not last more than twenty minutes at the most and five of that must be gone already. He put the handgun between his teeth, jerked the latch to the overhead hatch, and pulled it down and open.

He put both hands on the edge of the hatch opening and with one spring went upward into the salon cabin overhead.

He erupted into the open space between a pair of facing seats, each of which held a girl in her twenties. The one on his left was a rather plump, short, blond girl who was sitting curled up on her particular seat with a towel across her knees, an open bottle of pink nail polish on the towel, and the brush-cap to the bottle poised in her hand. The other was a tall, dark-haired, very pretty lass with a lap-desk pulled down from the wall and a hand-scriber on the desk where she was apparently writing a letter. For a moment both stared at him, and his gun; and then the blonde gave a muffled shriek, pulled the towel over her head, and lay still, while the brunette, staring at Cully, went slowly pale.

"Jim!" she said.

"Sorry," said Cully. "The real name's Cully When. Sorry about this, too, Lucy." He held the gun casually, but it was pointed in her general direction. "I didn't have any choice."

A little of the color came back. Her eyes were as still as fragments of green bottle glass.

"No choice about what?" she said.

"To come through this way," said Cully. "Believe me, if I'd known you were here, I'd have picked any other way. But there wasn't any other way; and I didn't know."

"I see," she said, and looked at the gun in his hand. "Do you have to point that at me?"

"I'm afraid," said Cully, gently, "I do."

She did not smile.

"I'd still like to know what you're doing here," she said.

"I'm just passing through," said Cully. He gestured with the gun to the emergency hatch to the Crew Section, overhead. "As I say, I'm sorry it has to be through your cabin. But I didn't even know you were serious about emigrating."

"People usually judge other people by themselves," she said expressionlessly. "As it happened, I believed you." She looked at the gun again. "How many of you are there on board?"

"I'm afraid I can't tell you that," said Cully.

"No. You couldn't, could you?" Her eyes held steady on him. "You know, there's an old poem about a man like you. He rides by a farm maiden and she falls in love with him, just like that. But he makes her guess what he is; and she guesses

. . . oh, all sorts of honorable things, like soldier, or forester. But he tells her in the end he's just an outlaw, slinking through the wood.''

Cully winced.

"Lucy—" he said. "Lucy—"

"Oh, that's all right," she said. "I should have known when you didn't call me or get in touch with me, after the boat docked." She glanced over at her friend, motionless under the towel. "You have the gun. What do you want us to do?"

"Just sit still," he said. "I'll go on up through here and be out of your way in a second. I'm afraid—" He reached over to the phone on the wall and pulled its cord loose. "You can buzz for the steward, still, after I'm gone," he said. "But he won't answer just a buzzer until after the maneuver period's over. And the stairway hatches are locked. Just sit tight and you'll be all right."

He tossed the phone aside and tucked the gun in the waist-band.

"Excuse me," he said, stepping up on the seat beside her. She moved stiffly away from him. He unlatched the hatch overhead, pulled it down, and went up through it. When he glanced back down through it, he saw her face stiffly upturned to him.

He turned away and found himself in an equipment room. It was what he had expected from the ship's plans he had memorized before coming aboard. He went quickly out of the room and scouted the section.

As he had expected, there was no one at all upon this level. Weight and space on interstellar liners being at the premium that they were, even a steward like the one who had locked him in his cabin did double duty. In overdrive, no one but the navigating officer had to do much of anything. But in ordinary operation, there were posts for all ship's personnel, and all ship's personnel were at them up in the Captain's Section at Control.

The stair hatch to this top and final section of the ship he found to be closed as the rest. This, of course, was routine. He had not expected this to be unlocked, though a few years back ships like this might have been that careless. There were emergency hatches from this level as well, of course, up to the final section. But it was no part of Cully's plan to come up in the middle of a Control Room or a Captain's Section filled with young, active, and almost certainly armed officers. The inside route was closed.

The outside route remained a possibility. Cully went down to the opposite end of the corridor and found the entry port closed, but sealed only by a standard lock. In an adjoining room there were outside suits. Cully spent a few minutes with his picks, breaking the lock of the seal; and then went in to put on the suit that came closest to fitting his six-foot-two frame.

A minute later he stepped out onto the outside skin of the ship.

As he watched the outer door of the entry port closing ponderously in the silence of airless space behind him, he felt the usual inner coldness that came over him at times like this. He had a mild but very definite phobia about open space with its myriads of unchanging stars. He knew what caused it —several psychiatrists had told him it was nothing to worry about, but he could not quite accept their unconcern. He knew he was a very lonely individual, underneath it all; and subconsciously he guessed he equated space with the final extinction in which he expected one day to disappear and be forgotten forever. He could not really believe it was possible for someone like him to make a dent in such a universe.

It was symptomatic, he thought now, plodding along with the magnetic bootsoles of his suit clinging to the metal hull, that he had never had any success with women—like Lucy. A sort of bad luck seemed to put him always in the wrong position with anyone he stood a chance of loving. Inwardly, he was just as starry-eyed as Lucy, he admitted to himself, alone with the vastness of space and the stars, but he'd never had much success bringing it out into the open. Where she went all right, he seemed to go all wrong. Well, he thought, that was life. She went her way and he would go his. And it was probably a good thing.

He looked ahead up the side of the ship, and saw the slight bulge of the observation window of the Navigator's Section. It was just a few more steps now.

Modern ships were sound insulated, thankfully, or the crew inside would have heard his dragging footsteps on the hull. He reached the window and peered in. The room he looked into was empty.

Beside the window was a small emergency port for cleaning

and repairs of the window. Clumsily, and with a good deal of effort, he got the lock-bolt holding it down unscrewed, and let himself in. The space between outer and inner ports here was just enough to contain a spacesuited man. He crouched in darkness after the outer port had closed behind him.

Incoming air screamed up to audibility. He cautiously cracked the interior door and looked into a room still empty of any crew members. He slipped inside and snapped the lock on the door before getting out of his suit.

As soon as he was out, he drew the handgun from his belt and cautiously opened the door he had previously locked. He looked out on a short corridor leading one way to the Control Room, and the other, if his memory of the ship plans had not failed him, to the central room above the stairway hatch from below. Opening off this small circular space surrounding the hatch would be another entrance directly to the Control Room, a door to the Captain's Quarters, and one to the Communications Room.

The corridor was deserted. He heard voices coming down it from the Control Room; and he slipped out the door that led instead to the space surrounding the stairway hatch. And checked abruptly.

The hatch was open. And it had not been open when he had checked it from the level below, ten minutes before.

For the first time he cocked an ear specifically to the kinds of voices coming from the Control Room. The acoustics of this part of the ship mangled all sense out of the words being said. But now that he listened, he had no trouble recognizing, among others, the voice of Lucy.

It occurred to him then with a kind of wonder at himself, that it would have been no feat for an active girl like herself to have followed him up through the open emergency hatch, and later mount the crew level stairs to the closed hatch there and pound on it until someone further opened up.

He threw aside further caution and sprinted across to the doorway of the Captain's Quarters. The door was unlocked. He ducked inside and looked around him. It was empty. It occurred to him that Lucy and the rest of the ship's complement would probably still be expecting him to be below in the Crew's Section. He closed the door and looked about him, at the room he was in.

The room was more lounge than anything else, being the place where the captain of a spaceship did his entertaining. But there was a large and businesslike desk in one corner of the room, and in the wall opposite was a locked, glassed-in case holding an assortment of rifles and handguns.

He was across the room in a moment, and in a few savage seconds had the lock to the case picked open. He reached in and took down a short-barreled, flaring-muzzled riot gun. He checked the chamber. It was filled with a full thousand-clip of the deadly steel darts. Holding this in one hand and his handgun in the other, he went back out the door and toward the other entrance to the Control Room—the entrance from the central room around the stairway hatch.

"... He wouldn't tell me if there were any others," Lucy was saying to a man in a captain's shoulder tabs, while eight other men, including the dour-faced steward who had locked Cully in his cabin, stood at their posts, but listening.

"There aren't any," said Cully, harshly. They all turned to him. He laid the handgun aside on a control table by the entrance to free his other hand, and lifted the heavy riot gun in both hands, covering them. "There's only me."

"What do you want?" said the man with the captain's tabs. His face was set, and a little pale. Cully ignored the question. He came into the room, circling to his right, so as to have a wall at his back.

"You're one man short," said Cully as he moved. "Where is he?"

"Off-shift steward's sleeping," said the steward who had locked Cully in his room.

"Move back," said Cully, picking up crew members from their stations at control boards around the room, and herding them before him back around the room's circular limit to the very entrance by which he had come in. "I don't believe you."

"Then I might as well tell you," said the captain, backing up now along with Lucy and the rest. "He's in Communications. We keep a steady contact with Solar Police right up until we go into overdrive. There are two of their ships pacing alongside us right now, lights off, a hundred miles each side of us."

"Tell me another," said Cully. "I don't believe that either." He was watching everybody in the room, but what he was most aware of were the eyes of Lucy, wide upon him. He spoke to her, harshly. "Why did you get into this?"

She was pale to the lips, and her eyes had a stunned look.

"I looked down and saw what you'd done to that child in the cabin below—" Her voice broke off into a whisper. "Oh, Cully—"

He laughed mournfully.

"Stop there," he ordered. He had driven them back into a corner near the entrance he had come in. "I've got to have all of you together. Now, one of you is going to tell me where that other man is—and I'm going to pick you off, one at a time, until somebody does."

"You're a fool," said the captain. A little of his color had come back. "You're all alone. You don't have a chance of controlling this ship by yourself. You know what happens to hilifters, don't you? It's not just a prison sentence. Give up now and we'll all put in a word for you. You might get off without mandatory execution."

"No thanks," said Cully. He gestured with the end of the riot gun. "We're going into overdrive. Start setting up the course as I give it to you."

"No," said the captain, looking hard at him.

"You're a brave man," said Cully. "But I'd like to point out something. I'm going to shoot you if you won't cooperate and then I'm going to work down the line of your officers. Sooner or later somebody's going to preserve his life by doing what I tell you. So getting yourself killed isn't going to save the ship at all. It just means somebody with less courage than you lives. And you die."

There was a sharp, bitter intake of breath from the direction of Lucy. Cully kept his eyes on the captain.

"How about it?" Cully asked.

"No brush-pants of a Colonial," said the captain, slowly and deliberately, "is going to stand in my Control Room and tell me where to take my ship."

"Did the captain and officers of the *Princess of Argyle* ever come back?" said Cully, somewhat cryptically.

"It's nothing to me whether they came or stayed."

"I take it all back," said Cully. "You're too valuable to lose." The riot gun shifted to come to bear on the First Officer, a tall, thin, younger man whose hair was already receding at the temples. "But you aren't, friend. I'm not even going to tell you what I'm going to do. I'm just going to start counting; and when I decide to stop you've had it. One . . . two . . .''

"Don't! Don't shoot!" The First Officer jumped across the few steps that separated him from the Main Computer Panel. "What's your course? What do you want me to set up—"

The captain began to curse the First Officer. He spoke slowly and distinctly and in a manner that completely ignored the presence of Lucy in the Control Room. He went right on as Cully gave the First Officer the course and the First Officer set it up. He stopped only as—abruptly—the lights went out, and the ship overdrove.

When the lights came on again—it was a matter of only a fraction of a second of real time—the captain was at last silent. He seemed to have sagged in the brief interval of darkness and his face looked older.

And then, slamming through the tense silence of the room, came the sound of the Contact Alarm Bell.

"Turn it on," said Cully. The First Officer stepped over and pushed a button below the room's communication screen. It cleared suddenly to show a man in a white jacket.

"We're alongside, Cully," he said. "We'll take over now. How're you fixed for casualties?"

"At the moment—" began Cully. But he got no further than that. Behind him, three hard, spaced words in a man's voice cut him off.

"Drop it, Hilifter!"

Cully did not move. He cocked his eyebrows a little sadly and grinned his untamable grin for the first time at the ship's officers, and Lucy and the figure in the screen. Then the grin went away.

"Friend," he said to the man hidden behind him, "your business is running a spaceship. Mine is taking them away from people who run them. Right now you're figuring how you make me give up or shoot me down and this ship dodges back into overdrive, and you become hero for saving it. But it isn't going to work that way."

He waited for a moment to hear if the off-watch steward behind him—or whoever the officer was—would answer. But there was only silence.

"You're behind me," said Cully. "But I can turn pretty fast. You may get me coming around, but unless you've got something like a small cannon, you're not going to stop me getting you at this short range, whether you've got me or not. Now, if you think I'm just talking, you better think again. For me, this is one of the risks of the trade."

He turned. As he did so he went for the floor and heard the first shot go by his ear. As he hit the floor another shot hit the deck beside him and ricocheted into his side. But by that time he had the heavy riot gun aimed and he pressed the firing button. The stream of darts knocked the man backward out of the entrance to the Control Room to lie, a still and huddled shape, in the corridor outside.

Cully got to his feet, feeling the single dart in his side. The room was beginning to waver around him, but he felt that he could hold on for the necessary couple of minutes before the people from the ship moving in alongside could breach the lock and come aboard. His jacket was loose and would hide the bleeding underneath. None of those facing him could know he had been hit.

"All right, folks," he said, managing a grin. "It's all over but the shouting—" And then Lucy broke suddenly from the group and went running across the room toward the entrance through which Cully had come a moment or so earlier.

"Lucy—" he barked at her. And then he saw her stop and turn by the control table near the entrance, snatching up the little handgun he had left them. "Lucy, do you want to get shot?"

But she was bringing up the little handgun, held in the grip of both her hands, and aiming it squarely at him. The tears were running down her face.

"It's better for you, Cully—" she was sobbing. "Better . . ."

He swung the riot gun to bear on her, but he saw she did not even see it.

"Lucy, I'll have to kill you!" he cried. But she no more heard him, apparently, than she saw the muzzle-on view of the riot gun in his hands. The wavering golden barrel in her grasp wobbled to bear on him.

"Oh, Cully!" she wept. "Cully—" And pulled the trigger.

"Oh, *hell!*" said Cully in despair. And let her shoot him down.

When he came back, things were very fuzzy there at first.

He heard the voice of the man in the white jacket, arguing with the voice of Lucy.

"Hallucination—" muttered Cully. The voices broke off.

"Oh, he said something!" cried the voice of Lucy.

"Cully?" said the man's voice. Cully felt a two-finger grip on his wrist in the area where his pulse should be—if, that was, he had a pulse. "How're you feeling?"

"Ship's doctor?" muttered Cully, with great effort. "You got the *Star of the North?*"

"That's right. All under control. How do you feel?"

"Feel fine," mumbled Cully. The doctor laughed.

"Sure you do," said the doctor. "Nothing like being shot a couple of times and having a pellet and a dart removed to put a man in good shape."

"Not Lucy's fault—" muttered Cully. "Not understand." He made another great effort in the interests of explanation. "Stars'n eyes."

"Oh, what does he mean?" wept Lucy.

"He means," said the voice of the doctor harshly, "that you're just the sort of fine young idealist who makes the best sort of sucker for the sort of propaganda the Old Worlds Confederation dishes out."

"Oh, you'd say that!" flared Lucy's voice. "Of course, you'd say that!"

"Young lady," said the doctor, "how rich do you think our friend Cully, here, is?"

Cully heard her blow her nose, weakly.

"He's got millions, I suppose," she said bitterly. "Hasn't he hilifted dozens of ships?"

"He's hilifted eight," said the doctor dryly, "which, incidentally, puts him three ships ahead of any other contender for the title of hilifting champion around the populated stars. The mortality rate among single workers—and you can't get any more than a single 'lifter aboard Confederation ships nowadays—hits ninety per cent with the third ship captured. But I doubt Cully's been able to save millions on a salary of six hundred a month, and a bonus of one tenth of one per cent of salvage value, at Colonial World rates."

There was a moment of profound silence.

"What do you mean?" said Lucy, in a voice that wavered a little.

"I'm trying," said the doctor, "for the sake of my patient

—and perhaps for your own—to push aside what Cully calls those stars in your eyes and let a crack of surface daylight through."

"But why would he work for a salary—like that?" Disbelief was strong in her voice.

"Possibly," said the doctor, "just possibly because the picture of a bloodstained hilifter with a knife between his teeth, carousing in Colonial bars, shooting down Confederation officers for the fun of it, and dragging women passengers off by the hair, has very little to do with the real facts of a man like Cully."

"Smart girl," managed Cully. "S'little mixed up, s'all—" He managed to get his vision cleared a bit. The other two were standing facing each other, right beside his bed. The doctor had a slight flush above his cheekbones and looked angry. Lucy, Cully noted anxiously, was looking decidedly pale. "Mixed up—" Cully said again.

"Mixed up isn't the word for it," said the doctor angrily, without looking down at him. "She and all ninety-nine out of a hundred people on the Old Worlds." He went on to Lucy, "You met Cully Earthside. Evidently you liked him there. He didn't strike you as the scum of the stars, then.

"But all you have to do is hear him tagged with the name 'hilifter' and immediately your attitude changes."

Lucy swallowed.

"No," she said, in a small voice, "it didn't . . . change."

"Then who do you think's wrong—you or Cully?" The doctor snorted. "If I have to give you reasons, what's the use? If you can't see things straight for yourself, who can help you? That's what's wrong with all the people back on the Old Worlds."

"I believe Cully," she said. "I just don't know why I should."

"Who has lots of raw materials—the raw materials to support trade—but hasn't any trade?" asked the doctor.

She frowned at him.

"Why . . . the New Worlds haven't any trade on their own," she said. "But they're too undeveloped yet, too young—"

"Young? There's three to five generations on most of them!"

"I mean they haven't got the industry, the commercial

organization—'' She faltered before the slightly satirical expression on the doctor's face. "All right, then, you tell me! If they've got everything they need for trade, why don't they? The Old Worlds did; why don't you?''

"In what?''

She stared at him.

"But the Confederation of the Old Worlds already has the ships for interworld trade. And they're glad to ship Colonial products. In fact they do,'' she said.

"So a load of miniaturized surgical power instruments made on Asterope in the Pleiades has to be shipped to Earth and then shipped clear back out to its destination on Electra, also in the Pleiades. Only by the time they get there they've doubled or tripled in price, and the difference is in the pockets of Earth shippers.''

She was silent.

"It seems to me,'' said the doctor, "that girl who was with you mentioned something about your coming from Boston, back in the United States on Earth. Didn't they have a tea party there once? Followed by a revolution? And didn't it all have something to do with the fact that England at that time would not allow its colonies to own and operate their own ships for trade—so that it all had to be funneled through England in English ships to the advantage of English merchants?''

"But why can't you build your own ships?'' she said. Cully felt it was time he got in on the conversation. He cleared his throat, weakly.

"Hey—'' he managed to say. They both looked at him; but he himself was looking only at Lucy.

"You see,'' he said, rolling over and struggling up on one elbow, "the thing is—''

"Lie down,'' said the doctor.

"Go jump out the air lock,'' said Cully. "The thing is, honey, you can't build spaceships without a lot of expensive equipment and tools, and trained personnel. You need a spaceship-building industry. And you have to get the equipment, tools, and people from somewhere else to start with. You can't get 'em unless you can trade for 'em. And you can't trade freely without ships of your own, which the Confederation, by forcing us to ship through them, makes it impossible for us to have.

"So you see how it works out," said Cully. "It works out you've got to have shipping before you can build shipping. And if people on the outside refuse to let you have it by proper means, simply because they've got a good thing going and don't want to give it up—then some of us just have to break loose and go after it any way we can."

"Oh, Cully!"

Suddenly she was on her knees by the bed and her arms were around him.

"Of course the Confederation news services have been trying to keep up the illusion we're sort of half jungle-jims, half wild-west characters," said the doctor. "Once a person takes a good look at the situation on the New Worlds, though, with his eyes open—" He stopped. They were not listening.

"I might mention," he went on, a little more loudly, "while Cully here may not be exactly rich, he does have a rather impressive medal due him, and a commission as Brevet-Admiral in the upcoming New Worlds Space Force. The New Worlds Congress voted him both at their meeting just last week on Asterope, as soon as they'd finished drafting their Statement of Independence—"

But they were still not listening. It occurred to the doctor then that he had better uses for this time—here on this vessel where he had been ship's doctor ever since she first lifted into space—than to stand around talking to deaf ears.

He went out, closing the door of the sick bay on the former *Princess of Argyle* quietly behind him.

BROTHER CHARLIE

I.

The matter of her standby burners trembled through the APC9 like the grumbling of an imminent and not entirely unominous storm. In the cramped, lightly grease-smelling cockpit, Chuck Wagnall sat running through the customary preflight check on his instruments and controls. There were a great many to check out—almost too many for the small cockpit space to hold; but then old number 9, like all of her breed, was equipped to operate almost anywhere but underwater. She could even have operated there as well, but she would have needed a little time to prepare herself, before immersion.

On his left-hand field screen the Tomah envoy escort was to be seen in the process of moving the Tomah envoy aboard. The Lugh, Binichi, was already in his bin. Chuck wasted neither time nor attention on these—but when his ship range screen lit up directly before him, he glanced at it immediately.

"Hold Seventy-nine," he said automatically to himself, and pressed the acknowledge button.

The light cleared to reveal the face of Roy Marlie, Advance Unit Supervisor. Roy's brown hair was neatly combed in place, his uniform closure pressed tight, and his blue eyes casual and relaxed—and at these top danger signals, Chuck felt his own spine stiffen.

78

"Yo, how's it going, Chuck?" Roy asked.

"Lift in about five minutes."

"Any trouble picking up Binichi?"

"A snap," said Chuck. "He was waiting for me right on the surface of the bay. For two cents' worth of protocol he could have boarded her here with the Tomah." Chuck studied the face of his superior in the screen. He wanted very badly to ask Roy what was up; but when and if the supervisor wanted to get to the point of his call, he would do so on his own initiative.

"Let's see your flight plan," said Roy.

Chuck played the fingers of his left hand over the keys of a charter to his right. There appeared superimposed on the face of the screen between himself and Roy an outline of the two continents of this planet that the Tomah called Mant and the Lugh called Vanyinni. A red line that was his projected course crept across a great circle arc from the dot of his present position, over the ocean gap to the dot well inside the coastline of the southern continent. The dot was the human Base camp position.

"You could take a coastal route," said Roy, studying it.

"This one doesn't put us more than eight hundred nautical miles from land at the midpoint between the continents."

"Well, it's your neck," said Roy, with a lightheartedness as ominous as the noise of the standby burners. "Oh, by the way, guess who we've got here? Just landed. Your uncle, Member Wagnall."

Aha! said Chuck. But he said it to himself.

"Tommy?" he said aloud. "Is he handy, there?"

"Right here," answered Roy, and backed out of the screen to allow a heavy, graying-haired man with a kind, broad face to take his place.

"Chuck, boy, how are you?" said the man.

"Never better, Tommy," said Chuck. "How's politicking?"

"The appropriations committee's got me out on a one-man junket to check up on you lads," said Earth District Member 439 Thomas L. Wagnall. "I promised your mother I'd say hello to you if I got to this Base. What's all this about having this project named after you?"

"Oh, not after me," said Chuck. "Its full name isn't Project Charlie, it's Project Big Brother Charlie. With us humans as Big Brother."

"I don't seem to know the reference."

"Didn't you ever hear that story?" said Chuck. "About three brothers—the youngest were twins and fought all the time. The only thing that stopped them was their big brother Charlie coming on the scene."

"I see," said Tommy. "With the Tomah and the Lugh as the two twins. Very apt. Let's just hope Big Brother can be as successful in this instance."

"Amen," said Chuck. "They're a couple of touchy peoples."

"Well," said Tommy. "I was going to run out where you are now and surprise you, but I understand you've got the only atmosphere pot of the outfit."

"You see?" said Chuck. "That proves we need more funds and equipment. Talk it up for us when you get back, Tommy. Those little airfoils you saw on the field when you came in have no range at all."

"Well, we'll see," said Tommy. "When do you expect to get here?"

"I'll be taking off in a few minutes. Say four hours."

"Good. I'll buy you a drink of diplomatic scotch when you get in."

Chuck grinned.

"Bless the governmental special supply. And you. See you, Tommy."

"I'll be waiting," said the Member. "You want to talk to your chief, again?"

He looked away outside the screen range. "He says nothing more. So long, Chuck."

"So long."

They cut connections. Chuck drew a deep breath. "Hold Seventy-nine," he murmured to his memory, and went back to check that item on his list.

He had barely completed his full check when a roll of drums from outside the ship, penetrating even over the sound of the burners, announced that the Tomah envoy was entering the ship. Chuck got up and went back through the door that separated the cockpit from the passenger and freight sections.

The envoy had just entered through the lock and was standing with his great claw almost in salute. He most nearly resembled, like all the Tomah, a very large ant with the front pair of legs developed into arms with six fingers each and double-opposed thumbs. In addition, however, a large, lobsterlike claw was hinged just behind and above the waist. When standing erect, as now, he measured about four feet from mandibles to the point where his rear pair of legs rested on the ground, although the great claw, fully extended, could have lifted something off a shelf a good foot or more above Chuck's head—and Chuck was over six feet in height. Completely unadorned as he was, this Tomah weighed possibly ninety to a hundred and ten Earth-pounds.

Chuck supplied him with a small throat-mike translator.

"Bright seasons," said the Tomah, as soon as this was adjusted. The translator supplied him with a measured, if uninflected, voice.

"Bright seasons," responded Chuck. "And welcome aboard, as we humans say. Now, if you'll just come over here—"

He went about the process of assisting the envoy into the bin across the aisle from the Lugh, Binichi. The Tomah had completely ignored the other; and all through the process of strapping in the envoy, Binichi neither stirred, nor spoke.

"There you are," said Chuck, when he was finished, looking down at the reclining form of the envoy. "Comfortable?"

"Pardon me," said the envoy. "Your throat-talker did not express itself."

"I said, comfortable?"

"You will excuse me," said the envoy. "You appear to be saying something I don't understand."

"Are you suffering any pain, no matter how slight, from the harness and bin I put you in?"

"Thank you," said the envoy. "My health is perfect."

He saluted Chuck from the reclining position. Chuck saluted back and turned to his other passenger. The similarity here was the throat-translator, that little miracle of engineering, which the Lugh, in common with the envoy and Chuck, wore as close as possible to his larynx.

"How about you?" said Chuck. "Still comfortable?"

"Like sleeping on a ground-swell," said Binichi. He grinned up at Chuck. Or perhaps he did not grin—like that of the dolphin he so much resembled, the mouth of the Lugh had a built-in upward twist at the corners. He lay. Extended at length in the bin he measured a few inches over five feet and weighed most undoubtedly over two hundred pounds. His wide-spreading tail was folded up like a fan into something resembling a club and his four short limbs were tucked in close to the short snowy fur of his belly. "I would like to see what the ocean looks like from high up."

"I can manage that for you," said Chuck. He went up front, unplugged one of the extra screens and brought it back. "When you look into this," he said, plugging it in above the bin, "it'll be like looking down through a hole in the ship's bottom."

"I will feel upside down," said Binichi. "That should be something new, too." He bubbled in his throat, an odd sound that the throat-box made no attempt to translate. Human sociologists had tried to equate this Lugh noise with laughter, but without much success. The difficulty lay in understanding what might be funny and what might not, to a different race. "You've got my opposite number tied down over there?"

"He's in harness," said Chuck.

"Good." Binichi bubbled again. "No point in putting temptation in my way."

He closed his eyes. Chuck went back to the cockpit, closed the door behind him, and sat down at the controls. The field had been cleared. He fired up and took off.

When the pot was safely airborne, he set the course on autopilot and leaned back to light a cigarette. For the first time he felt the tension in his neck and shoulder blades and stretched, to break its grip. Now was no time to be tightening up. But what had Binichi meant by this last remark? He certainly wouldn't be fool enough to attack the Tomah on dry footing?

Chuck shook off the ridiculous notion. Not that it was entirely ridiculous—the Lugh were individualists from the first moment of birth, and liable to do anything. But in this case both sides had given the humans their words (Binichi his personal word and the nameless Tomah their collective word) that there would be no trouble between the representatives of the two races. The envoy, Chuck was sure, would not violate the word of his people, if only for the reason that he would weigh his own life as nothing in comparison to the breaking of a promise. Binichi, on the other hand . . .

The Lugh were impeccably honest. The strange and difficult thing was, however, that they were much harder to understand than the Tomah, in spite of the fact that being warm-blooded and practically mammalian they appeared much more like the human race than the chitinous land-dwellers. Subtle shades and differences of meaning crept into every contact with the Lugh. They were a proud, strong, free, and oddly artistic people; in contradistinction to the intricately organized, highly logical Tomah, who took their pleasure in spectacle and group action.

But there was no sharp dividing line that placed some talents all on the Tomah side, and other all on the Lugh. Each people had musical instruments, each performed group dances, each had a culture and a science and a history. And, in spite of the fantastic surface sociological differences, each made the family unit a basic one, each was monogamous, each entertained the concept of a single deity, and each had very sensitive personal feelings.

The only trouble was, they had no use for each other—and a rapidly expanding human culture needed them both.

It so happened that this particular world was the only humanly habitable planet out of six circling a sun which was an ideal jumping-off spot for further spatial expansion. To use this world as a space depot of the size required, however, necessitated a local civilization of a certain type and level to support it. From a practical point of view this could be supplied only by a native culture both agreeable and sufficiently advanced to do so.

Both the Tomah and the Lugh were agreeable, as far as the humans were concerned. They were not advanced enough, and could not be, as long as they remained at odds.

It was not possible to advance one small segment of a civilization. It had to be upgraded as a whole. That meant cooperation, which was not now in effect. The Tomah had a science, but no trade. They were isolated on a few of the large landmasses by the seas that covered nine-tenths of their globe. Ironically, on a world which had great amounts of settlable land and vast untapped natural resources, they were cramped for living room and starved for raw materials. All this because to venture out on the Lugh-owned seas was sheer suicide. Their civilization was still in the candlelit, domestic-beast-powered stage, although they were further advanced in theory.

The Lugh, on the other hand, with the overwhelming resources of the oceans at their disposal, had by their watery environment been prohibited from developing a chemistry. The sea-girt islands and the uninhabited land masses were open to them; but, being already on the favorable end of the current status quo, they had had no great need or urge to develop further. What science they had come up with had been mainly for the purpose of keeping the Tomah in their place.

The human sociologists had given their opinion that the conflicts between the two races were no longer based on valid needs. They were, in fact, hangovers from competition in more primitive times when both peoples sought to control the seashores and marginal lands. To the Tomah in those days (and still), access to the seas had meant a chance to tap a badly needed source of food; and to the Lugh (no longer), access to the shore had meant possession of necessary breeding grounds. In the past the Tomah had attempted to clear the Lugh from their path by exterminating their helpless land-based young. And the Lugh had tried to starve the Tomah out, by way of retaliation.

The problem was to bury these ancient hatreds and prove cooperation was both practical and profitable. The latest step in this direction was to invite representatives of both races to a conference at the human Base on the uninhabited southern continent of this particular hemisphere. The humans would act as mediator, since both sides were friendly toward them. Which was what caused Chuck to be at the controls now, with his two markedly dissimilar passengers in the bins behind him.

Unfortunately, the sudden appearance of Member Thomas Wagnall meant they were getting impatient back home. In fact, he could not have come at a worse time. Human prestige with the two races was all humanity had to work with; and it was a delicate thing. And now had arisen this suddenly new question in Chuck's mind as to whether Binichi had regarded his promise to start no trouble with the Tomah as an ironclad guaranty, or a mere casual agreement contingent upon a number of unknown factors.

The question acquired its full importance a couple of hours later, and forty thousand feet above nothing but ocean, when the main burners abruptly cut out.

•   •   •

II.

Chuck wiped blood from his nose and shook his head to clear it. Underneath him, the life raft was rocking in soothing fashion upon the wide swell of the empty ocean; but, in spite of the fact that he knew better, he was having trouble accepting the reality of his present position.

Everything had happened a little too fast. His training for emergency situations of this sort had been semi-hypnotic. He remembered now a blur of action in which he had jabbed the distress button to send out an automatic signal on his position and predicament. Just at that moment the standby burners had cut in automatically—which was where he had acquired the bloody nose, when the unexpected thrust slammed him against the controls. Then he had cut some forty-two various switches, got back to the main compartment, unharnessed his passengers, herded them into the escape hatch, blown them all clear, hit the water, inflated the life raft, and got them aboard it just as the escape hatch itself sank gracefully out of sight. The pot, of course, had gone down like so much pig iron when it hit.

And here they were.

Chuck wiped his nose again and looked at the far end of the rectangular life raft. Binichi, the closer of the two, was half-lolling, half-sitting on the curved muscle of his tail. His curved mouth was half-open as if he might be laughing at them. And indeed, thought Chuck, he very well might. Chuck and the envoy, adrift on this watery waste, in this small raft, were castaways in a situation that threatened their very lives. Binichi the Lugh was merely and comfortably back at home.

"Binichi," said Chuck. "Do you know where we are?"

The curved jaw gaped slightly wider. The Lugh head turned this way and that on the almost nonexistent neck; then, twisting, he leaned over the edge of the raft and plunged his whole head briefly under water like a duck searching for food. He pulled his head out again, now slick with moisture.

"Yes," said Binichi.

"How far are we from the coast of the south continent?"

"A day's swim," said Binichi. "And most of a night."

He gave his information as a simple statement of fact. But Chuck knew the Lugh was reckoning in his own terms of speed and distance, which were roughly twelve nautical miles an hour as a steady pace. Undoubtedly it could be done in better time if a Lugh had wished to push himself. The human Base had clocked some of this race at up to eighty miles an hour through the water for short bursts of speed.

Chuck calculated. With the small outboard thrust unit provided for the raft, they would be able to make about four miles an hour if no currents went against them. Increase Binichi's estimate then by a factor of three—three days and nights with a slight possibility of its being less and a very great probability of its taking more. Thought of the thrust unit reminded him. He went to work unfolding it from its waterproof seal and attaching it in running position. Binichi watched him with interest, his head cocked a little on one side like an inquisitive bird's; but as soon as the unit began to propel the raft through the waves at its maximum cruising speed of four miles an hour, his attention disappeared.

With the raft running smoothly, Chuck had another question.

"Which way?"

Binichi indicated with a short thick-muscled forearm, and Chuck swung the raft in nearly a full turn. A slight shiver ran down his spine as he did so. He had been heading away from land out into nearly three thousand miles of open ocean.

"Now," said Chuck, locking the tiller, and looking at both of them. "It'll take us three days and nights to make the coast. And another three or four days to make it overland from there to the Base. The accident happened so quickly I didn't have time to bring along anything with which I could talk to my friends there." He paused, then added: "I apologize for causing you this inconvenience."

"There is no inconvenience," said Binichi, and bubbled in his throat. The envoy neither moved nor answered.

"This raft," said Chuck, "has food aboard it for me, but nothing, I think, that either one of you could use. There's water, of course. Otherwise, I imagine Binichi can make out with the sea all around him, the way it is; and I'm afraid there's not much to be done for you, Envoy, until we reach land. Then you'll be in Binichi's position of being able to forage for yourself."

The envoy still did not answer. There was no way of knowing what he was thinking. Sitting facing the two of them,

Chuck tried to imagine what it must be like for the Tomah, forced into a position inches away from his most deadly traditional enemy. And with the private preserves of that enemy, the deep-gulfed sea, source of all his culture's legends and terrors, surrounding him. True, the envoy was the pick of his people, a learned and intelligent being—but possibly there could be such a situation here that would try his self-control too far.

Chuck had no illusion about his ability to cope, barehanded, with either one of his fellow passengers—let alone come between them if they decided on combat. At the same time he knew that if it came to that, he would have to try. There could be no other choice; for the sake of humanity's future here on this world, all three races would hold him responsible.

The raft plodded on toward the horizon. Neither the Tomah nor Binichi had moved. They seemed to be waiting.

They traveled all through the afternoon, and the night that followed. When the sun came up the following morning they seemed not to have moved at all. The sea was all around them as before and unchanging. Binichi now lay half-curled upon the yielding bottom of the raft, his eyes all but closed. The envoy appeared not to have moved an inch. He stood tensely in his corner, claw at half-cock, like a statue carved from his native rock.

With the rising sun, the wind began to freshen. The gray rolling furrows of the sea's eternal surface deepened and widened. The raft tilted, sliding up one heavy slope and down another.

"Binichi!" said Chuck.

The Lugh opened his near eye lazily.

"Is it going to storm?"

"There will be wind," said Binichi.

"Much wind?" asked Chuck—and then realized that his question was too general. "How high will the waves be?"

"About my height," said Binichi. "It will be calmer in the afternoon."

It began to grow dark rapidly after that. By ten o'clock on Chuck's chronometer it was as murky as twilight. Then the rain came suddenly, and a solid sheet of water blotted out the rest of the raft from his eyes.

Chuck clung to the thrust unit for something to hang onto.

In the obscurity, the motion of the storm was eerie. The raft seemed to plunge forward, mounting a slope that stretched endlessly, until with a sudden twist and dip, it adopted a down-slant to forward—and then it seemed to fly backward in that position with increasing rapidity until its angle was as suddenly reversed again. It was like being on a monstrous seesaw that, even as it went up and down, was sliding back and forth on greased rollers.

At some indeterminate time later, Chuck began to worry about their being washed out of the raft. There were lines in the locker attached midway to the left-hand side of the raft. He crawled forward on hands and knees and found the box. It opened to his cold fingers, and he clawed out the coiled lines.

It struck him then, for the first time, that on this small, circumscribed raft, he should have bumped into Binichi or the envoy in making his way to the box. He lifted his face to the wind and the rain and darkness, but it told him nothing. And then he felt something nudge his elbow.

"He is gone," said the voice of the envoy's translator, in Chuck's ear.

"Gone?" yelled Chuck above the storm.

"He went over the side a little while ago."

Chuck clung to the box as the raft suddenly reversed its angle.

"How do you know?"

"I saw him," said the envoy.

"You—" Chuck yelled, "you can see in this?"

There was a slight pause.

"Of course," said the envoy. "Can't you?"

"No." Chuck unwound the lines. "We better tie ourselves into the raft," he shouted. "Keep from being washed overboard."

The envoy did not answer. Taking silence for assent, Chuck reached for him in the obscurity and passed one of the lines about the chitinous body. He secured the line tightly to the ring-handgrips fastened to the inner side of the raft's edge. Then he tied himself securely with a line around his waist to a handgrip further back by the thrust unit.

They continued to ride the pitching ocean. After some time, the brutal beating of the rain slackened off; and a little light began to filter through. The storm cleared then, as suddenly as it had commenced. Within minutes the raft heaved upon a metal-gray sea under thinning clouds in a sky from which the rain had ceased falling.

Teeth chattering, Chuck crawled forward to his single remaining passenger and untied the rope around him. The envoy was crouched down in his corner, his great claw hugging his back, as if he huddled for warmth. When Chuck untied him, he remained so motionless that Chuck was struck with the sudden throat-tightening fear that he was dead.

"Are you all right?" asked Chuck.

"Thank you," said the envoy; "I am in perfect health."

Chuck turned away to contemplate the otherwise empty raft. He was, he told himself, doing marvelously. Already, one of his charges had taken off . . . and then, before he could complete the thought, the raft rocked suddenly and the Lugh slithered aboard over one high side.

He and Chuck looked at each other. Binichi bubbled comfortably.

"Looks like the storm's over," said Chuck.

"It is blowing to the south of us now," said the Lugh.

"How far are we from land, now?"

"We should come to it," said Binichi, "in the morning."

Chuck blinked a little in surprise. This was better time than he had planned. And then he realized that the wind was blowing at their backs, and had been doing so all through the storm. He looked up at the sky. The sun was past its zenith, and a glance at his watch, which was corrected for local time, showed the hands at ten minutes to three. Chuck turned his attention back to Binichi, revolving the phraseology of his next question in his mind.

"Did you get washed overboard?" he asked, at last.

"Washed overboard?" Binichi bubbled. "I went into the water. It was more pleasant."

"Oh," said Chuck.

They settled down once more to their traveling.

A little over an hour later the raft jarred suddenly and rocked as if, without warning, it had found a rock beneath it, here in the middle of the ocean. For a second Chuck entertained the wild idea that it had. But such a notion was preposterous. There were undersea mountains all through this area, but the closest any came to the surface was a good forty fathoms down. At the same time the envoy's claw suddenly shot up and gaped above him, as he recoiled toward the center of the boat; and, looking overboard, Chuck came into view of the explanation for both occurrences.

A gray back as large around as an oil drum and ten to twelve feet in length was sliding by about a fathom and a half below them. At a little distance off Chuck could make out a couple more. As he watched, they turned slowly and came back toward the raft again.

Chuck recognized these sea-creatures. He had been briefed on them. They were the local counterpart of the Earthly shark —not as bloodthirsty, but they could be dangerous enough. They had wide catfishlike mouths, equipped with cartilaginous ridges rather than teeth. They were scavengers, rather than predators, generally feeding off the surface. As he watched now, the closest rose slowly to the surface in front of him, and suddenly an enormous jaw gaped a full six feet in width and closed over the high rim of the raft. The plastic material squealed to the rubbing of the horny ridges, giving but not puncturing. Temporarily defeated, the jaws opened again and the huge head sank back under the water.

Chuck's hand went instinctively to his belt for the handgun that was, of course, not there.

The raft jolted and twisted and rocked for several moments as the creatures tried to overturn it. The envoy's claw curved and jerked this way and that above him, like a sensitive antenna, at each new sound or jolt. Binichi rested lazy-eyed on the raft's bottom, apparently concerned only with the warmth of the sun upon his drying body.

After several minutes, the attacks on the raft ceased and the creatures drew off through the water. Chuck could catch a glimpse of them some thirty yards or so off, still following. Chuck looked back at Binichi, but the Lugh had his eyes closed as if he dozed. Chuck drew a deep breath and turned to the envoy.

"Would you like some water?" he asked.

The envoy's claw had relaxed slightly upon his back. He turned his head toward Chuck.

"If you have any you do not desire yourself," he said.

Chuck got out the water, debated offering some to the Lugh out of sheer form and politeness, then took his cue from the fact that Binichi appeared asleep, and confined his attentions to the envoy and himself. It surprised him now to remember that he had not thought of water up until this moment. He wondered if the Tomah had been suffering for it in silence, too polite or otherwise to ask for some.

This latter thought decided him against eating any of the food that the boat was also provided with. If they would reach land inside of another twelve or fourteen hours, he could last until then. It would hardly be kind, not to say politic, to eat in front of the Tomah when nothing was available for that individual. Even the Lugh, if he had eaten at all, had done so when he was out of the raft during the night and storm, when they could not see him.

Chuck and the envoy drank and settled down again. Sundown came quickly; and Chuck, making himself as comfortable as possible, went to sleep.

He woke with a start. For a second he merely lay still on the soft, yielding bottom of the raft without any clear idea as to what had brought him into consciousness. Then a very severe bump from underneath the raft almost literally threw him up into a sitting position.

The planet's small, close moon was pouring its brilliant light across the dark waters, from a cloudless sky. The night was close to being over, for the moon was low and its rays struck nearly level on the wave tops. The sea had calmed, but in its closer depths were great moving streaks and flashes of phosphorescence. For a moment these gleams only baffled and confused his eyes; and then Chuck saw that they were being made by the same huge scavengers that had bothered the raft earlier—only now there were more than a dozen of them, filling the water about and underneath the raft.

The raft rocked again as one of them struck it once more from below.

Chuck grabbed at the nearest ring-handhold and glanced at his fellow passengers. Binichi lay as if asleep, but in the dark shadow of his eye-sockets little reflected glints of light showed where his eyeballs gleamed in the darkness. Beyond him, the envoy was fully awake and up on all four feet, his claw extended high above him, and swaying with every shock like the balancing pole of a tightrope walker. His front pair of handed limbs were also extended on either side as if for balance. Chuck opened his mouth to call to the Tomah to take hold on one of the handgrips.

At that moment, however, there rose from out of the sea at

his elbow a pair of the enormous ridged jaws. Like the mouth of a trout closing over a fly, these clamped down, suddenly and without warning, on the small, bright metal box of the thrust unit where it was fastened to the rear end of the raft. And the raft itself was suddenly jerked and swung as the sea-creature tore the thrust unit screeching from its moorings into the sea. The raft was upended by the force of the wrench; and Chuck, holding on for dear life from sliding into the sea, saw the creature that had pulled the unit loose release it disappointedly, as if sensing its inedibility. It glittered down through the dark waters, falling from sight.

The raft slammed back down on the watery surface. And immediately on the heels of this came the sound of a large splash. Jerking his head around, Chuck saw the envoy struggling in the ocean.

His black body glittered among the waves, his thrashing limbs kicking up little dashes and glitters of phosphorescence. Chuck hurled himself to the far end of the raft and stretched out his hand, but the Tomah was already beyond his reach. Chuck turned, and dived back to the box at midraft, pawing through it for the line he had used to tie them in the boat earlier. It came up tangled in his hands. He lunged to the end of the raft nearest the envoy again, trying to unravel the line as he did so.

It came slowly and stubbornly out of its snarl. But when he got it clear at last and threw it, its unweighted end fell little more than halfway of the widening distance between the raft and the Tomah.

Chuck hauled it in, in a frenzy of despair. The raft, sitting high in the water, was being pushed by the night wind farther from the envoy with every second. The envoy himself had in all this time made no sound, only continuing to thrash his limbs in furious effort. His light body seemed in no danger of sinking; but his narrow limbs in uncoordinated effort barely moved him through the water—and now the scavengers were once more beginning to enter the picture.

These, like any fish suddenly disturbed, had scattered at the first splash of the Tomah's body. For a short moment it had seemed that they had been frightened away entirely. But now they were beginning to circle in, moving around the envoy, dodging close, then flirting away again—but always ending up a little closer than before.

Chuck twisted about to face Binichi.

"Can't you do something?" he cried.

Binichi regarded him with his race's usual unreadable expression.

"I?" he said.

"You could swim to him and let him hang on to you and tow him back," said Chuck. "Hurry!"

Binichi continued to look at him.

"You don't want the Tomah eaten?" he said at last.

"Of course not!"

"Then why don't you bring him back yourself to this thing?"

"I can't. I can't swim that well!" said Chuck. "You can."

"You can't?" echoed Binichi slowly. "I can?"

"You know that."

"Still," said the Lugh. "I would have thought you had some way—it's nothing to me if the Tomah is eaten."

"You promised."

"Not to harm him," said Binichi. "I have not. The Tomah have killed many children to get at the sea. Now this one has the sea. Let him drink it. The Tomah have been hungry for fish. This one has fish. Let him eat the fish."

Chuck brought his face close to the grinning dolphin head.

"You promised to sit down with us and talk to that Tomah," he said. "If you let him die, you're dodging that promise."

Binichi stared back at him for a short moment. Then he bubbled abruptly and went over the side of the raft in a soaring leap. He entered the water with his short limbs tucked in close to his body and his wide tail fanning out. Chuck had heard about, but never before seen, the swiftness of the Lugh, swimming. Now he saw it. Binichi seemed to give a single wriggle and then torpedo like a streak of phosphorescent lightning just under the surface of the water toward the struggling envoy.

One of the scavengers was just coming up under the Tomah. The streak of watery fire that was Binichi converged upon him and his heavy shape shot struggling from the surface, the sound of a dull impact heavy in the night. Then the phosphorescence of Binichi's path was among the others, striking right and left as a swordfish strikes on his run among a school of smaller feed fish. The scavengers scattered into darkness, all but the one Binichi had first hit, which was flopping upon the surface of the moonlit sea as if partially paralyzed.

Binichi broke surface himself, plowing back toward the Tomah. His head butted the envoy and a second later the envoy was skidding and skittering like a toy across the water's surface to the raft. A final thrust at the raft's edge sent him up and over it. He tumbled on his back on the raft's floor, glittering with wetness; and, righting himself with one swift thrust of his claw, he whirled, claw high, to face Binichi as the Lugh came sailing aboard.

Binichi sprang instantly erect on the curved spring of his tail; and Chuck, with no time for thought, thrust himself between the two of them.

For a second Chuck's heart froze. He found himself with his right cheek bare inches from the heavy double meat-choppers of the Tomah claw, while, almost touching him on the left, the gaping jaws of the Lugh glinted with thick, short scimitarlike teeth, and the fishy breath of the sea-dweller filled his nostrils. In this momentary, murderous tableau they all hung motionless for a long, breathless second. And then the Tomah claw sank backward to the shiny back below it and the Lugh slid backward and down upon his tail. Slowly, the two members of opposing races retreated each to his own end of the raft.

Chuck, himself, sat down. And the burst of relieved breath that expelled itself from his tautened lungs echoed in the black and moonlit world of the seascape night.

III.

Some two hours after sunrise, a line of land began to make its appearance upon their further horizon. It mounted slowly, as the onshore wind, and perhaps some current as well, drove them ahead. It was a barren, semiarid and tropical coastline, with a rise of what appeared to be hills—light green with a sparse vegetation—beyond it.

As they drifted closer, the shoreline showed itself in a thin pencil-mark of foam. No outer line of reefs was apparent, but the beaches themselves seemed to be rocky or nonexistent. Chuck turned to the Lugh.

"We need a calm, shallow spot to land in," he said. "Otherwise the raft's liable to upset in the surf, going in."

Binichi looked at him, but did not answer.

"I'm sorry," said Chuck. "I guess I didn't explain myself properly. What I mean is, I'm asking for your help again. If the raft upsets or has a hole torn in it when we're landing, the envoy and I will probably drown. Could you find us a fairly smooth beach somewhere and help us get to it?"

Binichi straightened up a little where he half-sat, half-lay propped against the end of the raft where the thrust unit had been attached.

"I had been told," he said, "that you had oceans upon your own world."

"That's right," said Chuck. "But we had to develop the proper equipment to move about on them. If I had the proper equipment here I wouldn't have to ask you for help. If it hadn't been for our crashing in the ocean none of this would be necessary."

"This 'equipment' of yours seems to have an uncertain nature," said Binichi. He came all the way erect. "I'll help you." He flipped overboard and disappeared.

Left alone in the raft with the envoy, Chuck looked over at him.

"The business of landing will probably turn out to be difficult and dangerous—at least we better assume the worst," he said. "You understand you may have to swim for your life when we go in?"

"I have given my word to accomplish this mission," replied the envoy.

A little while after that, it became evident from the angle at which the raft took the waves that they had changed course. Chuck, looking about for an explanation of this, discovered Binichi at the back of the raft, pushing them.

Within the hour, the Lugh had steered them to a small, rocky inlet. Picked up in the landward surge of the surf, the raft went, as Chuck had predicted, end over end in a smother of water up on the pebbly beach. Staggering to his feet with the solid land at last under him, Chuck smeared water from his eyes and took inventory of a gashed and bleeding knee. Binding the cut as best he could with a strip torn from his now-ragged pants, he looked about for his fellow travelers.

The raft was flung upside down between himself and them.

Just beyond it, the envoy lay with his claw arm flung limply out on the sand. Binichi, a little further on, was sitting up like a seal. As Chuck watched, the envoy stirred, pulled his claw back into normal position, and got shakily up on all four legs.

Chuck went over to the raft and, with some effort, managed to turn it back, right side up. He dug into the storage boxes and got out food and water. He was not sure whether it was the polite, or even the sensible thing to do, but he was shaky from hunger, parched from the salt water, dizzy from the pounding in the surf—and his knee hurt. He sat down and made his first ravenous meal since the pot had crashed in the sea, almost two days before.

As he was at it, the Tomah envoy approached. Chuck offered him some of the water, which the Tomah accepted.

"Sorry I haven't anything you could eat," said Chuck, a full belly having improved his manners.

"It doesn't matter," said the envoy. "There will be flora growing farther inland that will stay my hunger. It's good to be back on the land."

"I'll go along with you on that statement," said Chuck. Looking up from the food and water, he saw the Lugh approaching. Binichi came up, walking on his four short limbs, his tail folded into a club over his back for balance, and sat down with them.

"And now?" he said, addressing Chuck.

"Well," said Chuck, stretching his cramped back, "we'll head inland toward the Base." He reached into his right-hand pants pocket and produced a small compass. "That direction" —he pointed toward the hills without looking—"and some five hundred miles. Only we shouldn't have to cover it all on foot. If we can get within four hundred miles of Base, we'll be within the airfoils' cruising range, and one of them should locate us and pick us up."

"Your people will find us, but they can't find us here?" said Binichi.

"That's right." Chuck looked at the Lugh's short limbs. "Are you up to making about a hundred-mile trip overland?"

"As you've reminded me before," said Binichi, "I made a promise. It will help, though, if I can find water to go into from time to time."

Chuck turned to the envoy.

"Can we find bodies of water as we go?"

"I don't know this country," said the Tomah, speaking to Chuck. "But there should be water; and I'll watch for it."

"We two could go ahead," said Chuck, turning back to the Lugh. "And maybe we could work some way of getting a vehicle back here to carry you."

"I've never needed to be carried," said Binichi, and turned away abruptly. "Shall we go?"

They went.

Striking back from the stoniness of the beach, they passed through a belt of shallow land covered with shrub and coarse grass. Chuck, watching the envoy, half-expected him to turn and feed on some of this as they passed, but the Tomah went straight ahead. Beyond the vegetated belt, they came on dunes of coarse sand, where the Lugh—although he did not complain, any more than the envoy had when he fell overboard from the raft—had rough going with his short limbs. This stretched for a good five miles; but when they had come at last to firmer ground, the first swellings of the foothills seemed not so far ahead of them.

They were now in an area of small trees with numbers of roots sprouting from the trunk above ground level, and of sticklike plants resembling cacti. The envoy led them, his four narrow limbs propelling him with a curious smoothness over the uncertain ground as if he might at any moment break into a run. However, he regulated his pace to that of the Lugh, who was the slowest in the party, though he showed no signs as yet of discomfort or of tiring.

This even space was broken with dramatic suddenness as they crossed a sort of narrow earth-bridge or ridge between two of the gullies. Without any warning, the envoy wheeled suddenly and sprinted down the almost perpendicular slope on his left, zigzagging up the gully bed as if chasing something and into a large hole in the dry, crumbling earth of the further bank. A sudden thin screaming came from the hole and the envoy tumbled out into the open with a small furry creature roughly in the shape of a weasel and about the size of a large rabbit. The screaming continued for a few seconds. Chuck turned his head away, shaken.

He was aware of Binichi staring at him.

"What's wrong?" asked the Lugh. "You showed no emotion when I hurt the—" His translator failed on a word.

"What?" said Chuck. "I didn't understand. When you hurt what?"

"One of those who would have eaten the Tomah."

"I . . ." Chuck hesitated. He could not say that it was because this small land creature had had a voice to express its pain while the sea-dweller had not. "It's our custom to kill our meat before eating it."

Binichi bubbled.

"This will be too new to the Tomah for ritual," he said.

Reinforcement for this remark came a moment or two later when the envoy came back up the near wall of the gully to rejoin them.

"This is a paradise of plenty, this land," he said. "Only once in my life before was I ever lucky enough to taste meat." He lifted his head to them. "Shall we go on?"

"We should try to get to some water soon," said Chuck, glancing at Binichi.

"I have been searching for it," said the envoy. "Now I smell it not far off. We should reach it before dark."

They went on; and gradually the gullies thinned out and they found themselves on darker earth, among more and larger trees. Just as the sunset was reddening the sky above the upthrust outline of the near hills, they entered a small glen where a stream trickled down from a higher slope and spread out into a small pool. Binichi trotted past them without a word, and plunged in.

Chuck woke when the morning sun was just beginning to touch the glen. For a moment he lay still under the mass of small-leaved branches with which he had covered himself the night before, a little bewildered to find himself no longer on the raft. Then memory returned and with it sensation, spreading through the stiff limbs of his body.

For the first time, he realized that his strength was ebbing. He had had first the envoy and then Binichi to worry about, and so he had been able to keep his mind off his own state.

His stomach was hollow with hunger that the last night's meager rations he had packed from the raft had done little to assuage. His muscles were cramped from the unusual exercise and he had the sick, dizzy feeling that comes from general overexposure. Also, right now, his throat was dry and aching for water.

He pulled himself up out of the leaves, stumbled to the edge of the pond and fell to hands and knees on its squashy margin. He drank; and as he raised his head and ran a wrist across his lips after quenching his thirst, the head of Binichi parted the surface almost where his lips had been.

"Time to go?" said the Lugh. He turned to one side and heaved himself up out onto the edge of the bank.

"We'll leave in just a little while," Chuck said. "I'm not fully awake yet." He sat back stiffly and exhaustedly on the ground and stretched his arms out to bring some life back into them. He levered himself to his feet and walked up and down, swinging his arms. After a little while his protesting muscles began to warm a little and loosen. He got one of the high-calorie candy bars from his food pack and chewed on it.

"All right," he said. And the envoy turned to lead the way up, out of the glen.

With the bit of food, the exercise, and the new warmth of the sun, Chuck began to feel better as they proceeded. They were breasting the near slopes of the hills now, and shortly before noon they came over the top of them, and paused to rest.

The land did not drop again, but swelled away in a gently rising plateau, into distance. And on its far horizon, insubstantial as clouds, rose the blue peaks of mountains.

"Base is over those mountains," said Chuck.

"Will we have to cross them?" The envoy's translator produced the words evenly, like a casual and unimportant query.

"No." Chuck turned to the Tomah. "How far in from the coast have we come so far?"

"I would estimate"—the translator hesitated a second over the translation of units—"thirty-two and some fraction of a mile."

"Another sixty miles, then," said Chuck, "and we should be within the range of the airfoils they'll have out looking for us." He looked again at the mountains and they seemed to waver before his eyes. Reaching up in an automatic gesture to brush the waveriness away, the back of his hand touched his forehead; and, startled, he pressed the hand against it. It was burning hot.

Feverish! thought Chuck And his mind somersaulted at the impossibility of the fact.

He could see the two others looking at him with the completely remote and unempathetic curiosity of peoples who had nothing in common with either his life or his death. A small rat's-jaw of fear gnawed at him suddenly. It had never occurred to him since the crash that there could be any danger that *he* would not make it safely back to Base. Now, for the first time, he faced that possibility. If the worst came to the worst, it came home to him suddenly, he could count on no help from either the Tomah, or the Lugh.

"What will they look like, these airfoils?" asked Binichi.

"Like a circle made out of bright material," said Chuck. "A round platform about twelve feet across."

"And there will be others of your people in them?"

"On them. No," said Chuck. "Anyway, I don't think so. We're too short of personnel. They operate on remote-beamed power from the ship and flash back pictures of the ground they cover. Once they send back a picture of us, Base'll know where to find us."

He levered himself painfully to his feet.

"Let's travel," he said.

They started out again. The walking was more level and easy now than it had been coming up through the hills. Plodding along, Chuck's eyes were suddenly attracted by a peculiarity of Binichi's back and sides. The Lugh was completely covered by a short close hair, which was snow-white under the belly, but shaded to a gray on the back. It seemed to Chuck, now, however, that this gray back hair had taken on a slight hint of rosiness.

"Hey!" he said, stopping. "You're getting sunburned."

The other two halted also; and Binichi looked up at him, inquiringly. Chuck repeated himself in simpler terms that his translator could handle.

"Let's go on," said Binichi, taking up the march again.

"Wait!" said Chuck, as he and the envoy moved to follow up the Lugh. "Don't you know that can be dangerous? Here—" He fumbled out of his own jacket. "We humans get sunburned, too, but we evidently aren't as susceptible as you. Now, I can tie the arms of this around your neck and you'll have some protection—"

Binichi halted suddenly and wheeled to face the human.

"You're intruding," said Binichi, "on something that is my own concern."

"But—" Chuck looked helplessly at him. "The sun is quite

strong in these latitudes. I don't think you understand—'' He turned to appeal to the Tomah. ''Tell him what the sun's like in a country like this.''

''Surely,'' said the envoy, ''this has nothing to do with you or me. If his health becomes imperfect, it will be an indication that he isn't fit to survive. He's only a Lugh; but certainly he has the right, like all living things, to make such a choice for himself.''

''But he might be mistaken—''

''If he is mistaken, it will be a sign that he is unfit to survive. I don't agree with Lughs—as you people know. But any creature has the basic right to entertain death if he so wishes. To interfere with him in that would be the highest immorality.''

''But don't you want to—'' began Chuck, incredulously, turning toward the Lugh.

''Let's go on,'' said Binichi, turning away.

They went on again.

After a while, the grasslands of the early plateau gave way to more forest.

Chuck was plodding along in the late hours of the afternoon with his eyes on the ground a few feet in front of him and his head singing, when a new sound began to penetrate his consciousness. He listened to it, more idly than otherwise, for some seconds—and then abruptly, it registered.

It was a noise like yelping, back along the trail he had just passed.

He checked and straightened and turned about. Binichi was no longer in sight.

''Binichi!'' he called. There was no answer, only the yelping. He began to run clumsily, back the way he had come.

Some eight or so yards back, he traced the yelping to a small clearing in a hollow. Breaking through the brush and trees that grew about its lip, he looked down on the Lugh. Binichi was braced at bay upon his clubbed tail, jaws agape, and turning to face half a dozen weasel-shaped creatures the size of small dogs that yelped and darted in and out at him, tearing and slashing.

The Lugh's sharp, tooth-studded jaws were more than a match for the jaws of any one of his attackers, but—here on land—they had many times his speed. No matter which way he turned, one was always at his back, and harrying him. But, like the envoy when he had been knocked into the sea, Binichi made no sound; and, although his eyes met those of Chuck, standing at the clearing edge, he gave no call for help.

Chuck looked about him desperately for a stick or stone he could use as a club. But the ground was bare of everything but the light wands of the bushes, and the trees overhead had all green, sound limbs firmly attached to their trunks. There was a stir in the bushes beside him.

Chuck turned and saw the envoy. He pushed through to stand beside Chuck, and also looked down at the fight going on in the clearing.

"Come on!" said Chuck, starting down into the clearing. Then he halted, for the envoy had not moved. "What's the matter?"

"Matter?" said the envoy, looking at him. "I don't understand."

"Those things will kill him!"

"You"—the envoy turned his head as if peering at Chuck —"appear to think we should interfere. You people have this strange attitude to the natural occurrences of life that I've noticed before."

"Do *you* people just stand by and watch each other get killed?"

"Of course not. Where another Tomah is concerned, it is of course different."

"He saved *your* life from those fish!" cried Chuck.

"I believe you asked him to. You were perfectly free to ask, just as he was perfectly free to accept or refuse. I'm in no way responsible for anything either of you have done."

"He's an intelligent being!" said Chuck desperately. "Like you. Like me. We're all alike."

"Certainly we aren't," said the envoy, stiffening. "You and I are not at all alike, except that we are both civilized. He's not even that. He's a Lugh."

"I told him he'd promised to sit down at Base and discuss with you," cried Chuck, his tongue loosened by the fever. "I said he was dodging his promise if he let you die. And he went out and saved you. But you won't save him."

The envoy turned his head to look at Binichi, now all but swarmed under by the predators.

"Thank you for correcting me," he said. "I hadn't realized there could be honor in this Lugh."

He went down the slope of the hollow in a sudden, blurring rush that seemingly moved him off at top speed from a standing start. He struck the embattled group like a projectile and emerged coated by the predators. For a split second it seemed to Chuck that he had merely thrown another life into the jaws of the attackers. And then the Tomah claw glittered and flashed, right and left like a black scimitar, lightning-swift out of the ruck—and the clearing was emptied, except for four furry bodies that twitched or lay about the hollow.

The envoy turned to the nearest and began to eat. Without a glance or word directed at his rescuer, Binichi, bleeding from a score of superficial cuts and scratches, turned about and climbed slowly up the slope of the hollow to where Chuck stood.

"Shall we go on?" he said.

Chuck looked past him at the feeding envoy.

"Perhaps we should wait for him," he said.

"Why?" said Binichi. "It's up to him to keep up, if he wants to. The Tomah is no concern of ours."

He headed off in the direction they had been going. Chuck waggled his head despairingly, and plodded after.

IV.

The envoy caught up to them a little further on; and shortly after that, as the rays of the setting sun were beginning to level through the trees, giving the whole forest a cathedral look, they came on water, and stopped for the night.

It seemed to Chuck that the sun went down very quickly—quicker than it ever had before; and a sudden chill struck through to his very bones. Teeth chattering, he managed to start a fire and drag enough dead wood to it to keep it going while they slept.

Binichi had gone into the waters of the small lake a few yards off, and was not to be seen. But through the long, fever-ridden night hours that were a patchwork of dizzy wakefulness and dreams and half-dreams, Chuck was aware of the smooth, dark insectlike head of the Tomah watching him across the fire with what seemed to be an absorbing fascination.

Toward morning, he slept. He awoke to find the sun risen

and Binichi already out of the lake. Chuck did not feel as bad, now, as he had earlier. He moved in a sort of fuzziness; and, although his body was slow responding, as if it was something operated by his mind from such a remote distance that mental directions to his limbs took a long time to be carried out, it was not so actively uncomfortable.

They led off, Chuck in the middle as before. They were moving out of the forest now, into more open country where the trees were interspersed with meadows. Chuck remembered now that he had not eaten in some time; but when he chewed on his food, the taste was uninteresting and he put it back in his pack.

Nor was he too clear about the country he was traversing. It was there all right, but it seemed more than a little unreal. Sometimes things, particularly things far off, appeared distorted. And he began remarking expressions on the faces of his two companions that he would not have believed physically possible to them. Binichi's mouth, in particular, had become remarkably mobile. It was no longer fixed by physiology into a grin. Watching out of the corner of his eye, Chuck caught glimpses of it twisted into all sorts of shapes; sad, sly, cheerful, frowning. And the Tomah was not much better. As the sun mounted up the clear arch of the sky, Chuck discovered the envoy squinting and winking at him, as if to convey some secret message.

"S'all right—s'all right—" mumbled Chuck. "I won't tell." And he giggled suddenly at the joke that he couldn't tell because he really didn't know what all the winking was about.

"I don't understand," said the envoy, winking away like mad.

"S'all right—s'all right—" said Chuck.

He discovered after a time that the other two were no longer close beside him. Peering around, he finally located them walking together at some distance off from him. Discussing something, no doubt, something confidential. He wandered, taking the pitch and slope of the ground at random, stumbling a little now and then when the angle of his footing changed. He was aware in vague fashion that he had drifted into an area with little rises and unexpected sinkholes, their edges tangled with brush. He caught himself on one of the sinkholes, swayed back to safety, tacked off to his right . . .

Suddenly he landed hard on something. The impact drove

all the air out of his lungs, so that he fought to breathe—and in that struggle he lost the cobwebs surrounding him for the first time that day.

He had not been aware of his fall, but now he saw that he lay half on his back, some ten feet down from the edge of one of the holes. He tried to get up, but one leg would not work. Panic cut through him like a knife.

"Help!" he shouted. His voice came out hoarse and strange-sounding. "Help!"

He called again; and after what seemed a very long time, the head of the envoy poked over the edge of the sinkhole and looked down at him.

"Get me out of here!" cried Chuck. "Help me out."

The envoy stared at him.

"Give me a hand!" said Chuck. "I can't climb up by myself. I'm hurt."

"I don't understand," said the envoy.

"I think my leg's broken. What's the matter with you?" Now that he had mentioned it, as if it had been lying there waiting for its cue, the leg that would not work sent a sudden, vicious stab of pain through him. And close behind this came a swelling agony that pricked Chuck to fury. "Don't you hear me? I said, pull me out of here! My leg's broken. I can't stand on it!"

"You are damaged?" said the envoy

"Of course I'm damaged!"

The envoy stared down at Chuck for a long moment. When he spoke again, his words struck an odd, formalistic note in Chuck's fevered brain.

"It is regrettable," said the envoy, "that you are no longer in perfect health."

And he turned away, and disappeared. Above Chuck's straining eyes, the edges of the hole and the little patch of sky beyond them tilted, spun about like a scene painted on a whirling disk, and shredded away into nothingness.

At some time during succeeding events he woke up again; but nothing was really clear or certain until he found himself looking up into the face of Doc Burgis, who was standing over him, with a finger on his pulse.

"How do you feel?" said Burgis.

"I don't know," said Chuck. "Where am I?"

"Back at Base," said Burgis, letting go of his wrist. "Your leg is knitting nicely and we've knocked out your pneumonia. You've been under sedation. A couple more days' rest and you'll be ready to run again."

"That's nice," said Chuck; and went back to sleep.

V.

Three days later he was recovered enough to take a ride in his motorized go-cart over to Roy Marlie's office. He found Roy there, and his uncle.

"Hi, Tommy," said Chuck, wheeling through the door. "Hi, Chief."

"How you doing, son?" asked Member Thomas Wagnall. "How's the leg?"

"Doc says I can start getting around on surgical splints in a day or two," Chuck looked at them both. "Well, isn't anybody going to tell me what happened?"

"Those two natives were carrying you when we finally located the three of you," said Tommy, "and we—"

"They were?" said Chuck.

"Why, yes." Tommy looked closely at him. "Didn't you know that?"

"I—I was unconscious before they started carrying me, I guess," said Chuck.

"At any rate, we got you all back here in good shape." Tommy went across the room to a built-in cabinet and came back carrying a bottle of scotch, capped with three glasses, and a bowl of ice. "Ready for that drink now?"

"Try me," said Chuck, not quite licking his lips. Tommy made a second trip for charged water and brought it back. He passed the drinks around.

"How," he said, raising his glass. They all drank in appreciative silence.

"Well," said Tommy, setting his glass down on the top of Roy's desk, "I suppose you heard about the conference." Chuck glanced over at Roy, who was evincing a polite interest.

"I heard they had a brief meeting and put everything off for a while," said Chuck.

"Until they had a chance to talk things over *between them-*

selves, yes,'' said Tommy. He was watching his nephew somewhat closely. "Rather surprising development. We hardly
know where we stand now, do we?"

"Oh, I guess it'll work out all right," said Chuck.

"You do?"

"Why, yes," said Chuck. He slowly sipped at his glass
again and held it up to the light of the window. "Good
scotch."

"*All right!*" Tommy's thick fist came down with a sudden
bang on the desk top. "I'll quit playing around. I may be
nothing but a chairside Earth-lubber, but I'll tell you one
thing. There's one thing I've developed in twenty years of
politics and that's a nose for smells. And something about this
situation smells! I don't know what, but it smells. And I want
to find out what it is."

Chuck and Roy looked at each other.

"Why, Member," said Roy. "I don't follow you."

"You follow me all right," said Tommy. He took a gulp
from his glass and blew out an angry breath. "All right—off
the record. But tell me!"

Roy smiled.

"You tell him, Chuck," he said.

Chuck grinned in his turn.

"Well, I'll put it this way, Tommy," he said. "You remember how I explained the story about Big Brother Charlie
that gave us the name for this project?"

"What about it?" said the Member.

"Maybe I didn't go into quite enough detail. You see," said
Chuck, "the two youngest brothers were twins who lived right
next door to each other in one town. They used to fight regu-
larly until their wives got fed up with it. And when that happened, their wives would invite Big Brother Charlie from the
next town to come and visit them."

Tommy was watching him with narrowed eyes.

"What happened, of course," said Chuck, lifting his glass
again, "was that after about a week, the twins weren't fighting
each other at all." He drank.

"All right. All right," said Tommy. "I'll play straight man.
Why weren't they fighting with each other?"

"Because," said Chuck, putting his glass back down again,
"they were both too busy fighting with Big Brother Charlie."

Tommy stared for a long moment. Then he grunted and sat

back in his chair, as if he had just had the wind knocked out of him.

"You see," said Roy, leaning forward over his desk, "what we were required to do here was something impossible. You just *don't* change centuries-old attitudes of distrust and hatred overnight. Trying to get the Lugh and the Tomah to like each other by any pressures we could bring to bear was like trying to move mountains with toothpicks. Too much mass for too little leverage. But we *could* change the attitudes of both of them toward us."

"And what's that supposed to mean?" demanded Tommy, glaring at him.

"Why, we might—and did—arrange for them to find out that, like the twins, they had more in common with each other than either one of them had with Big Brother Charlie. Not that we wanted them, God forbid, to unite in actively *fighting* Big Brother: We do need this planet as a space depot. But we wanted to make them see that they two form one unit—with us on the outside. They don't like each other any better now, but they've begun to discover a reason for hanging together."

"I'm not sure I follow you," said Tommy dryly.

"What I'm telling you," said Roy, "is that we arranged a demonstration to bring home to them the present situation. They weren't prepared to share this world with each other. But when it came to their both sharing it with a third life form, they began to realize that the closer relative might see more eye-to-eye with them than the distant one. Chuck was under strict orders not to intervene, but to manage things so that each of them would be forced to solve the problems of the other, with no assistance from Earth or its technology."

"Brother," Chuck grunted, "the way it all worked out I didn't have to 'manage' a thing. The 'accident' was more thorough than we'd planned, and I was pretty much without the assistance of our glorious technology myself. Each of them had problems I couldn't have solved if I'd wanted to . . . but the other one could."

"Well," Roy nodded, "they are the natives, after all. We are the aliens. Just *how* alien, it was Chuck's job to demonstrate."

"You mean—" exploded Tommy, "that you threw away a half-million-dollar vehicle—that you made that crash-landing in the ocean—on purpose!"

"Off the record, Tommy," said Chuck, holding up a re-minding finger. "As for the pot, it's on an undersea peak in forty fathoms. As soon as you can get us some more equipment it'll be duck soup to salvage it."

"Off the record be hanged!" roared Tommy. "Why, you might have killed them. You might have had one or the other species up in arms! You might—"

"We thought it was worth the risk," said Chuck mildly. "After all, remember I was sticking my own neck into the same dangers."

"You thought!" Tommy turned a seething glance on his nephew. He thrust himself out of his chair and stamped up and down the office in a visible effort to control his temper.

"Progress is not made by rules alone," misquoted Chuck complacently, draining the last scotch out of his glass. "Come back and sit down, Tommy. It's all over now."

The older man came glowering back and wearily plumped in his chair.

"All right," he said. "I said off the record, but I didn't expect this. Do you two realize what it is you've just done? Risked the lives of two vital members of intelligent races necessary to our future! Violated every principle of ordinary diplomacy in a harebrained scheme that had nothing more than a wild notion to back it up! And to top it off, involved me—*me*, a Member of the Government! If this comes out nobody will ever believe I didn't know about it!"

"All right, Tommy," said Chuck. "We hear you. Now, what are you going to do about it?"

Earth District Member 439 Thomas L. Wagnall blew out a furious breath.

"Nothing!" he said, violently. "Nothing."

"That's what I thought," said Chuck. "Pass the scotch."

ACT OF CREATION

Now that I have had time to think it over, the quite commonsense explanation occurs to me that old Jonas Wellman must have added an extra, peculiar circuit to cause the one unusual response. He was quite capable of it, of course—technically, that is. And I don't know but that he was equally capable of it psychologically. Nevertheless, at the time, the whole thing shook me up badly.

I had gone up to see him on a traditionally unpleasant duty. His son, Alvin, had been in my outfit at the time of Flander's Charge, off the Vegan Warhold. The boy was liaison officer from the Earth Draft, and he went with the aft gun platform, the Communications Dorsai Regulars, when we got pinched between a light cruiser and one of those rearmed freighters the Vegans filled their assault line with.

The cruiser stood off at a little under a thousand kilometers and boxed us with her light guns. While we were occupied, the freighter came up out of the sun and hit us with a CO beam, before we caught her in our laterals and blew her to bits. It was their CO beam that did it for Alvin and the rest.

At any rate, Alvin had been on loan to us, so to speak, and, as commanding officer, I owed a duty-call to his surviving relatives. At that time, I hadn't connected his last name—

110

Wellman—with Jonas Wellman. Even if I had, I would have had to think a long minute before remembering just who Jonas Wellman was.

Most people using robots nowadays never heard of him. Of course, I had, because we Dorsai mercenaries were the first to use them in combat. When I did make the connection, I remember it struck me as rather odd, because I had never heard Alvin mention his father.

I had duty time-off after that—and, since we were in First Quadrant area, I shuttled to Arcturus and took the short hop to Sol. I had never been on the home world before and I was rather interested to see what Earth looked like. As usual, with such things, it was somewhat of a disappointment. It's a small world, anyway, and, since it lost its standing as a commercial power, a lot of the old city areas have been grubbed up and turned into residential districts.

In fact, the planet is hardly more than one vast suburb, nowadays. I was told that there's a movement under way to restore some of the old districts as historical shrines, but they'd need Outsystem funds for that, and I can't, myself, see many of the large powers sparing an appropriation at the present time.

Still, there's something about the planet. You can't forget that this was where we all started. I landed in the South Pacific, and took a commuter's rocket to the Mojave. From there, I put in a call to Jonas Wellman, who lived someplace north and west of the mountain range there—I forget the name of it. He was pleased to hear from me, and invited me up immediately.

I located one of these little automatic taxi-ships, and we puttered north by northwest for about half an hour and finally set down in a small parking area in the Oregon woods. There was nothing there but the glassy rectangle of the area itself, plus an automatic call station for the taxis. A few people were waiting around for their ships to arrive, and, as I sat down, what looked like an A-5 robot came across the field to meet me.

When he got close, I saw he wasn't an A-5, but something similar—possibly something a bit special that Jonas had designed for himself.

"Commandant Jiel?" he asked.

"That's right," I said.

I followed him across the parking area, toward a private

hopper. The few people we passed on the way turned their backs as we passed, with a deliberateness and uniformity that was too pointed to be accidental. For a moment, it occurred to me that I might be the cause of their reaction—certain creeds and certain peoples, who have experienced wars, have no use for the mercenary soldier.

But this was the home world nobody would think of attacking, even if they had a reason for doing so, which, of course, Earth will never be able to give them, as long as the large powers exist.

Belatedly, it occurred to me that the robot with me might be the cause. I turned to look at him. An A-5—particularly an A-5—is built to resemble the human form. This was, as I have said, a refined model. I mulled the matter over, trying to phrase the question, so I could get information out of the mechanical.

"Are there Anti-R's in the community here?" I asked finally.

"Yes, sir," he said.

Well, that explained it. The AR's are, in general, folk with an unpleasant emotional reaction to robots. They are psychopathic in my opinion and in that of any man who has used robots commercially or for military purposes. They find robots resembling the human form—particularly the A-5 model and the rest of the A- series—*obscene, disgusting,* and so forth. Some worlds which have experienced wars are almost completely AR.

I didn't, however, expect to find it on Earth, especially so close to the home of Jonas Wellman. Still, a prophet in his own country, or however the old saying goes.

We took a ground car, which the robot drove, and, eventually, reached a curious anachronism of a house, set off in the woods by itself. It was a long, rambling structure, made in frame of native stone and wood, the only civilized thing about it being vibratory weather-screens between the pillars of the frame, to keep out the rain and wind.

It had a strange aura about it, as if it were a dwelling place, old not so much in years as in memories, as if something about it went back to the very dawn of the race. The rain and the falling night, as we approached it, heightened this illusion so that the tall pines, clustered closely about house and lawn, seemed almost primeval, seemed to enclose us in an ancestral past.

Yet, the house itself was cheerful. Its lighting was inlaid in the archaic framing, and it glowed internally, with a subdued, casual illumination that did not dim the flames in a wide, central fireplace. Real flames from actual burning wood—not an illusion! It touched me, somehow. Few people, unless they have seen the real article, appreciate the difference between the actual flames of a real fire, and those of an illusion.

I, who have experienced the reality, on strange planets, of a need for warmth and light, know the difference very well. It is a subjective reaction, not easily put into words. Perhaps, if you will forgive my straining to be fanciful, who am not a fanciful man, it's this—there are stories in the real flames. I know it can mean nothing to those of you who have never seen it but—try it for yourself, sometime.

Jonas Wellman, himself, came forward to meet me, when we stepped through the front screen lens. He was a short, slim man, a little bent about the shoulders, who had let his hair go completely white. He had a gnome's face, all wrinkled, sad and merry in the same instant. He came forward and held out his hand.

"Commandant Jiel," he said.

His voice was as warm as the hissing flames of his fireplace. I took his hand without hesitation, for I am no hater of old traditions.

"Good of you to come," he said. "Sorry about the rain. The district requires it for our trees, and we like our trees around here."

He turned and led the way to a little conversation area. The robot glided on silent feet behind us, towering over both of us. Though I have the hereditary Dorsai height, the A-5 run to a two-and-a-quarter-meter length, which is possibly one of the reasons the AR dislike them so.

"Sit down, Commandant, sit down, please," Jonas said. "Adam, would you bring us some drinks, please? What would you like, Commandant?"

"Plain ethyl and water, thanks," I said. "It's what we get used to on duty."

He smiled at me in the light of the fire, which was dancing to our right and throwing ruddy lights on his time-marked face.

"Whatever is your pleasure," he said.

The robot brought the glasses. Jonas was drinking something also colorless. I remember I meant to ask him what it was, but never got around to doing so. Instead, I asked him about the robot.

"Adam?" I said.

Jonas chuckled.

"He was to be the first of a new series," he answered.

"I didn't mean that," I said. "I meant your naming him at all. Very few people do, nowadays."

"The vogue has passed," he said. "But I've had him for a long time, and I live alone here." The last words reminded us both of my errand, and he stopped rather abruptly. He hurried back into conversation, to bridge the gap. "I suppose you know about my connection with robotics and robots?"

"We used them on Kemelman for land scouts, first, eighty years or so back."

"That's right," he said, his gnome's face saddening a little. "I'd forgotten."

"They were very successful."

"I suppose they were—militarily." He looked squarely at me, suddenly. "No offense to you Dorsai, Commandant, but I was not in favor of military use of my robots. Only—the decision was taken out of my hands. I lost control of the manufacturing and licensing rights early."

"No offense," I said, but I looked at him curiously. "I didn't know that."

"Oh, yes," he said. "It was a little too big for one man, anyway. First the Earth Council grabbed it, then the Solar Commission. Then it went out in all directions, with every system grabbing a chunk and setting up their own manufactories and regulators."

"I'm sorry to hear that," I said.

"Don't be." He shook his head, sticking out his lower lip like someone deprecating something already so small as to be beneath notice. "It was probably inevitable. Then, I think my robots have done more harm than good in the long run, no matter what's been accomplished with them." He shook his head again, smiling. "Not that I was always so resigned to the situation."

"No?"

"No—I had my dreams, when I was younger. To build a better universe, to better people—I was an idealist."

"An idealist?" I repeated. "I don't know the word."

"It's an old one," he answered. "Almost lost its meaning, now. It means—well, that you have a very high opinion of the human race, or people. That you expect the best *of* them, and want the best *for* them."

I laughed. "It sounds like being in love with everyone at once."

He nodded, smiling.

"Something like that, Commandant—perhaps not so violent. Tone it down a little and call it being fond of people. I'm a fond sort of person, I suppose. I've been fond of a great many things. Of people, of my robots, of my first wife, of . . ." His voice trailed off and he looked into the firelight. He sighed. "Perhaps," he added, "you'd better tell me about my son, now, Commandant."

I told him briefly. It is always best that way. Make it like a news report, impersonal, then sit back for the questions. There are always the questions.

Jonas Wellman was no different. He sat a little longer than most, after I had finished, staring into the fire, but he came to it at last.

"Commandant," he said, "what did you think of Alvin?"

"Why," I told him, "I didn't know him too well, you know. He was liaison officer from another outfit—almost a visitor aboard our ship. We had different customs, and he kept pretty much to himself." I stopped, but when I saw him still waiting, I had to go on. "He was very quiet, a good sort of officer, not self-conscious with us Dorsai, the way a lot of outsiders are . . ."

I talked on, trying to bring my memory of Alvin Wellman back into focus, but it was not too good. You try to remember the best on these occasions, to forget the worst. The truth was, there was very little to remember. Young Wellman had been like a ghost among us. The only clear memory I could bring to mind was of his sitting back in his corner of the table at mess, his pale young features withdrawn from the place and the technical conversation that went on among the rest of us.

"He was a good man," I wound up finally. "We all liked him."

"Yes." The old man lifted his face from the flames. "He was drafted, you know."

"Oh?" I said—although, of course, I had known it perfectly well. It was why we had called the Solar Contingent the Earth Draft among ourselves. None of them had any real stake in the war, and few had wanted to come. It was Arcturus' doing, as everybody knew. The home system is under Arcturus' thumb, and probably always will be. But you don't tell that to an old man who has lost his only son in a war resulting from such a situation.

"His mother never wanted him to go—but there was no choice." Jonas picked up his drink, sipped it, as an old man will, then put it down again. But his voice was a little stronger when he went on.

"His mother was my second wife, you know. We separated when Alvin was six. That was—that was . . ." His voice took on a fretful note. For the first time a true note of his age rang through it. "When was that, Adam?"

"Eighteen years ago," said the robot suddenly, startling me. I had almost forgotten that he was still with us. His voice, coming unexpectedly out of the fire-cast shadows behind us, made me start.

"Oh, yes—yes. Eighteen years ago," said Jonas, with a sigh of pleasure and relief. He looked over at me with something that was almost like shyness. "Adam is my memory," he said. "Everything that I forget, he remembers—everything! Tell the Commandant what the house was like, then, Adam."

"It was as it is now," said the robot. "The lawn was the same, except that we had a bed of roses along the south edge."

"Ah, yes—those roses," said Jonas, nodding. "Alvin was very fond of those roses. Even as a baby—even when he stuck himself with the thorns."

"Did they have thorns?" I asked, surprised.

"Yes," he answered. "Yes, indeed. I'm very old-fashioned in some ways, Commandant, as you can tell by this house. Something in me has always yearned toward the past. That's why I like it here, with the trees all around me and the mountains standing over and behind them, unchanging, year after year."

"And you were the man who came up with the first practical humanoid robots," I said.

"Why should that surprise you?" He looked at me almost wonderingly. "I didn't intend them to lead us farther away from old virtues, but back to them again."

I shook my head. "I don't see how," I said.

"Why, I wanted to set people free," he said. "I wanted to unite their hands, and their minds. The average man is essentially good, Commandant. A hundred and forty years of life have never changed my mind about that. He wants to be fond of his fellowman and will, given half a chance."

I shook my head again, but without saying anything. I did not want to argue with him.

"Love is life," he said, "and life is love. All the accidents in the world can't prove that false. Did the accident that took my first wife's life prove that I didn't love her when she was alive? Did the accidental combination of political powers that took my robots from me negate the love for people that caused me to create those robots in the first place?

"Did the accident that my second wife never really loved me deny the life that was given to Alvin, or my love for him, or his for me—before she took him away? I tell you, he loved me as a baby—didn't he, Adam?"

"He loved you, Jonas."

"And I was very fond of him. I was already an old man then. I didn't remarry for many, many years, after my first— my Elaine—died. I thought I would never marry again. But then *she* came along—and she gave me Alvin. But then she took him away again, for no good reason, except that she knew I was fond of him, and wanted him. She was very bitter against me for not having what she believed I had when she married me." He paused.

"Money," said the robot quietly.

"Yes, money. She thought I still controlled some part of the robot franchise, here in the system, that no one knew about. She was too cautious, too clever, to check fully before she married me. After we were married, it was too late.

"She tried to make a go of it, though, which is much more than another woman might have done in her place. She gave me Alvin. But she had never really liked me, and her dislike grew worse and worse, until she couldn't stand it. So she left me, and took him."

He stopped. The fire flickered on the pillars of the house.

"That's too bad," I said awkwardly. "It—is she still alive?"

"No." He said it abruptly. "She died shortly after Alvin was drafted. I went to see her, but she wouldn't see me. And so, she died. It was then I learned that Alvin was gone. She hadn't told me about the draft.''

"I see," I said.

"I was fond of her, too—still," he went on. "But it hurt me that I had not been able to see my son, before he went off to die, so many millions and millions of miles away. If she had left him with me as a boy, I would have taught him to love people, to love everything as I myself have. Perhaps he would have been a success, where I have been a failure." He flung up his head and turned suddenly to the robot.

"Adam, I've been a failure!" he cried.

"No," said the robot.

The old man heaved a heavy sigh. Slowly, the tension leaked out of him, and he slumped back in his chair. His eyes were abstracted, and on the fire.

"No," I said. "In my opinion, you're no failure, Mr. Wellman. You have to judge success or failure by concrete things. You set out to give robots to people, and you did. That's the one big accomplishment of your life."

"No." He shook his head, his eyes still locked in the heart of the fire. "Love is life. Love should create life to some good, purposeful end. I poured out my love, and all I created came to a dead end. Not the theory, but I fell down. I have Adam tell me that I didn't—but this is the sort of soothing syrup an old man feeds himself. Well . . ."

He roused himself. He looked at me and I was surprised at the change in Wellman's face. The sad and merry lines were all fallen into the still mask of great age. It was a face which sees at once the empty future and the lid of the coffin closing soon upon it.

"I get tired quickly nowadays," he said. "If you'll forgive me, Commandant, I'll have Adam take you back to the taxi-area. Thank you for coming this long distance to tell me about Alvin."

He held out his hand. I took it briefly, and stood up. "It's nothing," I said. "We mercenaries spend our lives in moving from one place to another. I was close as star-distances go. Good-by, Mr. Wellman."

He looked up at me from the depths of his chair. "One thing, Commandant," he said. "Just one more thing—were people fond—did the men on your ship really *like* Alvin?"

"Why . . ." I said, fumbling, for the truth was that none of us had known the young man well enough to like or dislike him—and the question had caught me off balance. "Why—they liked him well enough."

The old man sagged. "Yes," he said. His downcast eyes, as if drawn by some force greater than the life within him, wandered back to the fire. "Well, thank you again, Commandant."

"It was nothing. Good-by," I said.

I offered my hand again, but he did not see it. He was seated staring into the flames, seeing something I could not imagine. I left him that way.

Outside, the robot opened the door of the ground car for me and slid behind the controls himself. The rain had stopped falling, but the night was heavy and dark. We moved silently down the road, man and mechanical, behind a little yellow pool of light dancing before us from the headlights.

For some time, I sat without saying anything, thinking to myself of odd things the old man's words had somehow conjured up within me—memories of the Dorsai Worlds, of Hevflum, my planet, of the cobalt seas beside our home in Tunisport, of the women of our family—of my grandfather, probably dead by now. What I thought about them, I don't know. I only know that I *did* think of them, one after the other, like a man counting over his possessions.

I roused myself at last, to become conscious of the robot beside me. We were almost at the parking area, and I could make out my waiting taxi, parked off to one side in the shadows.

"Over there," I directed the robot.

"Yes, sir," he said.

He turned the ground car a trifle in that direction, and we rolled up beside the taxi. He got out, went around to open the door on my side of the car, and let me out. I stepped from floor cushion to the glassy surface of the area and looked at the tall, black metal body of the robot, a full head above me in height.

"Adam . . ." I said.

"Sir?"

But I found I had no words for what seemed to be inside me.

"Nothing," I said.

I stepped up to the entrance of the taxi, closed the door behind me, and moved forward, into the pilot's seat. Out through the window beside me, I could see Adam standing silently, his head now at last a little below mine. I started the engine, then, on sudden impulse, throttled back to idling power and set the window down. I leaned out of it.

"Adam, come here," I ordered.

The robot took two steps forward, so that he was standing just below the window.

"When you get back to Mr. Wellman," I said, "give him the following message from me. Say that—that . . ."

But it was no use. There was still nothing for me to say. I wanted, with a strange desperation, to send some word to Jonas Wellman, to prove to him that he was not alone in the world, that his love had not failed in its task of creation as we both knew it had. But what could I say in the face of the facts?

"Never mind, *Cancel!*" I said angrily, and turned away, reaching for the throttle. But, just as my hand touched it, the robot's voice drew me back to the window.

"Commandant," it said.

I turned and looked out. The robot had taken a step nearer, and, as I looked, his head swiveled back on its smooth bearings, his face raised to mine. I remember the twin dull gleam of his red eye-lens scanners coming up to me in the shadowy dimness, like two embers in a fire uncovered by a breath and glowing into sudden life.

"Rest easy, Commandant," he said. "I love him."

IDIOT SOLVANT

The afternoon sun, shooting the gap of the missing slat in the venetian blind on the window of Art Willoughby's small rented room, splashed fair in Art's eyes, blinding him.

"Blast!" muttered Art. "Got to do something about that sun."

He flipped one long, lean hand up as an eyeshield and leaned forward once more over the university news sheet, unaware that he had reacted with his usual gesture and litany to the sun in his eyes. His mouth watered. He spread out his sharp elbows on the experiment-scarred surface of his desk and reread the ad.

Volunteers for medical research testing. $1.60 hr., rm., board. Dr. Henry Rapp, Room 432, A Bldg., University Hospital.

"Board—" echoed Art aloud, once more unaware he had spoken. He licked his lips hungrily. *Food,* he thought. Plus wages. And hospital food was supposed to be good. If they would just let him have all he wanted . . .

Of course, it would be worth it for the dollar-sixty an hour alone.

"I'll be sensible," thought Art. "I'll put it in the bank and just draw out what I need. Let's see—one week's work, say—seven times twenty-four times sixteen. Two-six-eight-eight—to the tenth. Two hundred sixty-eight dollars and eighty cents. . ."

That much would support him for—mentally, he toted up his daily expenses. Ordinary expenses, that was. Room, a dollar-fifty. One-and-a-half-pound loaf of day-old bread at half price—thirteen cents. Half a pound of peanut butter, at ninety-eight cents for the three-pound economy size jar—seventeen cents roughly. One all-purpose vitamin capsule—ten cents. Half a head of cabbage, or whatever was in season and cheap—approximately twelve cents. Total, for shelter with all utilities paid and a change of sheets on the bed once a week, plus thirty-two hundred calories a day—two dollars and two cents.

Two dollars and two cents. Art sighed. Sixty dollars and sixty cents a month for mere existence. It was heartbreaking. When sixty dollars would buy a fine double magnum of imported champagne at half a dozen of the better restaurants in town, or a 1954 used set of the Encyclopedia Britannica, or the parts from a mail-order house so that he could build himself a little ocean-hopper shortwave receiver so that he could tune in on foreign language broadcasts and practice understanding German, French, and Italian.

Art sighed. He had long ago come to the conclusion that since the two billion other people in the world could not very well all be out of step at the same time, it was probably he who was the odd one. Nowadays he no longer tried to fight the situation, but let himself reel uncertainly through life, sustained by the vague, persistent conviction that somewhere, somehow, in some strange fashion destiny would eventually be bound to call on him to have a profound effect on his fellowmen.

It was a good twenty-minute walk to the university. Art scrambled lankily to his feet, snatched an ancient leather jacket off the hook holding his bagpipes, put his slide rule up on top of the poetry anthologies in the bookcase so he would know where to find it again—that being the most unlikely place, Q.E.D.—turned off his miniature electric furnace in which he had been casting up a gold pawn for his chess set, left some bread and peanut butter for his pet raccoon, now asleep in the wastebasket, and hurried off, closing the door.

"There's one more," said Margie Hansen, Dr. Hank Rapp's lab assistant. She hesitated. "I think you'd better see him." Hank looked up from his desk, surprised. He was a short, cheerful, tough-faced man in his late thirties.

"Why?" he said. "Some difficulties? Don't sign him up if you don't want to."

"No. No . . . I just think maybe you'd better talk to him. He passed the physical all right. It's just . . . well, you have a look at him."

"I don't get it," said Hank. "But send him in."

She opened the door behind her and leaned out through it.

"Mr. Willoughby, will you come in now?" She stood aside and Art entered. "This is Dr. Rapp, Mr. Willoughby. Doctor, this is Art Willoughby." She went out rather hastily, closing the door behind her.

"Sit down," said Hank automatically. Art sat down, and Hank blinked a little at his visitor. The young man sitting opposite him resembled nothing so much as an unbearded Abe Lincoln. A *thin* unbearded Abe Lincoln, if it was possible to imagine our sixteenth President as being some thirty pounds lighter than he actually had been.

"*Are* you a student at the university here?" asked Hank, staring at the decrepit leather jacket.

"Well, yes," said Art, hoping the other would not ask him what college he was in. He had been in six of them, from Theater Arts to Engineering. His record in each was quite honorable. There was nothing to be ashamed of—it was just always a little bit difficult to explain.

"Well—" said Hank. He saw now why Margie had hesitated. But if the man was in good enough physical shape, there was no reason to refuse him. Hank made up his mind. "Has the purpose of this test been explained to you?"

"You're testing a new sort of stay-awake pill, aren't you?" said Art. "Your nurse told me all about it."

"Lab assistant," corrected Hank automatically. "There's no reason you can think of yourself, is there, why you shouldn't be one of the volunteers?"

"Well, no. I . . . I don't usually sleep much," said Art painfully.

"That's no barrier." Hank smiled. "We'll just keep you

awake until you get tired. How much do you sleep?" he asked, to put the younger man at his ease at least a little.

"Oh . . . six or seven hours."

"That's a little less than average. Nothing to get in our way . . . why, what's wrong?" said Hank, sitting up suddenly, for Art was literally struggling with his conscience, and his Abe Lincoln face was twisted unhappily.

"A . . . a week," blurted Art.

"A week! Are you—" Hank broke off, took a good look at his visitor and decided he was not kidding. Or at least, believed himself that he was not kidding. "You mean, less than an hour a night?"

"Well, I usually wait to the end of the week—Sunday morning's a good time. Everybody else is sleeping then, anyway. I get it over all at once—" Art leaned forward and put both his long hands on Hank's desk pleadingly. "But can't you test me, anyway, Doctor? I need this job. Really, I'm desperate. If you could use me as a control, or something—"

"Don't worry," said Hank grimly. "You've got the job. In fact if what you say is true, you've got more of a job than the rest of the volunteers. This is something we're all going to want to see!"

"Well," said Hank, ten days later. "Willoughby surely wasn't kidding."

Hank was talking to Dr. Arlie Bohn, of the Department of Psychology. Arlie matched Hank's short height, but outdid him otherwise to the tune of some fifty pounds and fifteen years. They were sitting in Hank's office, smoking cigarettes over the remains of their bag lunches.

"You don't think so?" said Arlie, lifting blond eyebrows toward his half-bare, round skull.

"Arlie! Ten days!"

"And no hallucinations?"

"None."

"Thinks his nurses are out to poison him? Doesn't trust the floor janitor?"

"No. No. No!"

Arlie blew out a fat wad of smoke.

"I don't believe it," he announced.

"I beg your pardon!"

"Oh—not you, Hank. No insults intended. But this boy of

yours is running some kind of a con. Sneaking some sort of stimulant when you aren't looking.''

"Why would he do that? We'd be glad to give him all the stimulants he wants. He won't take them. And even if he was sneaking something—ten days, Arlie! Ten days and he looks as if he just got up after a good eight hours in his own bed.'' Hank smashed his half-smoked cigarette out in the ashtray. "He's not cheating. He's a freak.''

"You can't be that much of a freak.''

"Oh, can't you?'' said Hank. "Let me tell you some more about him. Usual body temperature—about one degree above normal average.''

"Not unheard of. You know that.''

"Blood pressure a hundred and five systolic, sixty-five diastolic. Pulse, fifty-five a minute. Height, six feet four, weight when he came in here a hundred and forty-two. We've been feeding him upward of six thousand calories a day since he came in and I swear he still looks hungry. No history of childhood diseases. All his wisdom teeth. No cavities in any teeth. Shall I go on?''

"How is he mentally?''

"I checked up with the university testing bureau. They rate him in the genius range. He's started in six separate colleges and dropped out of each one. No trouble with grades. He gets top marks for a while, then suddenly stops going to class, accumulates a flock of incompletes, and transfers into something else. Arlie,'' said Hank, breaking off suddenly, lowering his voice and staring hard at the other, "I think we've got a new sort of man here. A mutation.''

"Hank,'' said Arlie, crossing his legs comfortably, "when you get to be my age, you won't be so quick to think that Gabriel's going to sound the last trump in your own particular backyard. This boy's got a few physical peculiarities, he's admittedly bright, and he's conning you. You know our recent theory about sleep and sanity.''

"Of course I—''

"Suppose,'' said Arlie, "I lay it out for you once again. The human being deprived of sleep for any length of time beyond what he's accustomed to begins to show signs of mental abnormality. He hallucinates. He exhibits paranoid behavior. He becomes confused, flies into reasonless rages, and over-reacts emotionally to trifles.''

"Arthur Willoughby doesn't."

"That's my point." Arlie held up a small, square slab of a hand. "Let me go on. How do we explain these reactions? We theorize that possibly sleep has a function beyond that of resting and repairing the body. In sleep we humans, at least, dream pretty constantly. In our dreams we act out our unhappiness, our frustrations, our terrors. Therefore sleep, we guess, may be the emotional safety valve by which we maintain our sanity against the intellectual pressures of our lives."

"Granted," said Hank, impatiently. "But Art—"

"Now, let's take something else. The problem-solving mechanism—"

"Damn it, Arlie—"

"If you didn't want my opinion, why did you ring me in on this . . . what was that you just said, Hank?"

"Nothing. Nothing."

"I'll pretend I didn't hear it. As I was saying—the problem-solving mechanism. It has been assumed for centuries that man attacked his intellectual problems consciously, and consciously solved them. Recent attention to this assumption has caused us to consider an alternate viewpoint, of which I may say I"—Arlie folded his hands comfortably over his bulging shirtfront—"was perhaps the earliest and strongest proponent. It may well be—I and some others now think—that man is inherently incapable of consciously solving any new intellectual problem."

"The point is, Art Willoughby—what?" Hank broke off suddenly and stared across the crumpled paper bags and wax paper on his desk, at Arlie's chubby countenance. "What?"

"Incapable. Consciously." Arlie rolled the words around in his mouth. "By which I mean," he went on, with a slight grin, "man has no *conscious* mechanism for the solution of new intellectual problems." He cocked his head at Hank, and paused.

"All right. All right!" fumed Hank. "Tell me."

"There seems to be a definite possibility," said Arlie, capturing a crumb from the piece of wax paper that had enwrapped his ham sandwich, and chewing on it thoughtfully, "that there may be more truth than poetry to the words *inspiration, illuminating flash,* and *stroke of genius.* It may well turn out that the new-problem solving mechanism is not under conscious control at all. Hm-m-m, yes. Did I tell you Marta wants me to try out one of these new all-liquid reducing diets? When a wife starts that—''

"Never mind Marta!" shouted Hank. "What about nobody being consciously capable of solving a problem?"

Arlie frowned.

"What I'm trying to say," he said, "is that when we try to solve a problem consciously, we are actually only utilizing an attention-focusing mechanism. Look, let me define a so-called 'new problem' for you—"

"One that you haven't bumped into before."

"No," said Arlie. "No. Now you're falling into a trap." He waggled a thick finger at Hank; a procedure intensely irritating to Hank, who suffered a sort of adrenalin explosion the moment he suspected anybody of lecturing down to him. "Does every hitherto undiscovered intersection you approach in your car constitute a new problem in automobile navigation? Of course not. A truly new problem is not merely some variation or combination of factors from problems you have encountered before. It's a problem that for you, at least, previously did not even exist. It is, in fact, *a problem created by the solution of a problem of equal value in the past.*"

"All right. Say it is," scowled Hank. "Then what?"

"Then," said Arlie, "a true problem must always pose the special condition that no conscious tools of education or experience yet exist for its solution. Ergo, it cannot be handled on the conscious level. The logic of conscious thought is like the limb structure of the elephant, which, though ideally adapted to allow seven tons of animal a six-and-a-half-foot stride, absolutely forbids it the necessary spring to jump across a seven-foot trench that bars its escape from the zoo. For the true problem, you've got to get from hyar to thar without any stepping stone to help you across the gap that separates you from the solution. So, you're up against it, Hank. You're in a position where you can't fly but you got to. What do you do?"

"You tell me," glowered Hank.

"The answer's simple," said Arlie, blandly. "You fly."

"But you just said I couldn't!" Hank snapped.

"What I said," said Arlie, "was two things. One, you can't fly; two, you got to fly. What you're doing is clinging to one, which forces you to toss out two. What I'm pointing out is that you should cling to two, which tosses out one. Now, your conscious, experienced, logical mind *knows* you can't fly. The whole idea's silly. It won't even consider the problem. But your unconscious—haa!"

"What about my unconscious?"

"Why, your unconscious isn't tied down by any ropes of logical process like that. When it wants a solution, it just goes looking for it."

"Just like that."

"Well," Arlie frowned, "not just like that. First it has to fire up a sort of little donkey-engine of its own which we might call the intuitive mechanism. And that's where the trickiness comes in. Because the intuitive mechanism seems to be all power and no discipline. Its great usefulness comes from the fact that it operates under absolutely no restrictions—and of course this includes the restriction of control by the conscious mind. It's a sort of idiot savant . . . no, idiot solvant would be a better term." He sighed.

"So?" said Hank, after eyeing the fat man for a moment. "What's the use of it all? If we can't control it, what good is it?"

"What good is it?" Arlie straightened up. "Look at art. Look at science! Look at civilization. You aren't going to deny the existence of inspirations, are you? They exist—and one day we're going to find some better method of sparking them than the purely inductive process of operating the conscious, attention-focusing mechanism in hopes that something will catch."

"You think that's possible?"

"I know it's possible."

"I see," said Hank. There was a moment or so of silence in the office. "Well," said Hank, "about this little problem of my own, which I hate to bring you back to, but you did say the other day you had some ideas about this Art Willoughby. Of course, you were probably only speaking inspirationally, or perhaps I should say, without restriction by the conscious mind—"

"I was just getting to that," interrupted Arlie. "This Art Willoughby obviously suffers from what educators like to call poor work habits. Hm-m-m, yes. Underdevelopment of the conscious, problem-focusing mechanism. He tries to get by on a purely intuitive basis. When this fails him, he is helpless. He gives up—witness his transfers from college to college. On the other hand, when it works good, it works very, very good. He has probably come up with some way of keeping himself abnormally stimulated, either externally or internally. The only trouble will be that he probably isn't even conscious of it, and he certainly has no control over it. He'll fall asleep any moment now. And when he wakes up you'll want him to duplicate his feat of wakefulness but he won't be able to do it.''

Hank snorted disbelievingly.

"All right," said Arlie. "All right. Wait and see."

"I will," said Hank. He stood up. "Want to come along and see him? He said he was starting to get foggy this morning. I'm going to try him with the monster."

"What," wondered Arlie, ingenuously, rising, "if it puts him to sleep?"

Hank threw him a glance of pure fury.

"Monster!" commanded Hank. He, Arlie, and Margie Hansen were gathered in Art's hospital room, which was a pleasant, bedless place already overflowing with books and maps. Art, by hospital rules deprived of such things as tools and pets, had discovered an interest in the wars of Hannibal of Carthage. At the present moment he was trying to pick the truth out of the rather confused reports following Hannibal's escape from the Romans, after Antiochus had been defeated at Magnesia and surrendered his great general to Rome.

Right now, however, he was forced to lay his books aside and take the small white capsule which Margie, at Hank's order, extended to him. Art took it; then hesitated.

"Do you think it'll make me very jittery?" he asked.

"It should just wake you up," said Hank.

"I told you how I am with things like coffee. That's why I never drink coffee, or take any stimulants. Half a cup and my eyes feel like they're going to pop out of my head."

"There wouldn't," said Hank a trifle sourly, "be much point in our paying you to test out the monster if you refused to take it, now would there?"

"Oh . . . oh, no," said Art, suddenly embarrassed. "Water?"

Margie gave him a full glass and threw an unkind glance at her superior.

"If it starts to bother you, Art, you tell us right away," she said.

Art gulped the capsule down. He stood there waiting as if he expected an explosion from the region of his stomach. Nothing happened, and after a second or two he relaxed.

"How long does it take?" he asked.

"About fifteen minutes," said Hank.

They waited. At the end of ten minutes, Art began to brighten up and said he was feeling much more alert. At fifteen minutes, he was sparkling-eyed and cheerful, almost, in fact, bouncy.

"Awfully sorry, Doctor," he said to Hank. "Awfully sorry I hesitated over taking the monster that way. It was just that coffee and things—"

"That's all right," said Hank, preparing to leave. "Margie'll take you down for tests now."

"Marvelous pill. I recommend it highly," said Art, going out the door with Margie. They could hear him headed off down the corridor outside toward the laboratory on the floor below, still talking.

"Well?" said Hank.

"Time will tell," said Arlie.

"Speaking of time," continued Hank, "I've got the plug-in coffeepot back at the office. Have you got time for a quick cup?"

". . . Don't deny it," Hank was saying over half-empty cups in the office a short while later. "I heard you; I read you loud and clear. If a man makes his mind up to it, he can fly, you said."

"Not at all. And besides, I was only speaking academically," retorted Arlie heatedly. "Just because I'm prepared to entertain fantastic notions academically doesn't mean I'm going to let you try to shove them down my throat on a practical basis. Of course nobody can fly."

"According to your ideas, someone like Willoughby could if we punched the right buttons in him."

"Nonsense. Certainly he can't fly."

There was the wild patter of feminine feet down the hallway outside the office, the door was flung open, and Margie tottered in. She clung to the desk and gasped, too out of wind to talk.

"What's wrong?" cried Hank.

"Art . . ." Margie managed, "flew out—lab window."

Hank jumped to his feet, and pulled his chair out for her. She fell into it gratefully.

"Nonsense!" said Arlie. "Illusion. Or"—he scowled at Margie—"collusion of some sort."

"Got your breath back yet? What happened?" Hank was demanding. Margie nodded and drew a deep breath.

"I was testing him," she said, still breathlessly. "He was talking a blue streak and I could hardly get him to stand still. Something about Titus Quintus Flamininius, the three-body problem, Sauce Countess Waleska, the family Syrphidae of the order Diptera—all mixed up. Oh, he was babbling! And all of a sudden he dived out an open window."

"Dived?" barked Arlie. "I thought you said he *flew*?"

"Well, the laboratory's on the third floor!" wailed Margie, almost on the verge of tears.

Further questioning elicited the information that when Margie ran to the window, expecting to see a shattered ruin on the grass three stories below, she perceived Art swinging by one arm from the limb of an oak outside the window. In response to sharp queries from Arlie, she asserted vehemently that the closest grabable limb of the oak was, however, at least eight feet from the window out which Art had jumped, fallen, or dived.

"And then what?" said Hank.

Then, according to Margie, Art had uttered a couple of Tarzan-like yodels, and swung himself to the ground. When last seen he had been running off across the campus through the cool spring sunlight, under the budding trees, in his slacks and shirt unbuttoned at the throat. He had been heading in a roughly northeasterly direction—*i.e.*, toward town—and occasionally bounding into the air as if from a sheer excess of energy.

"Come on!" barked Hank, when he had heard this. He led the way at a run toward the hospital parking lot three stories below and his waiting car.

On the other side of the campus, at a taxi stand, the three of them picked up Art's trail. A cab driver waiting there remembered someone like Art taking another cab belonging to the same company. When Hank identified the passenger as a patient under his, Hank's care, and further identified himself as a physician from the university hospital, the cab driver they were talking to agreed to call in for the destination of Art's cab.

The destination was a downtown bank. Hank, Arlie, and Margie piled back into Hank's car and went there.

When they arrived, they learned that Art had already come and gone, leaving some confusion behind him. A vice-president of the bank, it appeared, had made a loan to Art of two hundred and sixty-eight dollars and eighty cents; and was now, it seemed, not quite sure as to why he had done so.

"He just talked me into it, I guess," the vice-president was saying unhappily as Hank and the others came dashing up. It further developed that Art had had no collateral. The vice-president had been given the impression that the money was to be used to develop some confusing but highly useful discovery or discoveries concerning Hannibal, encyclopedias, the sweat fly, and physics—with something about champagne and a way of preparing trout for the gourmet appetite.

A further check with the cab company produced the information that Art's taxi had taken him on to a liquor store. They followed. At the liquor store they discovered Art had purchased the single jeroboam of champagne (Moët et Chandon) that the liquor store had on hand, and had mentioned that he was going on to a restaurant. What restaurant, the cab company was no longer able to tell them. Art's driver had just announced that he would not be answering his radio for the next half hour.

They began checking the better and closer restaurants. At the fourth one, which was called the Calice d'Or, they finally ran Art to ground. They found him seated alone at a large round table, surrounded by gold-tooled leather volumes of a brand-new encyclopedia, eating and drinking what turned out to be Truite Sauce Countess Waleska and champagne from the jeroboam, now properly iced.

"Yahoo!" yelped Art, as he saw them approaching. He waved his glass on high, sloshing champagne liberally about. "Champagne for everybody! Celebrate Dr. Rapp's pill!"

"You," said Hank, "are coming back to the hospital."

"Nonsense! Glasses! Champagne for m'friends!"

"Oh, Art!" cried Margie.

"He's fried to the gills," said Arlie.

"Not at all," protested Art. "Illuminated. Blinding flash.

Understand everything. D'you know all knowledge has a common point of impingement?''

"Call a taxi, Margie," commanded Hank.

"Encyclopedia. Champagne bubble. Same thing."

"Could I help you, sir?" inquired a waiter, approaching Hank.

"We want to get our friend here home—"

"All roads lead knowledge. Unnerstand ignorance, unnerstand everything—"

"I understand, sir. Yes sir, he paid the check in advance—"

"Would *you* like to speak three thousand, four hundred and seventy-one languages?" Art was asking Arlie.

"Of course," Arlie was saying soothingly.

"My assistant has gone to get a taxi, now. I'm Dr. Rapp of the university hospital, and—"

"When I was child," announced Art, "thought as child, played child; now man—put away childish things."

"Here's the young lady, sir."

"But who will take care of pet raccoon?"

"I flagged a taxi down. It's waiting out front."

"Hoist him up," commanded Hank.

He and Arlie both got a firm hold on a Willoughby arm and maneuvered Art to his feet.

"This way," said Hank, steering Art toward the door.

"The universe," said Art. He leaned confidentially toward Hank, almost toppling the three of them over. "Only two inches across."

"That so?" grunted Hank.

"Hang on to Arlie, Art, and you won't fall over. There—" said Margie. Art blinked and focused upon her with some difficulty.

"Oh . . . there you are—" he said. "Love you. Naturally. Only real woman in universe. Other four point seven to the nine hundred seventeenth women in universe pale imitations. Marry me week Tuesday, three P.M., courthouse, wear blue." Margie gasped.

"Open the door for us, will you?"

"Certainly, sir," said the waiter, opening the front door to the Calice d'Or. A pink and gray taxi was drawn up at the curb.

"Sell stock in Wehauk Cannery immediately," Art was saying to the waiter. "Mismanagement. Collapse." The waiter blinked and stared. "News out in ten days."

"But how did you know I had—" the waiter was beginning as they shoved Art into the back seat of the cab. Margie got in after him.

"Ah, there you are," came Art's voice from the cab. "First son Charles Jonas—blond hair, blue eyes. Second son, William—"

"I'll send somebody to pick up that encyclopedia and anything else he left," said Hank to the waiter and got into the taxi himself. The taxi pulled away from the curb.

"Well," said the waiter, after a long pause in which he stared after the receding cab, to the doorman who had just joined him on the sidewalk, "how do you like that? Ever see anything like that before?"

"No, and I never saw anyone with over a gallon of champagne in him still walking around, either," said the doorman.

". . . And the worst of it is," said Hank to Arlie, as they sat in Hank's office, two days later, "Margie *is* going to marry him."

"What's wrong with that?" asked Arlie.

"What's wrong with it? Look at that!" Hank waved his hand at an object in the center of his desk.

"I've seen it," said Arlie.

They both examined the object. It appeared to be an ordinary moveable telephone with a cord and wall plug. The plug, however, was plugged into a small cardboard box the size of a cheese carton, filled with a tangled mess of wire and parts cannibalized from a cheap portable radio. The box was plugged into nothing.

"What was that number again . . . oh, yes," said Arlie. He picked up the phone and dialed a long series of numbers. He held the phone up so that they could both hear. There was a faint buzzing ring from the earphone and then a small, tinny voice filled the office.

". . . The time is eight forty-seven. The temperature is eighteen degrees above zero, the wind westerly at eight miles an hour. The forecast for the Anchorage area is continued cloudy and some snow with a high of twenty-two degrees, a low tonight of nine above. Elsewhere in Alaska—"

Arlie sighed, and replaced the phone in its cradle.

"We bring him back here," said Hank, "stewed to the gills. In forty minutes, before he passed out, he builds this trick wastebasket of his that holds five times as much as it ought to. He sleeps seven hours and wakes up as good as ever. What should I do? Shoot him, or something? I must have some responsibility to the human race—if not to Margie."

"He seems sensible now?"

"Yes, but what do I do?"

"Hypnosis."

"You keep saying that. I don't see—"

"We must," said Arlie, "inhibit the connection of his conscious mind with the intuitive mechanism. The wall between the two—the normal wall—seems to have been freakishly thin in his case. Prolonged sleeplessness, combined with the abnormal stimulation of your monster, has caused him to break through—to say to the idiot solvant, *'Solve!'* And the idiot solvant in the back of his head has provided him with a solution."

"I still think it would be better for me to shoot him."

"You are a physician—"

"You would remind me of that. All right, so I can't shoot him. I don't even want to shoot him. But, Arlie, what's going to happen to everybody? Here I've raised up a sort of miracle worker who can probably move the North American continent down to the South Pacific if he wants to—only it just happens he's also a feather-headed butterfly who never lit on one notion for more than five minutes at a time in his life. Sure, I've got a physician's responsibility toward him. But what about my responsibility to the rest of the people in the world?"

"There is no responsibility being violated here," said Arlie patiently. "Simply put him back the way you found him."

"No miracles?"

"None. At least, except accidental ones."

"It might be kinder to shoot him."

"Nonsense," said Arlie sharply. "It's for the good of everybody." Hank sighed, and rose.

"All right," he said. "Let's go."

They went down the hall to Art's room. They found him seated thoughtfully in his armchair, staring at nothing, his books and maps ignored around him.

"Good morning, Art," said Arlie.

"Oh? Hello," said Art, waking up. "Is it time for tests?"

"In a way," said Arlie. He produced a small box surmounted by a cardboard disk on which were inked alternate spirals of white and black. He plugged the box into a handy electric socket by means of the cord attached to it, and set it on a small table in front of Art. The disk began to revolve. "I want you to watch that," said Arlie.

Art stared at it.

"What do you see?" asked Arlie.

"It looks like going down a tunnel," said Art.

"Indeed it does," said Arlie. "Just imagine yourself going down that tunnel. Down the tunnel. Faster and faster. . . ." He continued to talk quietly and persuasively for about a minute and a half, at the end of which Art was limply demonstrating a state of deep trance. Arlie brought him up a bit for questioning.

". . . And how do these realizations, these answers, come to you?" Arlie was asking a few minutes later.

"In a sort of a flash," replied Art. "A blinding flash."

"That is the way they have always come to you?"

"More lately," said Art.

"Yes," said Arlie, "that's the way it always is just before people outgrow these flashes—you know that."

There was a slight pause.

"Yes," said Art.

"You have now outgrown these flashes. You have had your last flash. Flashes belong to childhood. You have had a delayed growing-up, but from now on you will think like an adult. Logically. You will think like an adult. Repeat after me."

"I will think like an adult," intoned Art.

Arlie continued to hammer away at his point for a few more minutes; then he brought Art out of his trance, with a final command that if Art felt any tendency to a recurrence of his flashes he should return to Arlie for further help in suppressing them.

"Oh, hello, Doctor," said Art to Hank, as soon as he woke up. "Say, how much longer are you going to need me as a test subject?"

Hank made a rather unhappy grimace.

"In a hurry to leave?" he said.

"I don't know," said Art enthusiastically, rubbing his long

hands together as he sat up in the chair, "but I was just thinking maybe it's time I got to work. Settled down. As long as I'm
going to be a married man shortly."

"We can turn you loose today, if you want," said Hank.

When Art stepped once more into his room, closing the
door behind him and taking off his leather jacket to hang it up
on the hook holding his bagpipes, the place seemed so little
changed that it was hard to believe ten full days had passed.
Even the raccoon was back asleep in the wastebasket. It was
evident the landlady had been doing her duty about keeping
the small animal fed—Art had worried a little about that. The
only difference, Art thought, was that the room seemed to feel
smaller.

He sighed cheerfully and sat down at the desk, drawing pencil and paper to him. The afternoon sun, shooting the gap of
the missing slat on the venetian blind at the window, splashed
fair in Art's eyes, blinding him.

"Blast!" he said aloud. "Got to do something about
that—"

He checked himself suddenly with one hand halfway up to
shield his eyes, and smiled. Opening a drawer of the desk, he
took out a pair of heavy kitchen scissors. He made a single cut
into the rope slot at each end of the plastic slat at the bottom
of the blind, snapped the slat out of position, and snapped it
back in where the upper slat was missing.

Still smiling, he picked up the pencil and doodled the name
Margie with a heart around it in the upper left-hand corner as
he thought, with gaze abstracted. The pencil moved to the
center of the piece of paper and hovered there.

After a moment, it began to sketch.

What it sketched was a sort of device to keep the sun out of
Art's eyes. At the same time, however, it just happened to be a
dome-shaped all-weather shield capable of protecting a city
ten miles in diameter the year round. The "skin" of the dome
consisted of a thin layer of carbon dioxide such as one finds
in the bubbles of champagne, generated and maintained by
magnetic lines of force emanating from three heavily charged
bodies, in rotation about each other at the apex of the dome
and superficially housed in a framework the design of which
was reminiscent of the wing structure found in the family Syrphidae of the order Diptera.

Art continued to smile as the design took form. But it was a thoughtful smile, a mature smile. Hank and Arlie had been quite right about him. He had always been a butterfly, flitting from notion to notion, playing.

But then, too, he had always been a bad hypnotic subject, full of resistances.

And he was about to have a wife to care for. Consequently it is hard to say whether Arlie and Hank would have been reassured if they could have seen Art at that moment. His new thinking was indeed adult, much more so than the other two could have realized. Where miracles were concerned, he had given up *playing*.

Now, he was *working*.

CALL HIM LORD

> "He called and commanded me
> —Therefore, I knew him;
> But later on, failed me; and
> —Therefore, I slew him!"

"Songs of the Shield Bearer"

The sun could not fail in rising over the Kentucky hills, nor could Kyle Arnam in waking. There would be eleven hours and forty minutes of daylight. Kyle rose, dressed, and went out to saddle the gray gelding and the white stallion. He rode the stallion until the first fury was out of the arched and snowy neck; and then led both horses around to tether them outside the kitchen door. Then he went in to breakfast.

The message that had come a week before was beside his plate of bacon and eggs. Teena, his wife, was standing at the breadboard with her back to him. He sat down and began eating, rereading the letter as he ate.

". . . The Prince will be traveling incognito under one of his family titles, as Count Sirii North; and should not be addressed as 'Lord' . . ." *You will call him 'Lord' . . .*"

"Why does it have to be you?" Teena asked.

He looked up and saw how she stood with her back to him.

139

"Teena—" he said sadly.

"Why?"

"My ancestors were bodyguards to his—back in the wars of conquest against the aliens. I've told you that," he said. "My forefathers saved the lives of his, many times when there was no warning—a Rak spaceship would probably appear out of nowhere to lock on, even to a flagship. And even an Emperor found himself fighting for his life, hand to hand."

"The aliens are all dead now, and the Emperor's got a hundred other worlds! Why can't his son take his Grand Tour on them? Why does he have to come here to Earth—and you?"

"There's only one Earth."

"And only one you, I suppose?"

He sighed internally and gave up. He had been raised by his father and his uncle after his mother died, and in an argument with Teena he always felt helpless. He got up from the table and went to her, putting his hands on her and gently trying to turn her about. But she resisted.

He sighed inside himself again and turned away to the weapons cabinet. He took out a loaded slug pistol, fitted it into the stubby holster it matched, and clipped the holster to his belt at the left of the buckle, where the hang of his leather jacket would hide it. Then he selected a dark-handled knife with a six-inch blade and bent over to slip it into the sheath inside his boot top. He dropped the cuff of his trouser leg back over the boot top and stood up.

"He's got no right to be here," said Teena fiercely to the breadboard. "Tourists are supposed to be kept to the museum areas and the tourist lodges."

"He's not a tourist. You know that," answered Kyle patiently. "He's the Emperor's oldest son and his great-grandmother was from Earth. His wife will be, too. Every fourth generation the Imperial line has to marry back into Earth stock. That's the law—still." He put on his leather jacket, sealing it closed only at the bottom to hide the slug-gun holster, half-turned to the door—then paused.

"Teena?" he asked.

She did not answer.

"Teena!" he repeated. He stepped to her, put his hands on her shoulders, and tried to turn her to face him. Again, she resisted, but this time he was having none of it.

He was not a big man, being of middle height, round-faced, with sloping and unremarkable-looking, if thick, shoulders. But his strength was not ordinary. He could bring the white stallion to its knees with one fist wound in its mame—and no other man had ever been able to do that. He turned her easily to look at him.

"Now, listen to me—" he began. But, before he could finish, all the stiffness went out of her and she clung to him, trembling.

"He'll get you into trouble—I know he will!" she choked muffledly into his chest. "Kyle, don't go! There's no law making you go!"

He stroked the soft hair of her head, his throat stiff and dry. There was nothing he could say to her. What she was asking was impossible. Ever since the sun had first risen on men and women together, wives had clung to their husbands at times like this, begging for what could not be. And always the men had held them, as Kyle was holding her now—as if understanding could somehow be pressed from one body into the other—and saying nothing, because there was nothing that could be said.

So, Kyle held her for a few moments longer, and then reached behind him to unlock her intertwined fingers at his back, and loosen her arms around him. Then, he went. Looking back through the kitchen window as he rode off on the stallion, leading the gray horse, he saw her standing just where he had left her. Not even crying, but standing with her arms hanging down, her head down, not moving.

He rode away through the forest of the Kentucky hillside. It took him more than two hours to reach the lodge. As he rode down the valleyside toward it, he saw a tall bearded man, wearing the robes they wore on some of the Younger Worlds, standing at the gateway to the interior courtyard of the rustic, wooded lodge.

When he got close, he saw that the beard was graying and the man was biting his lips. Above a straight, thin nose, the eyes were bloodshot and circled beneath as if from worry or lack of sleep.

"He's in the courtyard," said the gray-bearded man as Kyle rode up. "I'm Montlaven, his tutor. He's ready to go." The darkened eyes looked almost pleadingly up at Kyle.

"Stand clear of the stallion's head," said Kyle. "And take me in to him."

"Not that horse, for him—" said Montlaven, looking distrustfully at the stallion, as he backed away.

"No," said Kyle. "He'll ride the gelding."

"He'll want the white."

"He can't ride the white," said Kyle. "Even if I let him, he couldn't ride this stallion. I'm the only one who can ride him. Take me in."

The tutor turned and led the way into the grassy courtyard, surrounding a swimming pool and looked down upon, on three sides, by the windows of the lodge. In a lounging chair by the pool sat a tall young man in his late teens, with a mane of blond hair, a pair of stuffed saddlebags on the grass beside him. He stood up as Kyle and the tutor came toward him.

"Majesty," said the tutor, as they stopped, "this is Kyle Arnam, your bodyguard for the three days here."

"Good morning, Bodyguard . . . Kyle, I mean." The Prince smiled mischievously. "Light, then. And I'll mount."

"You ride the gelding, Lord," said Kyle.

The Prince stared at him, tilted back his handsome head, and laughed.

"I can ride, man!" he said. "I ride well."

"Not this horse, Lord," said Kyle dispassionately. "No one rides this horse, but me."

The eyes flashed wide, the laugh faded—then returned.

"What can I do?" The wide shoulders shrugged. "I give in —always I give in. Well, almost always." He grinned up at Kyle, his lips thinned, but frank. "All right."

He turned to the gelding—and with a sudden leap was in the saddle. The gelding snorted and plunged at the shock; then steadied as the young man's long fingers tightened expertly on the reins and the fingers of the other hand patted a gray neck. The Prince raised his eyebrows, looking over at Kyle, but Kyle sat stolidly.

"I take it you're armed, good Kyle?" the Prince said slyly. "You'll protect me against the natives if they run wild?"

"Your life is in my hands, Lord," said Kyle. He unsealed the leather jacket at the bottom and let it fall open to show the slug pistol in its holster for a moment. Then he resealed the jacket again at the bottom.

"Will—" The tutor put his hand on the young man's knee. "Don't be reckless, boy. This is Earth and the people here don't have rank and custom like we do. Think before you—"

"Oh, cut it out, Monty!" snapped the Prince. "I'll be just as incognito, just as humble, as archaic and independent as the rest of them. You think I've no memory! Anyway, it's only for three days or so until my Imperial father joins me. Now, let me go!"

He jerked away, turned to lean forward in the saddle, and abruptly put the gelding into a bolt for the gate. He disappeared through it, and Kyle drew hard on the stallion's reins as the big white horse danced and tried to follow.

"Give me his saddlebags," said Kyle.

The tutor bent and passed them up. Kyle made them fast on top of his own, across the stallion's withers. Looking down, he saw there were tears in the bearded man's eyes.

"He's a fine boy. You'll see. You'll know he is!" Montlaven's face, upturned, was mutely pleading.

"I know he comes from a fine family," said Kyle slowly. "I'll do my best for him." And he rode off out of the gateway after the gelding.

When he came out of the gate, the Prince was nowhere in sight. But it was simple enough for Kyle to follow, by dinted brown earth and crushed grass, the marks of the gelding's path. This brought him at last through some pines to a grassy open slope where the Prince sat looking skyward through a single-lens box.

When Kyle came up, the Prince lowered the instrument, and without a word passed it over. Kyle put it to his eye and looked skyward. There was the whir of the tracking unit and one of Earth's three orbiting power stations swam into the field of vision of the lens.

"Give it back," said the Prince.

"I couldn't get a look at it earlier," went on the young man as Kyle handed the lens to him. "And I wanted to. It's a rather expensive present, you know—it and the other two like it—from our Imperial treasury. Just to keep your planet from drifting into another ice age. And what do we get for it?"

"Earth, Lord," answered Kyle. "As it was before men went out to the stars."

"Oh, the museum areas could be maintained with one station and a half-million caretakers," said the Prince. "It's the other two stations and you billion or so freeloaders I'm talking about. I'll have to look into it when I'm Emperor. Shall we ride?"

"If you wish, Lord." Kyle picked up the reins of the stallion and the two horses with their riders moved off across the slope.

". . . And one more thing," said the Prince, as they entered the farther belt of pine trees. "I don't want you to be misled —I'm really very fond of old Monty, back there. It's just that I wasn't really planning to come here at all—*Look at me, Bodyguard!*"

Kyle turned to see the blue eyes that ran in the Imperial family blazing at him. Then, unexpectedly, they softened. The Prince laughed.

"You don't scare easily, do you, Bodyguard . . . Kyle, I mean?" he said. "I think I like you after all. But look at me when I talk."

"Yes, Lord."

"That's my good Kyle. Now, I was explaining to you that I'd never actually planned to come here on my Grand Tour at all. I didn't see any point in visiting this dusty old museum world of yours with people still trying to live like they lived in the Dark Ages. But—my Imperial father talked me into it."

"Your father, Lord?" asked Kyle.

"Yes, he bribed me, you might say," said the Prince thoughtfully. "He was supposed to meet me here for these three days. Now, he's messaged there's a slight delay— but that doesn't matter. The point is, he belongs to the school of old men who still think your Earth is something precious and vital. Now, I happen to like and admire my father, Kyle. You approve of that?"

"Yes, Lord."

"I thought you would. Yes, he's the one man in the human race I look up to. And to please him, I'm making this Earth trip. And to please him—only to please *him*, Kyle—I'm going to be an easy Prince for you to conduct around to your natural wonders and watering spots and whatever. Now, you understand me—and how this trip is going to go. Don't you?" He stared at Kyle.

"I understand," said Kyle.

"That's fine," said the Prince, smiling once more. "So now you can start telling me all about these trees and birds and animals so that I can memorize their names and please my father when he shows up. What are those little birds I've been seeing under the trees—brown on top and whitish underneath? Like that one—there!"

"That's a Veery, Lord," said Kyle. "A bird of the deep woods and silent places. Listen—" He reached out a hand to the gelding's bridle and brought both horses to a halt. In the sudden silence, off to their right they could hear a silver bird-voice, rising and falling, in a descending series of crescendos and diminuendos, that softened at last into silence. For a moment after the song was ended the Prince sat staring at Kyle, then seemed to shake himself back to life.

"Interesting," he said. He lifted the reins Kyle had let go and the horses moved forward again. "Tell me more."

For more than three hours, as the sun rose toward noon, they rode through the wooded hills, with Kyle identifying bird and animal, insect, tree, and rock. And for three hours the Prince listened—his attention flashing and momentary, but intense. But when the sun was overhead the intensity flagged.

"That's enough," he said. "Aren't we going to stop for lunch? Kyle, aren't there any towns around here?"

"Yes, Lord," said Kyle. "We've passed several."

"Several?" The Prince stared at him. "Why haven't we come into one before now? Where are you taking me?"

"Nowhere, Lord," said Kyle. "You lead the way, I only follow."

"I?" said the Prince. For the first time he seemed to become aware that he had been keeping the gelding's head always in advance of the stallion. "Of course. But now it's time to eat."

"Yes, Lord," said Kyle. "This way."

He turned the stallion's head down the slope of the hill they were crossing and the Prince turned the gelding after him.

"And now listen," said the Prince, as he caught up. "Tell me I've got it all right." And to Kyle's astonishment he began to repeat, almost word for word, everything that Kyle had said. "Is it all there? Everything you told me?"

"Perfectly, Lord," said Kyle. The Prince looked slyly at him.

"Could you do that, Kyle?"

"Yes," said Kyle. "But these are things I've known all my life."

"You see?" The Prince smiled. "That's the difference between us, good Kyle. You spend your life learning something —I spend a few hours and I know as much about it as you do."

"Not as much, Lord," said Kyle slowly.

The Prince blinked at him, then jerked his hand dismissingly, and half-angrily, as if he were throwing something aside.

"What little else there is probably doesn't count," he said.

They rode down the slope and through a winding valley and came out at a small village. As they rode clear of the surrounding trees a sound of music came to their ears.

"What's that?" The Prince stood up in his stirrups. "Why, there's dancing going on, over there."

"A beer garden, Lord. And it's Saturday—a holiday here."

"Good. We'll go there to eat."

They rode around to the beer garden and found tables back away from the dance floor. A pretty, young waitress came and they ordered, the Prince smiling sunnily at her until she smiled back—then hurried off as if in mild confusion. The Prince ate hungrily when the food came and drank a stein and a half of brown beer, while Kyle ate more lightly and drank coffee.

"That's better," said the Prince, sitting back at last. "I had an appetite. . . . Look there, Kyle! Look, there are five, six . . . seven drifter platforms parked over there. Then you don't all ride horses?"

"No," said Kyle. "It's as each man wishes."

"But if you have drifter platforms, why not other civilized things?"

"Some things fit, some don't Lord," answered Kyle. The Prince laughed.

"You mean you try to make civilization fit this old-fashioned life of yours, here?" he said. "Isn't that the wrong way around—" He broke off. "What's that they're playing now? I like that. I'll bet I could do that dance." He stood up. "In fact, I think I will."

He paused, looking down at Kyle.

"Aren't you going to warn me against it?" he asked.

"No, Lord," said Kyle. "What you do is your own affair."

The young man turned away abruptly. The waitress who had served them was passing, only a few tables away. The

Prince went after her and caught up with her by the dance-floor railing. Kyle could see the girl protesting—but the Prince hung over her, looking down from his tall height, smiling. Shortly, she had taken off her apron and was out on the dance floor with him, showing him the steps of the dance. It was a polka.

The Prince learned with fantastic quickness. Soon, he was swinging the waitress around with the rest of the dancers, his foot stamping on the turns, his white teeth gleaming. Finally the number ended and the members of the band put down their instruments and began to leave the stand.

The Prince, with the girl trying to hold him back, walked over to the bandleader. Kyle got up quickly from his table and started toward the floor.

The bandleader was shaking his head. He turned abruptly and slowly walked away. The Prince started after him, but the girl took hold of his arm, saying something urgent to him.

He brushed her aside and she stumbled a little. A busboy among the tables on the far side of the dance floor, not much older than the Prince and nearly as tall, put down his tray and vaulted the railing onto the polished hardwood. He came up behind the Prince and took hold of his arm, swinging him around.

". . . can't do that here," Kyle heard him say, as Kyle came up. The Prince struck out like a panther—like a trained boxer—with three quick lefts in succession into the face of the busboy, the Prince's shoulder bobbing, the weight of his body in behind each blow.

The busboy went down. Kyle, reaching the Prince, herded him away through a side gap in the railing. The young man's face was white with rage. People were swarming onto the dance floor.

"Who was that? What's his name?" demanded the Prince, between clenched teeth. "He put his hand on me! Did you see that? *He put his hand on me!*"

"You knocked him out," said Kyle. "What more do you want?"

"He manhandled me—*me!*" snapped the Prince. "I want to find out who he is!" He caught hold of the bar to which the horses were tied, refusing to be pushed farther. "He'll learn to lay hands on a future Emperor!"

"No one will tell you his name," said Kyle. And the cold

note in his voice finally seemed to reach through to the Prince and sober him. He stared at Kyle.

"Including you?" he demanded at last.

"Including me, Lord," said Kyle.

The Prince stared a moment longer, then swung away. He turned, jerked loose the reins of the gelding, and swung into the saddle. He rode off. Kyle mounted and followed.

They rode in silence into the forest. After a while, the Prince spoke without turning his head.

"And you call yourself a bodyguard," he said, finally.

"Your life is in my hands, Lord," said Kyle. The Prince turned a grim face to look at him.

"Only my life?" said the Prince. "As long as they don't kill me, they can do what they want? Is that what you mean?"

Kyle met his gaze steadily.

"Pretty much so, Lord," he said.

The Prince spoke with an ugly note in his voice.

"I don't think I like you, after all, Kyle," he said. "I don't think I like you at all."

"I'm not here with you to be liked, Lord," said Kyle.

"Perhaps not," said the Prince, thickly. "But I know *your* name!"

They rode on in continued silence for perhaps another half hour. But then gradually the angry hunch went out of the young man's shoulders and the tightness out of his jaw. After a while he began to sing to himself, a song in a language Kyle did not know; and as he sang, his cheerfulness seemed to return. Shortly, he spoke to Kyle, as if there had never been anything but pleasant moments between them.

Mammoth Cave was close and the Prince asked to visit it. They went there and spent some time going through the cave. After that they rode their horses up along the left bank of the Green River. The Prince seemed to have forgotten all about the incident at the beer garden and be out to charm everyone they met. As the sun was at last westering toward the dinner hour, they came finally to a small hamlet back from the river, with a roadside inn mirrored in an artificial lake beside it, and guarded by oak and pine trees behind.

"This looks good," said the Prince. "We'll stay overnight here, Kyle."

"If you wish, Lord," said Kyle.

• • •

They halted, and Kyle took the horses around to the stable, then entered the inn to find the Prince already in the small bar off the dining room, drinking beer and charming the waitress. This waitress was younger than the one at the beer garden had been; a little girl with soft loose hair and round brown eyes that showed their delight in the attention of the tall, good-looking young man.

"Yes," said the Prince to Kyle, looking out of corners of the Imperial blue eyes at him, after the waitress had gone to get Kyle his coffee. "This is the very place."

"The very place?" said Kyle.

"For me to get to know the people better—what did you think, good Kyle?" said the Prince and laughed at him. "I'll observe the people here and you can explain them—won't that be good?"

Kyle gazed at him thoughtfully.

"I'll tell you whatever I can, Lord," he said.

They drank—the Prince his beer, and Kyle his coffee—and went in a little later to the dining room for dinner. The Prince, as he had promised at the bar, was full of questions about what he saw—and what he did not see.

". . . But why go on living in the past, all of you here?" he asked Kyle. "A museum world is one thing. But a museum people—" He broke off to smile and speak to the little, soft-haired waitress, who had somehow been diverted from the bar to wait upon their dining-room table.

"Not a museum people, Lord," said Kyle. "A living people. The only way to keep a race and a culture preserved is to keep it alive. So we go on in our own way, here on Earth, as a living example for the Younger Worlds to check themselves against."

"Fascinating . . ." murmured the Prince; but his eyes had wandered off to follow the waitress, who was glowing and looking back at him from across the now-busy dining room.

"Not fascinating. Necessary, Lord," said Kyle. But he did not believe the younger man had heard him.

After dinner, they moved back to the bar. And the Prince, after questioning Kyle a little longer, moved up to continue his researches among the other people standing at the bar. Kyle watched for a little while. Then, feeling it was safe to do so, he slipped out to have another look at the horses and to ask the innkeeper to arrange a saddle lunch put up for them the next day.

When he returned, the Prince was not to be seen.

Kyle sat down at a table to wait; but the Prince did not return. A cold, hard knot of uneasiness began to grow below Kyle's breastbone. A sudden pang of alarm sent him swiftly back out to check the horses. But they were cropping peacefully in their stalls. The stallion whickered, low-voiced, as Kyle looked in on him, and turned his white head to look back at Kyle.

"Easy, boy" said Kyle and returned to the inn to find the innkeeper.

But the innkeeper had no idea where the Prince might have gone.

". . .If the horses aren't taken, he's not far," the innkeeper said. "There's no trouble he can get into around here. Maybe he went for a walk in the woods. I'll leave word for the night staff to keep an eye out for him when he comes in. Where'll you be?"

"In the bar until it closes—then, my room," said Kyle.

He went back to the bar to wait, and took a booth near an open window. Time went by and gradually the number of other customers began to dwindle. Above the ranked bottles, the bar clock showed nearly midnight. Suddenly, through the window, Kyle heard a distant scream of equine fury from the stables.

He got up and went out quickly. In the darkness outside, he ran to the stables and burst in. There in the feeble illumination of the stable's night lighting, he saw the Prince, palefaced, clumsily saddling the gelding in the center aisle between the stalls. The door to the stallion's stall was open. The Prince looked away as Kyle came in.

Kyle took three swift steps to the open door and looked in. The stallion was still tied, but his ears were back, his eyes rolling, and a saddle lay tumbled and dropped on the stable floor beside him.

"Saddle up," said the Prince thickly from the aisle. "We're leaving." Kyle turned to look at him.

"We've got rooms at the inn here," he said.

"Never mind. We're riding. I need to clear my head." The young man got the gelding's cinch tight, dropped the stirrups and swung heavily up into the saddle. Without waiting for Kyle, he rode out of the stable into the night.

"So, boy . . ." said Kyle soothingly to the stallion. Hastily he untied the big white horse, saddled him, and set out after the Prince. In the darkness there was no way of ground-tracking the gelding; but he leaned forward and blew into the ear of the stallion. The surprised horse neighed in protest and the whinny of the gelding came back from the darkness of the slope up ahead and over to Kyle's right. He rode in that direction.

He caught the Prince on the crown of the hill. The young man was walking the gelding, reins loose, and singing under his breath—the same song in an unknown language he had sung earlier. But now, as he saw Kyle, he grinned loosely and began to sing with more emphasis. For the first time Kyle caught the overtones of something mocking and lusty about the incomprehensible words. Understanding broke suddenly in him.

"The girl!" he said. "The little waitress. Where is she?"

The grin vanished from the Prince's face, then came slowly back again. The grin laughed at Kyle.

"Why, where d'you think?" The words slurred on the Prince's tongue and Kyle, riding close, smelled the beer heavy on the young man's breath. "In her room, sleeping and happy. Honored . . . though she doesn't know it . . . by an Emperor's son. And expecting to find me there in the morning. But I won't be. Will we, good Kyle?"

"Why did you do it, Lord?" asked Kyle quietly.

"Why?" The Prince peered at him, a little drunkenly in the moonlight. "Kyle, my father has four sons. I've got three younger brothers. But I'm the one who's going to be Emperor; and Emperors don't answer questions."

Kyle said nothing. The Prince peered at him. They rode on together for several minutes in silence.

"All right, I'll tell you why," said the Prince, more loudly, after a while as if the pause had been only momentary. "It's because you're not *my* bodyguard, Kyle. You see, I've seen through you. I know whose bodyguard you are. You're *theirs!*"

Kyle's jaw tightened. But the darkness hid this reaction.

"All right—" The Prince gestured loosely, disturbing his balance in the saddle. "That's all right. Have it your way. I don't mind. So, we'll play points. There was that lout at the beer garden, who puts his hands on me. But no one would tell me his name, you said. All right, you managed to bodyguard him. One point for you. But you didn't manage to bodyguard the girl at the inn back there. One point for me. Who's going to win, good Kyle?''

Kyle took a deep breath.

"Lord," he said, "some day it'll be your duty to marry a woman from Earth—"

The Prince interrupted him with a laugh, and this time there was an ugly note in it.

"You flatter yourselves," he said. His voice thickened. "That's the trouble with you—all you Earth people—you flatter yourselves."

They rode on in silence. Kyle said nothing more, but kept the head of the stallion close to the shoulder of the gelding, watching the young man closely. For a little while the Prince seemed to doze. His head sank on his chest and he let the gelding wander. Then, after a while, his head began to come up again, his automatic horseman's fingers tightened on the reins, and he lifted his head to stare around in the moonlight.

"I want to drink," he said. His voice was no longer thick, but it was flat and uncheerful. "Take me where we can get some beer, Kyle."

Kyle took a deep breath.

"Yes, Lord," he said.

He turned the stallion's head to the right and the gelding followed. They went up over a hill and down to the edge of a lake. The dark water sparkled in the moonlight and the farther shore was lost in the night. Lights shone through the trees around the curve of the shore.

"There, Lord," said Kyle. "It's a fishing resort, with a bar."

They rode around the shore to it. It was a low, casual building, angled to face the shore; a dock ran out from it to which fishing boats were tethered, bobbing slightly on the black water. Light gleamed through the windows as they hitched their horses and went to the door.

The barroom they stepped into was wide and bare. A long bar faced them with several planked fish on the wall behind it. Below the fish were three bartenders—the one in the center, middle-aged, and wearing an air of authority with his apron.

The other two were young and muscular. The customers, mostly men, scattered at the square tables and standing at the bar wore rough working clothes, or equally casual vacationers' garb.

The Prince sat down at a table back from the bar and Kyle sat down with him. When the waitress came they ordered beer and coffee, and the Prince half-emptied his stein the moment it was brought to him. As soon as it was completely empty, he signaled the waitress again.

"Another," he said. This time, he smiled at the waitress when she brought his stein back. But she was a woman in her thirties, pleased but not overwhelmed by his attention. She smiled lightly back and moved off to return to the bar where she had been talking to two men her own age, one fairly tall, the other shorter, bullet-headed, and fleshy.

The Prince drank. As he put his stein down, he seemed to become aware of Kyle, and turned to look at him.

"I suppose," said the Prince, "you think I'm drunk?"

"Not yet," said Kyle.

"No," said the Prince, "that's right. Not yet. But perhaps I'm going to be. And if I decide I am, who's going to stop me?"

"No one, Lord."

"That's right," the young man said. "That's right." He drank deliberately from his stein until it was empty, and then signaled the waitress for another. A spot of color was beginning to show over each of his high cheekbones. "When you're on a miserable little world with miserable little people . . . hello, Bright Eyes!" he interrupted himself as the waitress brought his beer. She laughed and went back to her friends. ". . . you have to amuse yourself any way you can," he wound up.

He laughed to himself.

"When I think how my father, and Monty—everybody—used to talk this planet up to me—" He glanced aside at Kyle. "Do you know at one time I was actually scared—well, not scared exactly, nothing scares me . . . say *concerned*—about maybe having to come here, some day?" He laughed again. "Concerned that I wouldn't measure up to you Earth people! Kyle, have you ever been to any of the Younger Worlds?"

"No," said Kyle.

"I thought not. Let me tell you, good Kyle, the worst of the people there are bigger, and better looking, and smarter, and everything than anyone I've seen here. And I, Kyle, I—the Emperor-to-be—am better than any of them. So, guess how all you here look to me?" He stared at Kyle, waiting. "Well, answer me, good Kyle. Tell me the truth. That's an order."

"It's not up to you to judge, Lord," said Kyle.

"Not—? Not up to me?" The blue eyes blazed. *"I'm* going to be Emperor!"

"It's not up to any one man, Lord," said Kyle. "Emperor or not. An Emperor's needed, as the symbol that can hold a hundred worlds together. But the real need of the race is to survive. It took nearly a million years to evolve a survival-type intelligence here on Earth. And out on the newer worlds people are bound to change. If something gets lost out there, some necessary element lost out of the race, there needs to be a pool of original genetic material to replace it."

The Prince's lips grew wide in a savage grin.

"Oh, good, Kyle—good!" he said. "Very good. Only, I've heard all that before. Only, I don't believe it. You see—I've seen you people, now. And you don't outclass us, out on the Younger Worlds. *We* outclass *you.* We've gone on and got better, while you stayed still. And you know it."

The young man laughed softly, almost in Kyle's face.

"All you've been afraid of is that we'd find out. And I have." He laughed again. "I've had a look at you; and now I know. I'm bigger, better, and braver than any man in this room—and you know why? Not just because I'm the son of the Emperor, but because it's born in me! Body, brains, and everything else! I can do what I want here, and no one on this planet is good enough to stop me. Watch."

He stood up, suddenly.

"Now, I want that waitress to get drunk with me," he said. "And this time I'm telling you in advance. Are you going to try and stop me?"

Kyle looked up at him. Their eyes met.

"No, Lord," he said. "It's not my job to stop you."

The Prince laughed.

"I thought so," he said. He swung away and walked between the tables toward the bar and the waitress, still in conversation with the two men. The Prince came up to the bar on the far side of the waitress and ordered a new stein of beer from the middle-aged bartender. When it was given to him, he took it, turned around, and rested his elbows on the bar, leaning back against it. He spoke to the waitress, interrupting the taller of the two men.

"I've been wanting to talk to you," Kyle heard him say.

The waitress, a little surprised, looked around at him. She smiled, recognizing him—a little flattered by the directness of his approach, a little appreciative of his clean good looks, a little tolerant of his youth.

"*You* don't mind, do you?" said the Prince, looking past her to the bigger of the two men, the one who had just been talking. The other stared back, and their eyes met without shifting for several seconds. Abruptly, angrily, the man shrugged, and turned about with his back hunched against them.

"You see?" said the Prince, smiling back at the waitress. "He knows I'm the one you ought to be talking to, instead of—"

"All right, sonny. Just a minute."

It was the shorter, bullet-headed man, interrupting. The Prince turned to look down at him with a fleeting expression of surprise. But the bullet-headed man was already turning to his taller friend and putting a hand on his arm.

"Come on back, Ben," the shorter man was saying. "The kid's a little drunk, is all." He turned back to the Prince. "You shove off now," he said. "Clara's with us."

The Prince stared at him blankly. The stare was so fixed that the shorter man had started to turn away, back to his friend and the waitress, when the Prince seemed to wake.

"Just a minute—" he said, in the turn.

He reached out a hand to one of the fleshy shoulders below the bullet head. The man turned back, knocking the hand calmly away. Then, just as calmly, he picked up the Prince's full stein of beer from the bar and threw it in the young man's face.

"Get lost," he said unexcitedly.

The Prince stood for a second, with the beer dripping from his face. Then, without even stopping to wipe his eyes clear, he threw the beautifully trained left hand he had demonstrated at the beer garden.

But the shorter man, as Kyle had known from the first mo-

ment of seeing him, was not like the busboy the Prince had
decisioned so neatly. This man was thirty pounds heavier, fifteen years more experienced, and by build and nature a natural bar fighter. He had not stood there waiting to be hit, but
had already ducked and gone forward to throw his thick arms
around the Prince's body. The young man's punch bounced
harmlessly off the round head, and both bodies hit floor, rolling in among the chair and table legs.

Kyle was already more than halfway to the bar and the three
bartenders were already leaping the wooden hurdle that walled
them off. The taller friend of the bullet-headed man, hovering
over the two bodies, his eyes glittering, had his boot drawn
back ready to drive the point of it into the Prince's kidneys.
Kyle's forearm took him economically like a bar of iron across
the tanned throat.

He stumbled backward choking. Kyle stood still, hands
open and down, glancing at the middle-aged bartender.

"All right," said the bartender. "But don't do anything
more." He turned to the two younger bartenders. "All right.
Haul him off!"

The pair of younger, aproned men bent down and came up
with the bullet-headed man expertly hand-locked between
them. The man made one surging effort to break loose, and
then stood still.

"Let me at him," he said.

"Not in here," said the older bartender. "Take it outside."

Between the tables, the Prince staggered unsteadily to his
feet. His face was streaming blood from a cut on his forehead,
but what could be seen of it was white as a drowning man's.
His eyes went to Kyle, standing beside him; and he opened his
mouth—but what came out sounded like something between a
sob and a curse.

"All right," said the middle-aged bartender again. "Outside, both of you. Settle it out there."

The men in the room had packed around the little space by
the bar. The Prince looked about and for the first time seemed
to see the human wall hemming him in. His gaze wobbled to
meet Kyle's.

"Outside . . . ?" he said chokingly.

"You aren't staying in here," said the older bartender,

answering for Kyle. "I saw it. You started the whole thing.
Now, settle it any way you want—but you're both going outside. Now! Get moving!"

He pushed at the Prince, but the Prince resisted, clutching
at Kyle's leather jacket with one hand.

"Kyle—"

"I'm sorry, Lord," said Kyle. "I can't help. It's your
fight."

"Let's get out of here," said the bullet-headed man.

The Prince stared around at them as if they were some
strange set of beings he had never known to exist before.

"No . . ." he said.

He let go of Kyle's jacket. Unexpectedly, his hand darted in
toward Kyle's belly holster and came out holding the slug
pistol.

"Stand back!" he said, his voice high-pitched. "Don't try
to touch me!"

His voice broke on the last words. There was a strange
sound, half-grunt, half-moan, from the crowd; and it swayed
back from him. Manager, bartenders, watchers—all but Kyle
and the bullet-headed man drew back.

"You dirty slob . . ." said the bullet-headed man distinctly.
"I knew you didn't have the guts."

"Shut up!" The Prince's voice was high and cracking.
"Shut up! Don't any of you try to come after me!"

He began backing away toward the front door of the bar.
The room watched in silence, even Kyle standing still. As he
backed, the Prince's back straightened. He hefted the gun in
his hand. When he reached the door he paused to wipe the
blood from his eyes with his left sleeve, and his smeared face
looked with a first touch of regained arrogance at them.

"Swine!" he said.

He opened the door and backed out, closing it behind him.
Kyle took one step that put him facing the bullet-headed man.
Their eyes met and he could see the other recognizing the
fighter in him, as he had earlier recognized it in the bullet-
headed man.

"Don't come after us," said Kyle.

The bullet-headed man did not answer. But no answer was
needed. He stood still.

Kyle turned, ran to the door, stood on one side of it, and

flicked it open. Nothing happened; and he slipped through, dodging to his right at once, out of the line of any shot aimed at the opening door.

But no shot came. For a moment he was blind in the night darkness, then his eyes began to adjust. He went by sight, feel, and memory toward the hitching rack. By the time he got there, he was beginning to see.

The Prince was untying the gelding and getting ready to mount.

"Lord," said Kyle.

The Prince let go of the saddle for a moment and turned to look over his shoulder at him.

"Get away from me," said the Prince thickly.

"Lord," said Kyle, low-voiced and pleading, "you lost your head in there. Anyone might do that. But don't make it worse, now. Give me back the gun, Lord."

"Give you the gun?"

The young man stared at him—and then he laughed.

Give *you* the gun!" he said again. "So you can let some-one beat me up some more? So you can not-guard me with it?"

"Lord," said Kyle, "please. For your own sake—give me back the gun."

"Get out of here," said the Prince thickly, turning back to mount the gelding. "Clear out before I put a slug in you."

Kyle drew a slow, sad breath. He stepped forward and tapped the Prince on the shoulder.

"Turn around, Lord," he said.

"I warned you—" shouted the Prince, turning.

He came around as Kyle stooped, and the slug pistol flashed in his hand from the light of the bar windows. Kyle, bent over, was lifting the cuff of his trouser leg and closing his fingers on the hilt of the knife in his boot sheath. He moved simply, skillfully, and with a speed nearly double that of the young man, striking up into the chest before him until the hand holding the knife jarred against the cloth covering flesh and bone.

It was a sudden, hard-driven, swiftly merciful blow. The blade struck upward between the ribs lying open to an under-handed thrust, plunging deep into the heart. The Prince grunted with the impact driving the air from his lungs; and he was dead as Kyle caught his slumping body in leather-jacketed arms.

Kyle lifted the tall body across the saddle of the gelding and tied it there. He hunted on the dark ground for the fallen pistol and returned it to his holster. Then, he mounted the stallion and, leading the gelding with its burden, started the long ride back.

Dawn was graying the sky when at last he topped the hill overlooking the lodge where he had picked up the Prince almost twenty-four hours before. He rode down toward the courtyard gate.

A tall figure, indistinct in the predawn light, was waiting inside the courtyard as Kyle came through the gate; and it came running to meet him as he rode toward it. It was the tutor, Montlaven, and he was weeping as he ran to the gelding and began to fumble at the cords that tied the body in place.

"I'm sorry . . ." Kyle heard himself saying; and was dully shocked by the deadness and remoteness of his voice. "There was no choice. You can read it all in my report tomorrow morning—"

He broke off. Another, even taller figure had appeared in the doorway of the lodge giving on the courtyard. As Kyle turned toward it, this second figure descended the few steps to the grass and came to him.

"Lord—" said Kyle. He looked down into features like those of the Prince, but older, under graying hair. This man did not weep like the tutor, but his face was set like iron.

"What happened, Kyle?" he said.

"Lord," said Kyle, "you'll have my report in the morning . . ."

"I want to know," said the tall man. Kyle's throat was dry and stiff. He swallowed but swallowing did not ease it.

"Lord," he said, "you have three other sons. One of them will make an Emperor to hold the worlds together."

"What did he do? Whom did he hurt? Tell me!" The tall man's voice cracked almost as his son's voice had cracked in the bar.

"Nothing. No one," said Kyle, stiff-throated. "He hit a boy not much older than himself. He drank too much. He may have got a girl in trouble. It was nothing he did to anyone else. It was only a fault against himself." He swallowed. "Wait until tomorrow, Lord, and read my report."

"No!" The tall man caught Kyle's saddle horn with a grip

that checked even the white stallion from moving. "Your family and mine have been tied together by this for three hundred years. What was the flaw in my son to make him fail his test, back here on Earth? *I want to know!*"

Kyle's throat ached and was dry as ashes.

"Lord," he answered, "he was a coward."

The hand dropped from his saddle horn as if struck down by a sudden strengthlessness. And the Emperor of a hundred worlds fell back like a beggar, spurned in the dust.

Kyle lifted his reins and rode out of the gate, into the forest away on the hillside. The dawn was breaking.

TIGER GREEN

I.

A man with hallucinations he cannot stand, trying to strangle himself in a homemade straitjacket, is not a pretty sight. But after a while, grimly thought Jerry McWhin, the *Star Scout*'s navigator, the ugly and terrible seem to backfire in effect, filling you with fury instead of harrowing you further. Men in crowds and packs could be stampeded briefly, but after a while the individual among them would turn, get his back up, and slash back.

At least—the hyperstubborn individual in himself had finally so reacted.

Determinedly, with fingers that fumbled from lack of sleep, he got the strangling man—Wally Blake, an assistant ecologist —untangled and into a position where it would be difficult for him to try to choke out his own life again. Then Jerry went out of the sick-bay storeroom, leaving Wally and the other seven men out of the *Star Scout*'s complement of twelve who were in total restraint. He was lightheaded from exhaustion; but a berserk something in him snarled like a cornered tiger and refused to break like Wally and the others.

When all's said and done, he thought half-crazily, there's worse ways to come to the end of it than a last charge, win or lose, alone in the midst of all your enemies.

Going down the corridor, the sight of another figure jolted him a little back toward common sense. Ben Akham, the drive engineer, came trudging back from the air-lock corridor with a flame thrower on his back. Soot etched darkly the lines on his once-round face.

"Get the hull cleared?" asked Jerry. Ben nodded exhaustedly.

"There's more jungle on her every morning," he grunted. "Now those big thistles are starting to drip a corrosive liquid. The hull needs an antiacid washing. I can't do it. I'm worn out."

"We all are," said Jerry. His own five-eleven frame was down to a hundred and thirty-eight pounds. There was plenty of food—it was just that the four men left on their feet had no time to prepare it; and little enough time to eat it, prepared or not.

Exploration Team Five-Twenty-Nine, thought Jerry, had finally bitten off more than it could chew, here on the second planet of Star 83476. It was nobody's fault. It had been a gamble for Milt Johnson, the Team captain, either way—to land or not to land. He had landed; and it had turned out bad.

By such small things was the scale toward tragedy tipped. A communication problem with the natives, a native jungle evidently determined to digest the spaceship, and eight of twelve men down with something like suicidal delirium tremens—any two of these things the Team could probably have handled.

But not all three at once.

Jerry and Ben reached the entrance of the Control Room together and peered in, looking for Milt Johnson.

"Must be ootside, talking to that native again," said Jerry.

"Ootside?—*oot*-side!" exploded Ben, with a sudden snapping of frayed nerves. "Can't you say 'out-side'?—'*out*-side,' like everybody else?"

The berserk something in Jerry lunged to be free, but he caught it and hauled it back.

"Get hold of yourself!" he snapped.

"Well . . . I wouldn't mind you sounding like a blasted Scotchman all the time!" growled Ben, getting himself, nevertheless, somewhat under control. "It's just you always do it when I don't expect it!"

"If the Lord wanted us all to sound alike, he'd have

propped up the Tower of Babel,'' said Jerry wickedly. He was not particularly religious himself, but he knew Ben to be a table-thumping atheist. He had the satisfaction now of watching the other man bite his lips and control himself in his turn.

Academically, however, Jerry thought as they both headed out through the ship to find Milt, he could not really blame Ben. For Jerry, like many Scot-Canadians, appeared to speak a very middle-western American sort of English most of the time. But only as long as he avoided such vocabulary items as "house" and "out," which popped off Jerry's tongue as "hoose" and "oot." However, every man aboard had his personal peculiarities. You had to get used to them. That was part of spaceship—in fact, part of human—life.

They emerged from the lock, rounded the nose of the spaceship, and found themselves in the neat little clearing on one side of the ship where the jungle paradoxically refused to grow. In this clearing stood the broad-shouldered figure of Milt Johnson, his whitish-blond hair glinting in the yellow-white sunlight.

Facing Milt was the thin, naked, and saddle-colored humanoid figure of one of the natives from the village, or whatever it was, about twenty minutes away by jungle trail. Between Milt and the native was the glittering metal console of the translator machine.

". . . Let's try it once more," they heard Milt saying as they came up and stopped behind him.

The native gabbled agreeably.

"Yes, yes. Try it again," translated the voice of the console.

"I am Captain Milton Johnson. I am in authority over the crew of the ship you see before me."

"Gladly would I not see it," replied the console on translation of the native's gabblings. "However—I am Communicator, messenger to you sick ones."

"I will call you Communicator, then," began Milt.

"Of course. What else could you call me?"

"Please," said Milt, wearily. "To get back to it—I also am a Communicator."

"No, no," said the native. "You are not a Communicator. It is the sickness that makes you talk this way."

"But," said Milt, and Jerry saw the big, white-haired captain swallow in an attempt to keep his temper. "You will notice, I am communicating with you."

"No, no."

"I see," said Milt patiently. "You mean, we aren't communicating in the sense that we aren't understanding each other. We're talking, but you don't understand me—"

"No, no. I understand you perfectly."

"Well," said Milt, exhaustedly. "I don't understand you."

"That is because you are sick."

Milt blew out a deep breath and wiped his brow.

"Forget that part of it, then," he said. "Many of my crew are upset by nightmares we all have been having. They *are* sick. But there are still four of us who are well—"

"No, no. You are all sick," said Communicator earnestly. "But you should love what you call nightmares. All people love them."

"Including you and your people?"

"Of course. Love your nightmares. They will make you well. They will make the little bit of proper life in you grow, and heal you."

Ben snorted beside Jerry. Jerry could sympathize with the other man. The nightmares he had been having during his scant hours of sleep, the past two weeks, came back to his mind, with the indescribably alien, terrifying sensation of drifting in a sort of environmental soup with identifiable things changing shape and identity constantly around him. Even pumped full of tranquilizers, he thought—which reminded Jerry.

He had not taken his tranquilizers lately.

When had he taken some last? Not since he woke up, in any case. Not since . . . yesterday, sometime. Though that was now hard to believe.

"Let's forget that, too, then," Milt was saying. "Now, the jungle is growing all over our ship, in spite of all we can do. You tell me your people can make the jungle do anything you want."

"Yes, yes," said Communicator agreeably.

"Then, will you please stop it from growing all over our spaceship?"

"We understand. It is your sickness, the poison that makes you say this. Do not fear. We will never abandon you." Communicator looked almost ready to pat Milt consolingly on the head. "You are people, who are more important than any cost. Soon you will grow and cast off your poisoned part and come to us."

"But we can come to you right now!" said Milt, between his teeth. "In fact—we've come to your village a dozen times."

"No, no." Communicator sounded distressed. "You approach, but you do not come. You have never come to us."

Milt wiped his forehead with the back of a wide hand. "I will come back to your village now, with you," he said. "Would you like that?" he asked.

"I would be so happy!" said Communicator. "But—you will not come. You say it, but you do not come."

"All right. Wait—" About to take a hand transceiver from the console, Milt saw the other two men. "Jerry," he said, "you go this time. Maybe he'll believe it if it's you who goes to the village with him."

"I've been there before. With you, the second time you went," objected Jerry. "And I've got to feed the men in restraint, pretty soon," he added.

"Try going again. That's all we can do—try things. Ben and I'll feed the men," said Milt. Jerry, about to argue further, felt the pressure of a sudden wordless, exhausted appeal from Milt. Milt's basic berserkedness must be just about ready to break loose, too, he realized.

"All right," said Jerry.

"Good," said Milt, looking grateful. "We have to keep trying. I should have lifted ship while I still had five well men to lift it with. Come on, Ben—you and I better go feed those men now, before we fall asleep on our feet."

II.

They went away around the nose of the ship. Jerry unhooked the little black-and-white transceiver that would radio-relay his conversations with Communicator back to the console of the translator for sense-making during the trip.

"Come on," he said to Communicator, and led off down the pleasantly wide jungle trail toward the native village.

They passed from under the little patch of open sky above the clearing and into green-roofed stillness. All about them, massive limbs, branches, ferns, and vines intertwined in a majestic maze of growing things. Small flying creatures, looking half-animal and half-insect, flittered among the branches overhead. Some larger, more animallike creatures sat on the heavier limbs and moaned off-key like abandoned puppies. Jerry's head spun with his weariness, and the green over his head seemed to close down on him like a net flung by some giant, crazy fisherman, to take him captive.

He was suddenly and bitterly reminded of the Team's high hopes, the day they had set down on this world. No other Team or Group had yet to turn up any kind of alien life much more intelligent than an anthropoid ape. Now they, Team 529, had not only uncovered an intelligent, evidently semi-cultured alien people, but an alien people eager to establish relations with the humans and communicate. Here, two weeks later, the natives were still apparently just as eager to communicate, but what they said made no sense.

Nor did it help that, with the greatest of patience and kindness, Communicator and his kind seemed to consider that it was the humans who were irrational and uncommunicative.

Nor that, meanwhile, the jungle seemed to be mounting a specifically directed attack on the human spaceship.

Nor that the nightmare afflicting the humans had already laid low eight of the twelve crew and were grinding the four left on their feet down to a choice between suicidal delirium or collapse from exhaustion.

It was a miracle, thought Jerry, lightheadedly trudging through the jungle, that the four of them had been able to survive as long as they had. A miracle based probably on some individual chance peculiarity of strength that the other eight men in straitjackets lacked. Although, thought Jerry now, that strength that they had so far defied analysis. Dizzily, like a man in a high fever, he considered their four surviving personalities in his mind's eye. They were, he thought, the four men of the team with what you might call the biggest mental crotchets.

—or ornery streaks.

Take the fourth member of the group—the medician, Arthyr Loy, who had barely stuck his nose out of the sick-bay lab in the last forty-eight hours. Not only because he was the closest thing to an M.D. aboard the ship was Art still determined to put the eight restrained men back on their feet again. It just happened, in addition, that Art considered himself the only true professional man aboard, and was not the kind to admit any inability to the lesser mortals about him.

And Milt Johnson—Milt made an excellent captain. He was a tower of strength, a great man for making decisions. The only thing was, that having decided, Milt could hardly be brought to consider the remote possibility that anyone else might have wanted to decide differently.

Ben Akham was another matter. Ben hated religion and loved machinery—and the jungle surrounding was attacking *his* spaceship. In fact, Jerry was willing to bet that by the time he got back, Ben would be washing the hull with an acid-counteractant in spite of what he had told Jerry earlier.

And himself? Jerry? Jerry shook his head woozily. It was hard to be self-analytical after ten days of three and four hours sleep per twenty. He had what his grandmother had once described as the curse of the Gael—black stubbornness and red rages.

All of these traits, in all four of them, had normally been buried safely below the surfaces of their personalities and had only colored them as individuals. But now, the last two weeks had worn those surfaces down to basic personality bedrock. Jerry shoved the thought out of his mind.

"Well," he said, turning to Communicator, "we're almost to your village now. . . . You can't say someone didn't come with you, this time."

Communicator gabbled. The transceiver in Jerry's hand translated.

"Alas," the native said, "but you are not with me."

"Cut it out!" said Jerry wearily. "I'm right here beside you."

"No," said Communicator. "You accompany me, but you are not here. You are back with your dead things."

"You mean the ship, and the rest of it?" asked Jerry.

"There is no ship," said Communicator. "A ship must have grown and been alive. Your thing has always been dead. But we will save you."

• • •

III.

They came out of the path at last into a clearing dotted with whitish, pumpkinlike shells some ten feet in height above the brown earth in which they were half-buried. Wide cracks in the out-curving sides gave view of tangled roots and plants inside, among which other natives could be seen moving about, scratching, tasting, and making holes in the vegetable surfaces.

"Well," said Jerry, making an effort to speak cheerfully, "here I am."

"You are not here."

The berserk tigerishness in Jerry leaped up unawares and took him by the inner throat. For a long second he looked at Communicator through a red haze. Communicator gazed back patiently, evidently unaware how close he was to having his neck broken by a pair of human hands.

"Look—" said Jerry, slowly, between his teeth, getting himself under control, "if you will just tell me what to do to join you and your people, here, I will do it."

"That is good!"

"Then," said Jerry, still with both hands on the inner fury that fought to tear loose inside him, "what do I do?"

"But you know—" The enthusiasm that had come into Communicator a moment before wavered visibly. "You must get rid of the dead things, and set yourself free to grow, inside. Then, after you have grown, your unsick self will bring you here to join us!"

Jerry stared back. Patience, he said harshly to himself.

"Grow? How? In what way?"

"But you have a little bit of proper life in you," explained Communicator. "Not much, of course . . . but if you will rid yourself of dead things and concentrate on what you call nightmares, it will grow and force out the poison of the dead life in you. The proper life and the nightmares are the hope for you—"

"Wait a minute!" Jerry's exhaustion-fogged brain cleared suddenly and nearly miraculously at the sudden surge of excitement into his bloodstream. "This proper life you talk about—does it have something to do with the nightmares?"

"Of course. How could you have what you call nightmares

without a little proper life in you to give them to you? As the proper life grows, you will cease to fight so against the 'nightmares' . . .''

Communicator continued to talk earnestly. But Jerry's spinning brain was flying off on a new tangent. What was it he had been thinking earlier about tranquilizers—that he had not taken any himself for some time? Then, what about the nightmares in his last four hours of sleep?

He must have had them—he remembered now that he *had* had them. But evidently they had not bothered him as much as before—at least, not enough to send him scrambling for tranquilizers to dull the dreams' weird impact on him.

"Communicator!" Jerry grabbed at the thin, leathery-skinned arm of the native. "Have I been chang—growing?"

"I do not know, of course," said the native, courteously. "I profoundly hope so. Have you?"

"Excuse me—" gulped Jerry. "I've got to get oot of here—back to th' ship!"

He turned, and raced back up the trail. Some twenty minutes later, he burst into the clearing before the ship to find an ominous silence hanging over everything. Only the faint rustle and hissing from the ever-growing jungle swallowing up the ship sounded on his eardrums.

"Milt—Ben!" he shouted, plunging into the ship. "Art!"

A hail from farther down the main corridor reassured him, and he followed it up to find all three unrestrained members of the crew in the sick bay. But—Jerry brought himself up short, his throat closing on him—there was a figure on the table.

"Who . . .'' began Jerry. Milt Johnson turned around to face him. The captain's body mercifully hid most of the silent form on the table.

"Wally Blake," said Milt emptily. "He managed to strangle himself after all. Got twisted up in his restraint jacket. Ben and I heard him thumping around in there, but by the time we got to him, it was too late. Art's doing an autopsy."

"Not exactly an autopsy," came the soft, Virginia voice of the medician from beyond Milt. "Just looking for something I suspected . . . and here it is!"

Milt spun about and Jerry pushed between the big captain and Ben. He found himself looking at the back of a human head from which a portion of the skull had been removed.

What he saw before him was a small expanse of whitish, soft inner tissue that was the brainstem; and fastened to it almost like a grape growing there, was a small, purplish mass.

Art indicated the purple shape with the tip of a sharp, surgical instrument.

"There," he said. "And I bet we've each got one."

"What is it?" asked Ben's voice, hushed and a little nauseated.

"I don't know," said Art harshly. "How the devil would I be able to tell? But I found organisms in the bloodstreams of those of us I've taken blood samples from—organisms like spores, that look like this, only smaller, microscopic in size."

"You didn't tell me that!" said Milt, turning quickly to face him.

"What was the point?" Art turned toward the Team captain. Jerry saw that the medician's long face was almost bloodless. "I didn't know what they were. I thought if I kept looking, I might know more. Then I could have something positive to tell you, as well as the bad news. But—it's no use now."

"Why do you say that?" snapped Milt.

"Because it's the truth." Art's face seemed to slide apart, go loose and waxy with defeat. "As long as it was something nonphysical we were fighting, there was some hope we could throw it off. But—you see what's going on inside us. We're being changed physically. That's where the nightmares come from. You can't overcome a physical change with an effort of will!"

"What about the Grotto at Lourdes?" asked Jerry. His head was whirling strangely with a mass of ideas. His own great-grandfather—the family story came back to mind—had been judged by his physician in 1896 to have advanced pulmonary tuberculosis. Going home from the doctor's office, Simon Fraser McWhin had decided that he could not afford to have tuberculosis at this time. That he would not, therefore, have tuberculosis at all. And he had dismissed the matter fully from his mind.

One year later, examined by the same physician, he had no signs of tuberculosis whatsoever.

But in this present moment, Art, curling up in his chair at the end of the table, seemed not to have heard Jerry's question. And Jerry was suddenly reminded of the question that had brought him pelting back from the native village.

"Is it growing—I mean was it growing when Wally strangled himself—that growth on his brain?" he asked.

Art roused himself.

"Growing?" he repeated dully. He climbed to his feet and picked up an instrument. He investigated the purple mass for a moment.

"No," he said, dropping the instrument wearily and falling back into his chair. "Looks like its outer layer has died and started to be reabsorbed—I think." He put his head in his hands. "I'm not qualified to answer such questions. I'm not trained . . ."

"Who is?" demanded Milt, grimly, looming over the table and the rest of them. "And we're reaching the limit of our strength as well as the limits of what we know—"

"We're done for," muttered Ben. His eyes were glazed, looking at the dissected body on the table. "It's not my fault—"

"Catch him! Catch Art!" shouted Jerry, leaping forward.

But he was too late. The medician had been gradually curling up in his chair since he had sat down in it again. Now, he slipped out of it to the floor, rolled in a ball, and lay still.

"Leave him alone." Milt's large hand caught Jerry and held him back. "He may as well lie there as someplace else." He got to his feet. "Ben's right. We're done for."

"Done for?" Jerry stared at the big man. The words he had just heard were words he would never have imagined hearing from Milt.

"Yes," said Milt. He seemed somehow to be speaking from a long distance off.

"Listen—" said Jerry. The tigerishness inside him had woken at Milt's words. It tugged and snarled against the words of defeat from the captain's lips. "We're winning. We aren't losing!"

"Quit it, Jerry," said Ben dully, from the far end of the room.

"Quit it—?" Jerry swung on the engineer. "You lost your temper with me before I went down to the village, about the way I said 'oot'! How could you lose your temper if you were full of tranquilizers? I haven't been taking any myself, and I feel better because of it. Don't tell me you've been taking yours!—and that means we're getting stronger than the nightmares."

"The tranquilizers've been making me sick, if you must know! That's why I haven't been taking them—" Ben broke off, his face graying. He pointed a shaking finger at the purplish mass. "I'm being changed, that's why they made me sick! I'm changing already!" His voice rose toward a scream. "Don't you see, it's changing me—" He broke off, suddenly screaming and leaping at Milt with clawing fingers. "We're all changing! And it's your fault for bringing the ship down here. You did it—"

Milt's huge fist slammed into the side of the smaller man's jaw, driving him to the floor beside the still shape of the medician, where he lay quivering and sobbing.

Slowly Milt lifted his gaze from the fallen man and faced Jerry. It was the standard seventy-two degrees centigrade in the room, but Jerry saw perspiration standing out on Milt's calm face as if he had just stepped out of a steam bath.

"But he may be right," said Milt emotionlessly. His voice seemed to come from the far end of some lightless tunnel. "We may be changing under the influence of those growths right now—each of us."

"Milt!" said Jerry sharply. But Milt's face never changed. It was large, and calm, and pale—and drenched with sweat. "Now's the last time we ought to give up! We're starting to understand it now. I tell you, the thing is to meet Communicator and the other natives head on! Head to head we can crack them wide open. One of us has to go down to that village."

"No. I'm the captain," said Milt, his voice unchanged. "I'm responsible, and I'll decide. We can't lift ship with less than five men and there's only two of us—you and I—actually left. I can't risk one of us coming under the influence of the growth in him, and going over to the alien side."

"Going over?" Jerry stared at him.

"That's what all this has been for—the jungle, the natives, the nightmare. They want to take us over." Sweat ran down Milt's cheeks and dripped off his chin, while he continued to talk tonelessly and gaze straight ahead. "They'll send us— what's left of us—back against our own people. I can't let that happen. We'll have to destroy ourselves so there's nothing for them to use."

"Milt—" said Jerry.

"No." Milt swayed faintly on his feet like a tall tree under a wind too high to be felt on the ground at its base. "We can't risk leaving ship or crew. We'll blow the ship up with ourselves in it—"

"*Blow up my ship!*"

It was a wild-animal scream from the floor at their feet; and Ben Akham rose from almost under the table like a demented wildcat, aiming for Milt's jugular vein. So unexpected and powerful was the attack that the big captain tottered and fell. With a noise like worrying dogs, they rolled together under the table.

The changed tiger inside Jerry broke its bonds and flung free.

He turned and ducked through the door into the corridor. It was a heavy pressure door with a wheel lock, activating metal dogs to seal it shut in case of a hull blowout and sudden loss of air. Jerry slammed the door shut, and spun the wheel.

The dogs snicked home. Snatching down the portable fire extinguisher hanging on the wall alongside, Jerry dropped the foam container on the floor and jammed the metal nozzle of its hose between a spoke of the locking wheel and the unlocking stop on the door beneath it.

He paused. There was silence inside the sick-bay lab. Then the wheel jerked against the nozzle and the door tried to open.

"What's going on?" demanded the voice of Milt. There was a pause. "Jerry, what's going on out there? Open up!"

A wild, crazy impulse to hysterical laughter rose inside Jerry without warning. It took all his willpower to choke it back.

"You're locked in, Milt," he said.

"Jerry!" The wheel spoke clicked against the jamming metal nozzle, in a futile effort to turn. "Open up! That's an order!"

"Sorry, Milt," said Jerry softly and lightheadedly. "I'm not ready yet to burn the hoose about my ears. This business of you wanting to blow up the ship's the same sort of impulse to suicide that got Wally and the rest. I'm off to face the natives now and let them have their way with me. I'll be back later, to let you oot."

"Jerry!"

Jerry heard Milt's voice behind him as he went off down the corridor.

"*Jerry!*" There was a fusillade of pounding fists against the door, growing fainter as Jerry moved away. "Don't you see?—that growth in you is finally getting you! Jerry, come back! Don't let them take over one of us! Jerry . . ."

Jerry left the noise and the ship together behind him as he stepped out of the air lock. The jungle, he saw, was covering the ship's hull again, already hiding it for the most part. He went on out to the translator console and began taking off his clothes. When he was completely undressed, he unhooked the transceiver he had brought back from the native village, slung it on a loop of his belt, and hung the belt around his neck.

He headed off down the trail toward the village, wincing a little as the soles of his shoeless feet came into contact with pebbles along the way.

When he got to the village clearing, a naked shape he recognized as that of Communicator tossed up its arms in joy and came running to him.

"Well," said Jerry. "I've grown. I've got rid of the poison of dead things and the sickness. Here I am to join you!"

"At last!" gabbled Communicator. Other natives were running up. "Throw away the dead thing around your neck!"

"I still need it to understand you," said Jerry. "I guess I need a little help to join you all the way."

"Help? We will help!" cried Communicator. "But you must throw that away. You have rid yourself of the dead things that you kept wrapped around your limbs and body," gabbled Communicator. "Now rid yourself of the dead thing hanging about your neck."

"But I tell you, if I do that," objected Jerry, "I won't be able to understand you when you talk, or make you understand me!"

"Throw it away. It is poisoning you! Throw it away!" said Communicator. By this time three or four more natives had come up and others were headed for the gathering. "Shortly you will understand all, and all will understand you. Throw it away!"

"Throw it away!" chorused the other natives.

"Well . . ." said Jerry. Reluctantly, he took off the belt with the transceiver, and dropped it. Communicator gabbled unintelligibly.

". . . come with me . . ." translated the transceiver like a faint and tinny echo from the ground where it landed.

Communicator took hold of Jerry's hand and drew him toward the nearest whitish structure. Jerry swallowed unobtrusively. It was one thing to make up his mind to do this; it was something else again to actually do it. But he let himself be led to and in through a crack in the structure.

Inside, the place smelled rather like a mixture of a root cellar and a hayloft—earthy and fragrant at the same time. Communicator drew him in among the waist-high tangle of roots rising and reentering the packed earth floor. The other natives swarmed after them. Close to the center of the floor they reached a point where the roots were too thick to allow them to pick their way any further. The roots rose and tangled into a mat, the irregular surface of which was about three feet off the ground. Communicator patted the root surface and gabbled agreeably.

"You want me to get up there?" Jerry swallowed again, then gritted his teeth as the chained fury in him turned suddenly upon himself. There was nothing worse, he snarled at himself, than a man who was long on planning a course of action, but short on carrying it out.

Awkwardly, he clambered up onto the matted surface of the roots. They gave irregularly under him and their rough surfaces scraped his knees and hands. The natives gabbled, and he felt leathery hands urging him to stretch out and lie down on his back.

He did so. The root scored and poked the tender skin of his back. It was exquisitely uncomfortable.

"Now what—?" he gasped. He turned his head to look at the natives and saw that green tendrils, growing rapidly from the root mass, were winding about and garlanding the arms and legs of Communicator and several other of the natives standing by. A sudden pricking at his left wrist made him look down.

Green garlands were twining around his own wrists and ankles, sending wire-thin tendrils into his skin. In unconscious reflex of panic he tried to heave upward, but the green bonds held him fast.

"*Gabble-gabble-gabble* . . ." warbled Communicator reassuringly.

With sudden alarm, Jerry realized that the green tendrils

were growing right into the arms and legs of the natives as well. He was abruptly conscious of further prickings in his own arms and legs.

"What's going on—" he started to say, but found his tongue had gone unnaturally thick and unmanageable. A wave of dizziness swept over him as if a powerful general anesthetic was taking hold. The interior of the structure seemed to darken; and he felt as if he was swooping away toward its ceiling on the long swing of some monster pendulum . . .

It swung him on into darkness. And nightmare.

It was the same old nightmare, but more so. It was nightmare experienced *awake* instead of asleep; and the difference was that he had no doubt about the fact that he was experiencing what he was experiencing, nor any tucked-away certainty that waking would bring him out of it.

Once more he floated through a changing soup of uncertainty, himself a changing part of it. It was not painful, it was not even terrifying. But it was hideous—it was an affront to nature. He was not himself. He was a thing, a part of the whole—and he must reconcile himself to being so. He must accept it.

Reconcile himself to it—no! It was not possible for the unbending, solitary, individualistic part that was *him* to do so. But accept it—maybe.

Jerry set a jaw that was no longer a jaw and felt the determination in him to blast through, to comprehend this incomprehensible thing, become hard and undeniable as a sword-point of tungsten steel. He drove through—

And abruptly the soup fell into order. It slid into focus like a blurred scene before the gaze of a badly myopic man who finally gets his spectacles before his eyes. Suddenly, Jerry was aware that what he observed was a scene not just before his eyes, but before his total awareness. And it was not the interior of the structure where he lay on a bed of roots, but the whole planet.

It was a landscape of factories. Countless factories, interconnected, intersupplying, integrated. It lacked only that he find his own working place among them.

Now, said this scene. *This is the sane universe, the way it really is. Reconcile yourself to it.*

The hell I will!

It was the furious, unbending, solitary, individualistic part that was essentially *him* speaking again. Not just speaking. Roaring—snarling its defiance, like a tiger on a hillside.

And the scene went—*pop*.

Jerry opened his eyes. He sat up. The green shoots around and in his wrists and ankles pulled prickingly at him. But they were already dying and not able to hold him. He swung his legs over the edge of the mat of roots and stood down. Communicator and the others who were standing there, backed fearfully away from him, gabbling.

He understood their gabbling no better than before, but now he could read the emotional overtones in it. And those overtones were now of horror and disgust, overlying a wild, atavistic panic and terror. He walked forward. They scuttled away before him, gabbling, and he walked through the nearest crack in the wall of the structure and out into the sunlight, toward the transceiver and the belt where he had dropped them.

"Monster!" screamed the transceiver tinnily, faithfully translating the gabbling of the Communicator, who was following a few steps behind like a small dog barking behind a larger. "Brute! Savage! Unclean . . ." It kept up a steady denunciation.

Jerry turned to face Communicator, and the native tensed for flight.

"You know what I'm waiting for," said Jerry, almost smiling, hearing the transceiver translate his words into gabbling —though it was not necessary. As he had said, Communicator knew what he was waiting for.

Communicator cursed a little longer in his own tongue, then went off into one of the structures, and returned with a handful of what looked like lengths of green vine. He dropped them on the ground before Jerry and backed away, cautiously, gabbling.

"Now will you go? And never come back! Never . . ."

"We'll see," said Jerry. He picked up the lengths of green vine and turned away up the path to the ship.

The natives he passed on his way out of the clearing huddled away from him and gabbled as he went.

When he stepped back into the clearing before the ship, he saw that most of the vegetation touching or close to the ship was already brown and dying. He went on into the ship, carefully avoiding the locked sick-bay door, and wound lengths of the green vine around the wrists of each of the men in restraints.

Then he sat down to await results. He had never been so tired in his life. The minute he touched the chair, his eyes started to close. He struggled to his feet and forced himself to pace the floor until the green vines, which had already sent hair-thin tendrils into the ulnar arteries of the arms around which they were wrapped, pumped certain inhibitory chemicals into the bloodstreams of the seven men.

When the men started to blink their eyes and look about sensibly, he went to work to unfasten the homemade straitjackets that had held them prisoner. When he had released the last one, he managed to get out his final message before collapsing.

"Take the ship on," croaked Jerry. "Then, let yourself into the sick bay and wrap a vine piece around the wrists of Milt, and Art, and Ben. Ship up first—then when you're safely in space, take care of them, in the sick bay. Do it the other way and you'll never see Earth again."

They crowded around him with questions. He waved them off, slumping into one of the abandoned bunks.

"Ship up—" he croaked. "Then release and fix the others. Ask me later. Later—"

. . . And that was all he remembered, then.

IV.

At some indefinite time later, not quite sure whether he had woken by himself, or whether someone else had wakened him, Jerry swam back up to consciousness. He was vaguely aware that he had been sleeping a long time; and his body felt sane again, but weak as the body of a man after a long illness.

He blinked and saw the large face of Milt Johnson, partly obscured by a cup of something. Milt was seated in a chair by the side of the bunk Jerry lay in, and the Team captain was offering the cup of steaming black liquid to Jerry. Slowly, Jerry understood that this was coffee and he struggled up on one elbow to take the cup.

He drank from it slowly for a little while, while Milt watched and waited.

"Do you realize," said Milt at last, when Jerry finally put down the three-quarters-empty cup on the nightstand by the bunk, "that what you did in locking me in the sick bay was mutiny?"

Jerry swallowed. Even his vocal cords seemed drained of strength and limp.

"You realize," he croaked, "what would have happened if I hadn't?"

"You took a chance. You followed a wild hunch—"

"No hunch," said Jerry. He cleared his throat. "Art found that growth on Wally's brain had quit growing before Wally killed himself. And I'd been getting along without tranquilizers—handling the nightmares better than I had with them."

"It could have been the growth in your own brain," said Milt, "taking over and running you—working better on you than it had on Wally."

"Working better—talk sense!" said Jerry weakly, too pared down by the past two weeks to care whether school kept or not, in the matter of service courtesy to a superior. "The nightmares had broken Wally down to where we had to wrap him in a straitjacket. They hadn't even knocked me off my feet. If Wally's physiological processes had fought the alien invasion to a standstill, then I, you, Art, and Ben—all of us—had to be doing even better. Besides—I'd figured out what the aliens were after."

"What were they after?" Milt looked strangely at him.

"Curing us—of something we didn't have when we landed, but they thought we had."

"And what was that?"

"Insanity," said Jerry grimly.

Milt's blond eyebrows went up. He opened his mouth as if to say something disbelieving—then closed it again. When he did speak, it was quite calmly and humbly.

"They thought," he asked, "Communicator's people thought that we were insane, and they could cure us?"

Jerry laughed; not cheerfully, but grimly.

"You saw that jungle around us back there?" he asked. "That was a factory complex—an infinitely complex factory complex. You saw their village with those tangles of roots inside the big whitish shells?—that was a highly diversified laboratory.''

Milt's blue eyes slowly widened, as Jerry watched.

"You don't mean that—seriously?" said Milt, at last.

"That's right." Jerry drained the cup and set it aside. "Their technology is based on organic chemistry, the way ours is on the physical sciences. By our standards, they're chemical wizards. How'd you like to try changing the mind of an alien organism by managing to grow an extra part on to his brain— the way they tried to do to us humans? To them, it was the simplest way of convincing us."

Milt stared again. Finally, he shook his head.

"Why?" he said. "Why would they want to change our minds?"

"Because their philosophy, their picture of life and the universe around them grew out of a chemically oriented science," answered Jerry. "The result is, they see all life as part of a closed, intra-acting chemical circuit with no loose ends; with every living thing, intelligent or not, a part of the whole. Well, you saw it for yourself in your nightmare. That's the cosmos as they see it—and to them it's beautiful."

"But why did they want us to see it the way they did?"

"Out of sheer kindness," said Jerry and laughed barkingly. "According to their cosmology, there's no such thing as an alien. Therefore we weren't alien—just sick in the head. Poisoned by the lumps of metal like the ship and the translator we claimed were so important. And our clothes and everything else we had. The kind thing was to cure and rescue us."

"Now, wait a minute," said Milt. "They saw those things of ours *work—*"

"What's the fact they worked got to do with it? What you don't understand, Milt," said Jerry, lying back gratefully on the bunk, "is that Communicator's peoples' minds were *closed.* Not just unconvinced, not just refusing to see—but *closed!* Sealed, and welded shut from prehistoric beginnings right down to the present. The fact our translator worked meant nothing to them. According to their cosmology, it shouldn't work, so it didn't. Any stray phenomena tending to prove it did were simply the product of diseased minds."

Jerry paused to emphasize the statement and his eyes drifted shut. The next thing he knew Milt was shaking him.

". . . Wake up!'' Milt was shouting at him. "You can dope off after you've explained. I'm not going to have any crew back in straitjackets again, just because you were too sleepy to warn me they'd revert!''

". . . Won't revert,'' said Jerry thickly. He roused himself. "Those lengths of vine released chemicals into their blood-streams to destroy what was left of the growths. I wouldn't leave until I got them from Communicator.'' Jerry struggled up on one elbow again. "And after a short walk in a human brain—mine—he and his people couldn't get us out of sight and forgotten fast enough.''

"Why?'' Milt shook him again as Jerry's eyelids sagged. "Why should getting their minds hooked in with yours shake them up so?''

". . . Bust—bust their cosmology open. Quit shaking . . . I'm awake.''

"Why did it bust them wide open?''

"Remember—how it was for you with the nightmares?'' said Jerry. "The other way around? Think back, about when you slept. There you were, a lone atom of humanity, caught up in a nightmare like one piece of stew meat in a vat stewing all life together—just one single chemical bit with no indepen-dent existence, and no existence at all except as part of the whole. Remember?''

He saw Milt shiver slightly.

"It was like being swallowed up by a soft machine,'' said the Team captain in a small voice. "I remember.''

"All right,'' said Jerry. "That's how it was for you in Com-unicator's cosmos. But remember something about that cos-mos? It was warm, and safe. It was all-embracing, all-settling, like a great, big, soft, woolly comforter.''

"It was too much like a woolly comforter,'' said Milt, shud-dering. "It was unbearable.''

"To you. Right,'' said Jerry. "But to Communicator, it was ideal. And if that was ideal, think what it was like when he had to step into a human mind—mine.''

Milt stared at him.

"Why?'' Milt asked.

"Because,'' said Jerry, "he found himself *alone* there!''

Milt's eyes widened.

"Think about it, Milt,'' said Jerry. "From the time we're

born, we're individuals. From the moment we open our eyes on the world, inside we're alone in the universe. All the emotional and intellectual resources that Communicator draws from his identity with the stewing vat of his cosmos, each one of us has to dig up for and out of himself!''

Jerry stopped to give Milt a chance to say something. But Milt was evidently not in possession of something to say at the moment.

''That's why Communicator and the others couldn't take it, when they hooked into my human mind,'' Jerry went on. ''And that's why, when they found out what we were like inside, they couldn't wait to get rid of us. So they gave me the vines and kicked us out. That's the whole story.'' He lay back on the bunk.

Milt cleared his throat.

''All right,'' he said.

Jerry's heavy eyes closed. Then the other man's voice spoke, still close by his ear.

''But,'' said Milt, ''I still think you took a chance, going down to butt heads with the natives that way. What if Communicator and the rest had been able to stand exposure to your mind. You'd locked me in and the other men were in restraint. Our whole team would have been part of that stewing vat.''

''Not a chance,'' said Jerry.

''You can't be sure of that.''

''Yes I can.'' Jerry heard his own voice sounding harshly beyond the darkness of his closed eyelids. ''It wasn't just that I knew my cosmological view was too tough for them. It was the fact that their minds were closed—in the vat they had no freedom to change and adapt themselves to anything new.''

''What's that got to do with it?'' demanded the voice of Milt.

''Everything,'' said Jerry. ''Their point of view only made us more uncomfortable—but our point of view, being individually adaptable, and open, threatened to destroy the very laws of existence as they saw them. An open mind can always stand a closed one, if it has to—by making room for it in the general picture. But a closed mind can't stand it near an open one without risking immediate and complete destruction in its own terms. In a closed mind, there's no more room.''

He stopped speaking and slowly exhaled a weary breath.

"Now," he said, without opening his eyes, "will you finally get oot of here and let me sleep?"

For a long second more, there was silence. Then, he heard a chair scrape softly, and the muted steps of Milt tiptoeing away.

With another sigh, at last Jerry relaxed and let consciousness slip from him.

He slept.

—as sleep the boar upon the plain, the hawk upon the crag, and the tiger on the hill . . .

_____ OF THE PEOPLE _____

But you know, I could sense it coming a long time off. It was a little extra time taken in drinking a cup of coffee, it was lingering over the magazines in a drugstore as I picked out a handful. It was a girl I looked at twice as I ran out and down the steps of a library.

And it wasn't any good and I knew it. But it kept coming and it kept coming, and one night I stayed working at the design of a power cruiser until it was finished, before I finally knocked off for supper. Then, after I'd eaten, I looked ahead down twelve dark hours to daylight, and I knew I'd had it.

So I got up and I walked out of the apartment. I left my glass half-full and the record player I had built playing the music I had written to the pictures I had painted. Left the organ and the typewriter, left the darkroom and the lab. Left the jammed-full filing cabinets. Took the elevator and told the elevator boy to head for the ground floor. Walked out into the deep snow.

"You going out in January without an overcoat, Mr. Crossman?" asked the doorman.

"Don't need a coat," I told him. "Never no more, no coats."

"Don't you want me to phone the garage for your car, then?"

"Don't need a car."

I left him and set out walking. After a while it began to snow, but not on me. And after a little more while people started to stare, so I flagged down a cab.

"Get out and give me the keys," I told the driver.

"You drunk?" he said.

"It's all right, son," I said. "I own the company. But you'll get out nonetheless and give me the keys." He got out and gave me the keys and I left him standing there.

I got in the cab and drove it off through the nightlit downtown streets, and I kissed the city good-by as I went. I blew a kiss to the grain exchange and a kiss to the stockyards. And a kiss to every one of the fourteen offices in the city that knew me each under a different title as head of a different business. You've got to get along without me now, city and people, I said, because I'm not coming back, no more, no more.

I drove out of downtown and out past Longview Acres and past Manor Acres and past Sherman Hills and I blew them all a kiss, too. Enjoy your homes, you people, I told them, because they're good homes—not the best I could have done you by a damn sight, but better than you'll see elsewhere in a long time, and your money's worth. Enjoy your homes and don't remember me.

I drove out to the airport and there I left the cab. It was a good airport. I'd laid it out myself and I knew. It was a good airport and I got eighteen days of good hard work out of the job. I got myself so lovely and tired doing it I was able to go out to the bars and sit there having half a dozen drinks—before the urge to talk to the people around me became unbearable and I had to get up and go home.

There were planes on the field. A good handful of them. I went in and talked to one of the clerks. "Mr. Crossman!" he said, when he saw me.

"Get me a plane," I said. "Get me a plane headed east and then forget I was in tonight."

He did; and I went. I flew to New York and changed planes and flew to London; and changed again and came in by jet to Bombay.

By the time I reached Bombay, my mind was made up for

good, and I went through the city as if it were a dream of buildings and people and no more. I went through the town and out of the town and I hit the road north, walking. And as I walked, I took off my coat and my tie. And I opened my collar to the open air and I started my trek.

I was six weeks walking it. I remember little bits and pieces of things along the way—mainly faces, and mainly the faces of the children, for they aren't afraid when they're young. They'd come up to me and run alongside, trying to match the strides I'd take, and after a while they'd get tired and drop back—but there were always others along the way. And there were adults, too, men and women, but when they got close they'd take one look at my face and go away again. There was only one who spoke to me in all that trip, and that was a tall, dark brown man in some kind of uniform. He spoke to me in English and I answered him in dialect. He was scared to the marrow of this bones, for after he spoke I could hear the little grinding of his teeth in the silence as he tried to keep them from chattering. But I answered him kindly, and told him I had business in the north that was nobody's business but my own. And when he still would not move—he was well over six feet and nearly as tall as I—I opened my right hand beneath his nose and showed him himself, small and weak as a caterpillar in the palm of it. And he fell out of my path as if his legs had all the strength gone out of them, and I went on.

I was six weeks walking it. And when I came to the hills, my beard was grown out and my pants and my shirt were in tatters. Also, by this time, the word had gone ahead of me. Not the official word, but the little words of little people, running from mouth to mouth. They knew I was coming and they knew where I was headed—to see the old man up behind Mutteeanee Pass, the white-bearded, holy man of the village between two peaks.

He was sitting on his rock out on the hillside, with his blind eyes following the sun and the beard running white and old between his thin knees and down to the brown earth.

I sat down on a smaller rock before him and caught my breath.

"Well, Erik," I said. "I've come."

"I'm aware you have, Sam."

"By foot," I said. "By car and plane, too, but mostly by foot, as time goes. All the way from the lowlands by foot,

Erik. And that's the last I do for any of them."

"For them, Sam?"

"For me, then."

"Nor for you, either, Sam," he said. And then he sighed. "Go back, Sam," he said.

"Go back!" I echoed. "Go back to hell again? No thank you, Erik."

"You faltered," he said. "You weakened. You began to slow down, to look around. There was no need to, Sam. If you hadn't started to slacken off, you would have been all right."

"All right? Do you call the kind of life I lead, that? What do you use for a heart, Erik?"

"A heart?" And with that he lowered his blind old eyes from the sun and turned them right on me. "Do you accuse me, Sam?"

"With you it's choice," I said. "You can go."

"No." He shook his head. "I'm bound by choice, just as you are bound by the greater strength in me. Go back, Sam."

"Why?" I cried. And I pounded my chest like a crazy man. "Why me? Why others go and I have to stay? There's no end to the universe. I don't ask for company. I'll find some lost hole somewhere and bury myself. Anywhere, just so I'm away."

"Would you, Sam?" He asked. And at that, there was pity in his voice. When I did not answer, he went on gently. "You see, Sam, that's exactly why I can't let you go. You're capable of deluding yourself, of telling youself that you'll do what we both know you will not, cannot do. So you must stay."

"No," I said. "All right." I got up and turned to go. "I came to you first and gave you your chance. But now I'll go on my own, and I'll get off somehow."

"Sam, come back," he said. And abruptly, my legs were mine no longer.

"Sit down again," he said. "And listen for a minute."

My traitorous legs took me back, and I sat.

"Sam," he said, "you know the old story. Now and then, at rare intervals, one like us will be born. Nearly always, when they are grown, they leave. Only a few stay. But only once in thousands of years does one like yourself appear who must be chained against his will to our world."

"Erik," I said, between my teeth. "Don't sympathize."

"I'm not sympathizing, Sam," he said. "As you said

yourself, there is no end to the universe, but I have seen it all and there is no place in it for you. For the others that have gone out, there are places that are no places. They sup at alien tables, Sam, but always and forever as a guest. They left themselves behind when they went and they don't belong any longer to our Earth.''

He stopped for a moment, and I knew what was coming.

''But you, Sam,'' he said, and I heard his voice with my head bowed, staring at the brown dirt. He spoke tenderly. ''Poor Sam. You'd never be able to leave the Earth behind. You're one of us, but the living cord binds you to the others. Never a man speaks to you, but your hands yearn toward him in friendship. Never a woman smiles your way, but love warms that frozen heart of yours. You can't leave them, Sam. If you went out now, you'd come back, in time, and try to take them with you. You'd hurry them on before they are ripe. And there's no place out there in the universe for them—yet.''

I tried to move, but could not. Tried to lift my face to his, but I could not.

''Poor Sam,'' he said, ''trapped by a common heart that chains the lightning of his brain. Go back, Sam. Go back to your cities and your people. Go back to a thousand little jobs, and the work that is no greater than theirs, but many times as much so that it drives you without a pause twenty, twenty-two hours a day. Go back, Sam, to your designing and your painting, to your music and your business, to your engineering and your landscaping, and all the other things. Go back and keep busy, so busy your brain fogs and you sleep without dreaming. And wait. Wait for the necessary years to pass until they grow and change and at last come to their destiny.

''When that time comes, Sam, they will go out. And you will go with them, blood of their blood, flesh of their flesh, kin and comrade to them all. You will be happier than any of us have ever been, when that time comes. But the years have still to pass, and now you must go back. Go back, Sam. Go back, go back, go back.''

And so I have come back. O people that I hate and love!

DOLPHIN'S WAY

Of course, there was no reason why a woman coming to Dolphin's Way—as the late Dr. Edwin Knight had named the island research station—should not be beautiful. But Mal had never expected such a thing to happen.

Castor and Pollux had not come to the station pool this morning. They might have left the station, as other wild dolphins had in the past—and Mal nowadays carried always with him the fear that the Willernie Foundation would seize on some excuse to cut off their funds for further research. Ever since Corwin Brayt had taken over, Mal had known this fear. Though Brayt had said nothing. It was only a feeling Mal got from the presence of the tall, cold man. So it was that Mal was out in front of the station, scanning the ocean when the water-taxi from the mainland brought the visitor.

She stepped out on the dock, as he stared down at her. She waved as if she knew him, and then climbed the stairs from the dock to the terrace in front of the door to the main building of the station.

"Hello," she said, smiling as she stopped in front of him. "You're Corwin Brayt?"

Mal was suddenly sharply conscious of his own lean and ordinary appearance in contrast to her startling beauty. She was brown-haired and tall for a girl—but these things did not describe her. There was a perfection to her—and her smile stirred him strangely.

"No," he said. "I'm Malcolm Sinclair. Corwin's inside."

"I'm Jane Wilson," she said. "*Background Monthly* sent me out to do a story on the dolphins. Do you work with them?"

"Yes," Mal said. "I started with Dr. Knight in the beginning."

"Oh, good," she said. "Then, you can tell me some things. You were here when Dr. Brayt took charge after Dr. Knight's death?"

"Mr. Brayt," he corrected automatically. "Yes." The emotion she moved in him was so deep and strong it seemed she must feel it too. But she gave no sign.

"Mr. Brayt?" she echoed. "Oh. How did the staff take to him?"

"Well," said Mal, wishing she would smile again "everyone took to him."

"I see," she said. "He's a good research head?"

"A good administrator," said Mal. "He's not involved in the research end."

"He's not?" She stared at him. "But didn't he replace Dr. Knight, after Dr. Knight's death?"

"Why, yes," said Mal. He made an effort to bring his attention back to the conversation. He had never had a woman affect him like this before. "But just as administrator of the station, here. You see—most of our funds for work here come from the Willernie Foundation. They had faith in Dr. Knight, but when he died . . . well, they wanted someone of their own in charge. None of us mind."

"Willernie Foundation," she said. "I don't know it."

"It was set up by a man named Willernie, in St. Louis, Missouri," said Mal. "He made his money manufacturing kitchen utensils. When he died he left a trust and set up the Foundation to encourage basic research." Mal smiled. "Don't ask me how he got from kitchen utensils to that. That's not much information for you, is it?"

"It's more than I had a minute ago." She smiled back. "Did you know Corwin Brayt before he came here?"

"No." Mal shook his head. "I don't know many people outside the biological and zoological fields."

"I imagine you know him pretty well now, though, after the six months he's been in charge."

"Well—" Mal hesitated. "I wouldn't say I know him *well*, at all. You see, he's up here in the office all day long and I'm down with Pollux and Castor—the two wild dolphins we've got coming to the station, now. Corwin and I don't see each other much."

"On this small island?"

"I suppose it seems funny—but we're both pretty busy."

"I guess you would be." She smiled again. "Will you take me to him?"

"Him?" Mal awoke suddenly to the fact they were still standing on the terrace. "Oh, yes—it's Corwin you came to see."

"Not just Corwin," she said. "I came to see the whole place."

"Well, I'll take you in to the office. Come along."

He led her across the terrace and in through the front door into the air-conditioned coolness of the interior. Corwin Brayt ran the air conditioning constantly, as if his own somewhat icy personality demanded the dry, distant coldness of a mountain atmosphere. Mal led Jane Wilson down a short corridor and through another door into a large wide-windowed office. A tall, slim, broad-shouldered man with black hair and a brown, coldly handsome face looked up from a large desk and got to his feet on seeing Jane.

"Corwin," said Mal. "This is Miss Jane Wilson from *Background Monthly*."

"Yes," said Corwin expressionlessly to Jane, coming around the desk to them. "I got a wire yesterday you were coming." He did not wait for Jane to offer her hand, but offered his own. Their fingers met.

"I've got to be getting down to Castor and Pollux," said Mal, turning away.

"I'll see you later then," Jane said, looking over at him.

"Why, yes. Maybe—" he said. He went out. As he closed the door of Brayt's office behind him, he paused for a moment in the dim, cool hallway, and shut his eyes. *Don't be a fool,* he told himself, *a girl like that can do a lot better than someone like you. And probably has already.*

He opened his eyes and went back down to the pool behind the station and the nonhuman world of the dolphins.

• • •

When he got there, he found that Castor and Pollux were back. Their pool was an open one, with egress to the open blue water of the Caribbean. In the first days of the research at Dolphin's Way, the dolphins had been confined in a closed pool like any captured wild animal. It was only later on, when the work at the station had come up against what Knight had called "the environmental barrier," that the notion was conceived of opening the pool to the sea so that the dolphins they had been working with could leave or stay, as they wished.

They had left—but they had come back. Eventually, they had left for good. But strangely, wild dolphins had come from time to time to take their place, so that there were always dolphins at the station.

Castor and Pollux were the latest pair. They had showed up some four months ago after a single dolphin frequenting the station had disappeared. Free, independent—they had been most cooperative. But the barrier had not been breached.

Now, they were sliding back and forth past each other underwater utilizing the full thirty-yard length of the pool, passing beside, over, and under each other, their seven-foot, nearly identical bodies almost, but not quite, rubbing as they passed. The tape showed them to be talking together up in the supersonic range, eighty to a hundred and twenty kilocycles per second. Their pattern of movement in the water now was something he had never seen before. It was regular and ritualistic as a dance.

He sat down and put on the earphones connected to the hydrophones, underwater at each end of the pool. He spoke into the microphone, asking them about their movements, but they ignored him and kept on with the patterned swimming.

The sound of footsteps behind him made him turn. He saw Jane Wilson approaching down the concrete steps from the back door of the station, with the stocky, overalled figure of Pete Adant, the station mechanic.

"Here he is," said Pete, as they came up. "I've got to get back, now."

"Thank you." She gave Pete the smile that had so moved Mal earlier. Pete turned and went back up the steps. She turned to Mal. "Am I interrupting something?"

"No." He took off the earphones. "I wasn't getting any answers, anyway."

She looked at the two dolphins in their underwater dance with the liquid surface swirling above them as they turned now this way, now that, just under it.

"Answers?" she said. He smiled a little ruefully.

"We call them answers," he said. He nodded at the two smoothly streamlined shapes turning in the pool. "Sometimes we can ask questions and get responses."

"Informative responses?" she asked.

"Sometimes. You wanted to see me about something?"

"About everything," she said. "It seems you're the man I came to talk to—not Brayt. He sent me down here. I understand you're the one with the theory."

"Theory?" he said warily, feeling his heart sink inside him.

"The notion, then," she said. "The idea that, if there is some sort of interstellar civilization, it might be waiting for the people of Earth to qualify themselves before making contact. And that test might not be a technological one like developing a faster-than-light means of travel, but a sociological one—"

"Like learning to communicate with an alien culture—a culture like that of the dolphins," he interrupted harshly. "Corwin told you this?"

"I'd heard about it before I came," she said. "I'd thought it was Brayt's theory, though."

"No," said Mal, "it's mine." He looked at her. "You aren't laughing."

"Should I laugh?" she said. She was attentively watching the dolphins' movements. Suddenly he felt sharp jealousy of them for holding her attention; and the emotion pricked him to something he might not otherwise have had the courage to do.

"Fly over to the mainland with me," he said, "and have lunch. I'll tell you all about it."

"All right." She looked up from the dolphins at him at last and he was surprised to see her frowning. "There's a lot I don't understand," she murmured. "I thought it was Brayt I had to learn about. But it's you—and the dolphins."

"Maybe we can clear that up at lunch, too," Mal said, not quite clear what she meant, but not greatly caring, either. "Come on, the helicopters are around the north side of the building."

They flew a copter across to Carúpano, and sat down to

lunch looking out at the shipping in the open roadstead of the azure sea before the town, while the polite Spanish of Venezuelan voices sounded from the tables around them.

"Why should I laugh at your theory?" she said again, when they were settled, and eating lunch.

"Most people take it to be a crackpot excuse for our failure at the station," he said.

Her brown arched brows rose. "Failure?" she said. "I thought you were making steady progress."

"Yes. And no." he said. "Even before Dr. Knight died, we ran into something he called the environmental barrier."

"Environmental barrier?"

"Yes." Mal poked with his fork at the shrimp in his seafood cocktail. "This work of ours all grew out of the work done by Dr. John Lilly. You read his book, *Man and Dolphin*?"

"No," she said. He looked at her, surprised.

"He was the pioneer in this research with dolphins," Mal said. "I'd have thought reading his book would have been the first thing you would have done before coming down here."

"The first thing I did," she said, "was try to find out something about Corwin Brayt. And I was pretty unsuccessful at that. That's why I landed here with the notion that it was he, not you, who was the real worker with the dolphins."

"That's why you asked me if I knew much about him?"

"That's right," she answered. "But tell me about this environmental barrier."

"There's not a great deal to tell," he said. "Like most big problems, it's simple enough to state. At first, in working with the dolphins, it seemed the early researchers were going great guns, and communication was just around the corner—a matter of interpreting the sounds they made to each other, in the humanly audible range and above it; and teaching the dolphins human speech."

"It turned out those things couldn't be done?"

"They could. They were done—or as nearly so as makes no difference. But then we came up against the fact that communication doesn't mean understanding." He looked at her. "You and I talk the same language, but do we really understand perfectly what the other person means when he speaks to us?"

She looked at him for a moment, and then slowly shook her head without taking her eyes off his face.

"Well," said Mal, "that's essentially our problem with the dolphins—only on a much larger scale. Dolphins, like Castor and Pollux, can talk with me, and I with them, but we can't understand each other to any great degree."

"You mean intellectually understood, don't you?" Jane said. "Not just mechanically?"

"That's right," Mal answered. "We agree on denotation of an auditory or other symbol, but not on connotation. I can say to Castor, *'the Gulf Stream is a strong ocean current,'* and he'll agree exactly. But neither of us really has the slightest idea of what the other really means. My mental image of the Gulf Stream is not Castor's image. My notion of 'powerful' is relative to the fact I'm six feet tall, weigh a hundred and seventy-five pounds, and can lift my own weight against the force of gravity. Castor's is relative to the fact that he is seven feet long, can speed up to forty miles an hour through the water, and as far as he knows weighs nothing, since his four hundred pounds of body weight are balanced out by the equal weight of the water he displaces. And the concept of lifting something is all but unknown to him. My mental abstraction of 'ocean' is not his, and our ideas of what a current is may coincide, or be literally worlds apart in meaning. And so far we've found no way of bridging the gap between us."

"The dolphins have been trying as well as you?"

"I believe so," said Mal. "But I can't prove it. Any more than I can really prove the dolphin's intelligence to hard-core skeptics until I can come up with something previously outside human knowledge that the dolphins have taught me. Or have them demonstrate that they've learned the use of some human intellectual process. And in these things we've all failed—because, as I believe and Dr. Knight believed, of the connotative gap, which is a result of the environmental barrier."

She sat watching him. He was probably a fool to tell her all this, but he had had no one to talk to like this since Dr. Knight's heart attack, eight months before, and he felt words threatening to pour out of him.

"We've got to learn to think like the dolphins," he said, "or the dolphins have to learn to think like us. For nearly six years now we've been trying and neither side's succeeded." Almost before he thought, he added the one thing he had been determined to keep to himself. "I've been afraid our research funds will be cut off any day now."

"Cut off? By the Willernie Foundation?" she said. "Why would they do that?"

"Because we haven't made any progress for so long," Mal said bitterly. "Or, at least, no provable progress. I'm afraid time's just about run out. And if it runs out, it may never be picked up again. Six years ago, there was a lot of popular interest in the dolphins. Now, they've been discounted and forgotten, shelved as merely bright animals."

"You can't be sure the research won't be picked up again."

"But I feel it," he said. "It's part of my notion about the ability to communicate with an alien race being the test for us humans. I feel we've got this one chance and if we flub it, we'll never have another." He pounded the table softly with his fist. "The worst of it is, I *know* the dolphins are trying just as hard to get through from their side—if I could only recognize what they're doing, how they're trying to make me understand!"

Jane had been sitting watching him.

"You seem pretty sure of that," she said. "What makes you so sure?"

He unclenched his fist and forced himself to sit back in his chair.

"Have you ever looked into the jaws of a dolphin?" he said. "They're this long." He spread his hands apart in the air to illustrate. "And each pair of jaws contains eighty-eight sharp teeth. Moreover, a dolphin like Castor weights several hundred pounds and can move at water speeds that are almost incredible to a human. He could crush you easily by ramming you against the side of a tank, if he didn't want to tear you apart with his teeth, or break your bones with blows of his flukes." He looked at her grimly. "In spite of all this, in spite of the fact that men have caught and killed dolphins—even we killed them in our early, fumbling researches, and dolphins are quite capable of using their teeth and strength on marine enemies—no dolphin has ever been known to attack a human being. Aristotle, writing in the fourth century B.C., speaks of the quote gentle and kindly end quote nature of the dolphin."

He stopped, and looked at Jane sharply.

"You don't believe me," he said.

"Yes," she said. "Yes, I do." He took a deep breath.

"I'm sorry," he said, "I've made the mistake of mentioning all this before to other people and been sorry I did. I told this to one man who gave me his opinion that it indicated that the dolphin instinctively recognized human superiority and the value of human life.'' Mal grinned at her harshly. ''But it was just an instinct. *'Like dogs,'* he said. *'Dogs instinctively admire and love people—'* and he wanted to tell me about a dachshund he'd had, named Poochie, who could read the morning newspaper and wouldn't bring it in to him if there was a tragedy reported on the front page. He could prove this, and Poochie's intelligence, by the number of times he'd had to get the paper off the front step himself.''

Jane laughed. It was a low, happy laugh; and it took the bitterness suddenly out of Mal.

''Anyway,'' said Mal, ''the dolphin's restraint with humans is just one of the indications, like the wild dolphins coming to us here at the station, that've convinced me the dolphins are trying to understand us, too. And have been, maybe, for centuries.''

''I don't see why you worry about the research stopping,'' she said. ''With all you know, can't you convince people—''

''There's only one person I've got to convince,'' said Mal. ''And that's Corwin Brayt. And I don't think I'm doing it. It's just a feeling—but I feel as if he's sitting in judgment upon me, and the work. I feel . . .'' Mal hesitated, ''almost as if he's a hatchet man.''

''He isn't,'' Jane said. ''He can't be. I'll find out for you, if you like. There're ways of doing it. I'd have the answer for you right now, if I'd thought of him as an administrator. But I thought of him as a scientist, and I looked him up in the wrong places.''

Mal frowned at her unbelievingly.

''You don't actually mean you can find out that for me?'' he asked.

She smiled.

''Wait and see,'' she replied. ''I'd like to know, myself, what his background is.''

''It could be important,'' he said eagerly. ''I know it sounds fantastic—but if I'm right, the research with the dolphins could be important, more important than anything else in the world.''

She stood up suddenly from the table.

''I'll go and start checking up right now,'' she said. ''Why don't you go on back to the island? It'll take me a few hours and I'll take the water-taxi over.''

"But you haven't finished lunch yet," he said. "In fact you haven't even started lunch. Let's eat first, then you can go.''

"I want to call some people and catch them while they're still at work," she said. "It's the time difference on these long-distance calls. I'm sorry. We'll have dinner together, will that do?''

"It'll have to," he said. She melted his disappointment with one of her amazing smiles, and went.

With her gone, Mal found he was not hungry himself. He got hold of the waiter and managed to cancel the main course of their meals. He sat and had two more drinks—not something usual for him. Then he left and flew the copter back to the island.

Pete Adant encountered him as he was on his way from the copter park to the dolphin pool.

"There you are," said Pete. "Corwin wants to see you in an hour—when he gets back, that is. He's gone over to the mainland himself.''

Ordinarily, such a piece of news would have awakened the foreboding about cancellation of the research that rode always like a small, cold metal weight inside Mal. But the total of three drinks and no lunch had anesthetized him somewhat. He nodded and went on to the pool.

The dolphins were still there, still at their patterned swimming. Or was he just imagining the pattern? Mal sat down on his chair by the poolside before the tape recorder which set down a visual pattern of the sounds made by the dolphins. He put the earphones to the hydrophones on, switching on the mike before him.

Suddenly, it struck him how futile all this was. He had gone through these same motions daily for four years now. And what was the sum total of results he had to show for it? Reel on reel of tape recording a failure to hold any truly productive conversation with the dolphins.

He took the earphones off and laid them aside. He lit a cigarette and sat gazing with half-seeing eyes at the underwater ballet of the dolphins. To call it ballet was almost to libel their actions. The gracefulness, the purposefulness of their movements, buoyed up by the salt water, was beyond that of any human in air or on land. He thought again of what he had told

Jane Wilson about the dolphin's refusal to attack their human captors, even when the humans hurt or killed them. He thought of the now-established fact that dolphins will come to the rescue of one of their own who has been hurt or knocked unconscious, and hold him up on top of the water so he would not drown—the dolphin's breathing process requiring conscious control, so that it failed if the dolphin became unconscious.

He thought of their playfulness, their affection, the wide and complex range of their speech. In any of those categories, the average human stacked up beside them looked pretty poor. In the dolphin culture there was no visible impulse to war, to murder, to hatred and unkindness. No wonder, thought Mal, they and we have trouble understanding each other. In a different environment, under different conditions, they're the kind of people we've always struggled to be. We have the technology, the tool-using capability, but with it all in many ways we're more animal than they are.

Who's to judge which of us is better, he thought, looking at their movements through the water with the slight hazy melancholy induced by the three drinks on an empty stomach. I might be happier myself, if I were a dolphin. For a second, the idea seemed deeply attractive. The endless open sea, the freedom, an end to all the complex structure of human culture on land. A few lines of poetry came back to him.

"*Come Children,*" he quoted out loud to himself, "*let us away! Down and away, below . . . !*"

He saw the two dolphins pause in their underwater ballet and saw that the microphone before him was on. Their heads turned toward the microphone underwater at the near end of the pool. He remembered the following lines, and he quoted them aloud to the dolphins.

> "*. . . Now my brothers call from the bay,*
> *Now the great winds shoreward blow,*
> *Now the salt tides seaward flow;*
> *Now the wild white horses play,*
> *Champ and chafe and toss in the spray—*"*

He broke off suddenly, feeling self-conscious. He looked

* "The Forsaken Merman," by Matthew Arnold, 1849.

down at the dolphins. For a moment they merely hung where they were under the surface, facing the microphone. Then Castor turned and surfaced. His forehead with its blowhole broke out into the air and then his head as he looked up at Mal. His airborne voice from the blowhole's sensitive lips and muscles spoke quacking words at the human.

"*Come, Mal,*" he quacked, "*let us away! Down and away! Below!*"

The head of Pollux surfaced beside Castor's. Mal stared at them for a long second. Then he jerked his gaze back to the tape of the recorder. There on it was the rhythmic record of his own voice as it had sounded in the pool, and below it on their separate tracks, the tapes showed parallel rhythms coming from the dolphins. They had been matching his speech largely in the inaudible range while he was quoting.

Still staring, Mal got to his feet, his mind trembling with a suspicion so great he hesitated to put it into words. Like a man in a daze he walked to the near end of the pool, where three steps led down into the shallow part. Here the water was only three feet deep.

"*Come, Mal!*" quacked Castor, as the two still hung in the water with their heads out, facing him. "*Let us away! Down and away! Below!*"

Step by step, Mal went down into the pool. He felt the coolness of the water wetting his pants legs, rising to his waist as he stood at last on the pool floor. A few feet in front of him, the two dolphins hung in the water, facing him, waiting. Standing with the water rippling lightly above his belt buckle, Mal looked at them, waiting for some sign, some signal of what they wanted him to do.

They gave him no clue. They only waited. It was up to him to go forward on his own. He sloshed forward into deeper water, put his head down, held his breath, and pushed himself off underwater.

In the forefront of his blurred vision, he saw the grainy concrete floor of the pool. He glided slowly over it, rising a little, and suddenly the two dolphins were all about him—gliding over, above, around his own underwater floating body, brushing lightly against him as they passed, making him a part of their underwater dance. He heard the creaking that was one of the underwater sounds they made and knew that they were probably talking in ranges he could not hear. He could not know what they were saying, he could not sense the meaning of their movements about him, but the feeling that they were trying to convey information to him was inescapable.

He began to feel the need to breathe. He held out as long as he could, then let himself rise to the surface. He broke water and gulped air, and the two dolphin heads popped up nearby, watching him. He dove under the surface again. *I am a dolphin*—he told himself almost desperately—*I am not a man, but a dolphin, and to me all this means—what?*

Several times he dove, and each time the persistent and disciplined movements of the dolphins about him underwater convinced him more strongly that he was on the right track. He came up, blowing, at last. He was not carrying the attempt to be like them far enough, he thought. He turned and swam back to the steps at the shallow end of the pool, and began to climb out.

"*Come, Mal—let us away!*" quacked a dolphin voice behind him, and he turned to see the heads of both Castor and Pollux out of the water, regarding him with mouths open urgently.

"*Come Children—down and away!*" he repeated, as reassuringly as he could intonate the words.

He hurried up to the big cabinet of the supply locker at the near end of the pool, and opened the door of the section on skin-diving equipment. He needed to make himself more like a dolphin. He considered the air tanks and the mask of the scuba equipment, and rejected them. The dolphins could not breathe underwater any more than he could. He started jerking things out of the cabinet.

A minute or so later he returned to the steps in swimming trunks, wearing a glass mask with a snorkel tube, and swim fins on his feet. In his hand he carried two lengths of soft rope. He sat down on the steps and with the rope tied his knees and ankles together. Then, clumsily, he hopped and splashed into the water.

Lying face down in the pool, staring at the bottom through his glass faceplate, he tried to move his bound legs together like the flukes of a dolphin, to drive himself slantingly down under the surface.

After a moment or two he managed it. In a moment the dolphins were all about him as he tried to swim underwater, dolphinwise. After a little while his air ran short again and he had to surface. But he came up like a dolphin and lay on the surface filling his lungs, before fanning himself down fluke-fashion with his swim fins. *Think like a dolphin,* he kept repeating to himself over and over. *I am a dolphin. And this is my world. This is the way it is.*

. . . And Castor and Pollux were all about him.

The sun was setting in the far distance of the ocean when at last he dragged himself, exhausted, up the steps of the pool and sat down on the poolside. To his water-soaked body, the twilight breeze felt icy. He unbound his legs, took off his fins and mask and walked wearily to the cabinet. From the nearest compartment he took a towel and dried himself, then put on an old bathrobe he kept hanging there. He sat down in an alu-minum deckchair beside the cabinet and sighed with weari-ness.

He looked out at the red sun dipping its lower edge in the sea, and felt a great warm sensation of achievement inside him. In the darkening pool, the two dolphins still swam back and forth. He watched the sun descending . . .

"Mal!"

The sound of Corwin Brayt's voice brought his head around. When he saw the tall, cold-faced man was coming toward him with the slim figure of Jane alongside, Mal got up quickly from his chair. They came up to him.

"Why didn't you come in to see me as I asked?" Brayt said. "I left word for you with Pete. I didn't even know you were back from the mainland until the water-taxi brought Miss Wilson out just now, and she told me."

"I'm sorry," said Mal. "I think I've run into something here—"

"Never mind telling me now," Brayt's voice was hurried and sharpened with annoyance. "I had a good deal to speak to you about but there's not time now if I'm to catch the main-land plane to St. Louis. I'm sorry to break it this way—" He checked himself and turned to Jane. "Would you excuse us, Miss Wilson? Private business. If you'll give us a second—"

"Of course," she said. She turned and walked away from them alongside the pool, into the deepening twilight. The dolphins paced her in the water. The sun was just down now, and with the sudden oncoming of tropical night, stars could be seen overhead.

"Just let me tell you," said Mal. "It's about the research."

"I'm sorry," said Brayt. "There's no point in your telling me now. I'll be gone a week and I want you to watch out for this Jane Wilson, here." He lowered his voice slightly. "I talked to *Background Monthly* on the phone this afternoon, and the editor I spoke to there didn't know about the article, or recognize her name—"

"Somebody new," said Mal. "Probably someone who didn't know her."

"At any rate it makes no difference," said Brayt. "As I say, I'm sorry to tell you in such a rushed fashion, but Willernie has decided to end its grant of funds to the station. I'm flying to St. Louis to settle details." He hesitated. "I'm sure you knew something like this was coming, Mal."

Mal stared, shocked.

"It was inevitable," said Brayt coldly. "You know that." He paused. "I'm sorry."

"But the station'll fold without the Willernie support!" said Mal, finding his voice. "You know that. And just today I found out what the answer is! Just this afternoon! Listen to me!" He caught Brayt's arm as the other started to turn away. "The dolphins have been trying to contact us. Oh, not at first, not when we experimented with captured specimens. But since we opened the pool to the sea. The only trouble was we insisted on trying to communicate by sound alone—and that's all but impossible for them."

"Excuse me," said Brayt, trying to disengage his arm.

"Listen, will you!" said Mal desperately. "Their communication process is an incredibly rich one. It's as if you and I communicated by using all the instruments in a symphony orchestra. They not only use sound from four to a hundred and fifty kilocycles per second, they use movement, and touch —and all of it in reference to the ocean conditions surrounding them at the moment."

"I've got to go."

"Just a minute. Don't you remember what Lilly hypothecated about the dolphin's methods of navigation? He suggested that it was a multivariable method, using temperature, speed, taste of the water, position of the stars, sun, and so forth, all fed into their brains simultaneously and instantaneously. Obviously, it's true, and obviously their process of communication is also a multivariable method utilizing sound, touch, position, place, and movement. Now that we know this, we can go into the sea with them and try to operate across their whole spectrum of communication. No wonder we weren't able to get across anything but the most primitive exchanges, restricting ourselves to sound. It's been equivalent to restricting human communication to just the nouns in each sentence, while maintaining the sentence structure—"

"I'm very sorry!" said Brayt firmly. "I tell you, Mal. None of this makes any difference. The decision of the Foundation is based on financial reasons. They've got just so much money available to donate, and this station's allotment has already gone in other directions. There's nothing that can be done, now."

He pulled his arm free.

"I'm sorry," he said again. "I'll be back in a week at the outside. You might be thinking of how to wind up things, here."

He turned with that, and went away, around the building toward the parking spot of the station copters. Mal, stunned, watched the tall, slim, broad-shouldered figure move into darkness.

"It doesn't matter," said the gentle voice of Jane comfortably at his ear. He jerked about and saw her facing him. "You won't need the Willernie funds any more."

"He told you?" Mal stared at her as she shook her head, smiling in the growing dimness. "You heard? From way over there?"

"Yes," she said. "And you were right about Brayt. I got your answer for you. He was a hatchet man—sent here by the Willernie people to decide whether the station deserved further funds."

"But we've got to have them!" Mal said. "It won't take much more, but we've got to go into the sea and work out ways to talk to the dolphins in their own mode. We've got to expand to their level of communication, not try to compress them to ours. You see, this afternoon, I had a breakthrough—"

"I know," she said. "I know all about it."

"You know?" He stared at her. "How do you know?"

"You've been under observation all afternoon," she said. "You're right. You did break through the environmental barrier. From now on it's just a matter of working out methods."

"Under observation? How?" Abruptly, that seemed the least important thing at hand. "But I have to have money," he said. "It'll take time and equipment, and that costs money—"

"No." Her voice was infinitely gentle. "You won't need to work out your own methods. Your work is done, Mal. This afternoon the dolphins and you broke the bars to communication between the two races for the first time in the history of either. It was the job you set out to do and you were part of it. You can be happy knowing that."

"Happy?" He almost shouted at her, suddenly. "I don't understand what you're talking about."

"I'm sorry." There was a ghost of a sigh from her. "We'll show you how to talk to the dolphins, Mal, if men need to. As well as some other things—perhaps." Her face lifted to him under the star-marked sky, still a little light in the west. "You see, you were right about something more than dolphins, Mal. Your idea that the ability to communicate with another intelligent race, an alien race, was a test that had to be passed before the superior species of a planet could be contacted by the intelligent races of the galaxy—that was right, too."

He stared at her. She was so close to him, he could feel the living warmth of her body, although they were not touching. He saw her, he felt her, standing before him; and he felt all the strange deep upwelling of emotion that she had released in him the moment he first saw her. The deep emotion he felt for her still. Suddenly understanding came to him.

"You mean you're not from Earth—" His voice was hoarse and uncertain. It wavered to a stop. "But you're human!" he cried desperately.

She looked back at him a moment before answering. In the dimness he could not tell for sure, but he thought he saw the glisten of tears in her eyes.

"Yes," she said, at last, slowly. "In the way you mean that—you can say I'm human."

A great and almost terrible joy burst suddenly in him. It was the joy of a man who, in the moment when he thinks he has lost everything, finds something of infinitely greater value.

"But how?" he said excitedly, a little breathlessly. He pointed up at the stars. "If you come from someplace—up there? How can you be human?"

She looked down, away from his face.

"I'm sorry," she said. "I can't tell you."

"Can't tell me? Oh," he said with a little laugh, "you mean I wouldn't understand."

"No—" Her voice was almost inaudible. "I mean I'm not allowed to tell you."

"Not allowed—" He felt an unreasoning chill about his heart. "But Jane—" He broke off, fumbling for words. "I don't know quite how to say this, but it's important to me to know. From the first moment I saw you there, I . . . I mean, maybe you don't feel anything like this, you don't know what I'm talking about—"

"Yes," she whispered. "I do."

"Then—" He stared at her. "You could at least say something that would set my mind at rest. I mean . . . it's only a matter of time now. We're going to be getting together, your people and I, aren't we?"

She looked up at him out of darkness.

"No," she said, "we aren't, Mal. Ever. And that's why I can't tell you anything."

"We aren't?" he cried. "We aren't? But you came and saw us communicate—why aren't we?"

She looked up at him for the last time, then, and told him. He, having heard what she had to say, stood still; still as a stone, for there was nothing left to do. And she, turning slowly and finally away from him, went off to the edge of the pool and down the steps into the shallow water, where the dolphins came rushing to meet her, their foamy tearing of the surface making a wake as white as snow.

Then the three of them moved, as if by magic, across the surface of the pool and out the entrance of it to the ocean. And so they continued to move off until they were lost to sight in darkness and the starlit, glinting surface of the waves.

It came to Mal then, as he stood there, that the dolphins must have been waiting for her all this time. All the wild dolphins, who had come to the station after the first two captives, were set free to leave or stay as they wanted. The dolphins had known, perhaps for centuries, that it was to them alone on Earth that the long-awaited visitors from the stars would finally come.

IN THE BONE

I.

Personally, his name was Harry Brennan.

Officially, he was the *John Paul Jones,* which consisted of four billion dollars' worth of irresistible equipment—the latest and best of human science—designed to spread its four thousand components out through some fifteen cubic meters of space under ordinary conditions—designed also to stretch across light-years under extraordinary conditions (such as sending an emergency messenger-component home) or to clump into a single magnetic unit in order to shift through space and explore the galaxy. Both officially and personally —but most of all personally—he represents a case in point.

The case is one having to do with the relative importance of the made thing and its maker.

It was, as we know, the armored horseman who dominated the early wars of the Middle Ages in Europe. But, knowing this, it is still wise to remember that it was not the iron shell that made the combination of man and metal terrible to the enemy—but rather the essentially naked man inside the shell. Later, French knights depending on their armor went down before the clothyard shafts of unarmored footmen with bows, at Crécy and Poitiers.

And what holds true for armor holds true for the latest

developments of our science as well. It is not the spacecraft or
the laser on which we will find ourselves depending when a
time of ultimate decision comes, but the naked men within and
behind these things. When that time comes, those who rank
the made thing before its maker will die as the French knights
died at Crécy and Poitiers. This is a law of nature as wide as
the universe, which Harry Brennan, totally unsuspecting, was
to discover once more for us, in his personal capacity.

Personally, he was in his mid-twenties, unremarkable except
for two years of special training with the *John Paul Jones* and
his superb physical condition. He was five eleven, a hundred
seventy-two pounds, with a round, cheerful face under his
brown crew-cut hair. I was Public Relations Director of the
Project that sent him out; and I was there with the rest to slap
him on the back the day he left.

"Don't get lost, now," said someone. Harry grinned.

"The way you guys built this thing," he answered, "if I got
lost the galaxy would just have to shift itself around to get me
back on plot."

There was an unconscious arrogance hidden in that answer,
but no one marked it at the time. It was not the hour of suspi-
cions.

He climbed into the twelve-foot-tall control-suit that with
his separate living tank were the main components of the *John
Paul Jones,* and took off. Up in orbit, he spent some thirty-
two hours testing to make sure all the several thousand other
component parts were responding properly. Then he left the
solar system.

He clumped together his components, made his first shift to
orbit Procyon—and from there commenced his explorations
of the stars. In the next nine weeks, he accumulated literally
amazing amounts of new information about the nearby stars
and their solar systems. And—this is an even better index of
his success—located four new worlds on which men could step
with never a spacesuit or even a water canteen to sustain them.
Worlds so like Earth in gravity, atmosphere, and even flora
and fauna, that they could be colonized tomorrow.

Those were his first four worlds. On the fifth he encountered his fate—a fate for which he was unconsciously ripe.

The fact was the medical men and psychologists had over-
looked a factor—a factor having to do with the effect of

Harry's official *John Paul Jones* self upon his entirely human personal self. And over nine weeks this effect changed Harry without his ever having suspected it.

You see, nothing seemed barred to him. He could cross light-years by touching a few buttons. He could send a sensing element into the core of the hottest star, into the most poisonous planetary atmospheres or crushing gravities, to look around as if he were down there in person. From orbit, he could crack open a mountain, burn off a forest, or vaporize a section of icecap in search of information just by tapping the energy of a nearby sun. And so, subtly, the unconscious arrogance born during two years of training, that should have been noted in him at take-off from Earth, emerged and took him over—until he felt that there was nothing he could not do; that all things must give way to him; that he was, in effect, master of the universe.

The day may come when a man like Harry Brennan may hold such a belief and be justified. But not yet. On the fifth Earth-like world he discovered—World 1242 in his records—Harry encountered the proof that his belief was unjustified.

II.

The world was one which, from orbit, seemed to be the best of all the planets which he had discovered were suitable for human settlement; and he was about to go down to its surface personally in the control-suit, when his instruments picked out something already down there.

It was a squat, metallic pyramid about the size of a fourplex apartment building; and it was radiating on a number of interesting frequencies. Around its base there was mechanical movement and an area of cleared ground. Further out, in the native forest, were treaded vehicles taking samples of the soil, rock, and vegetation.

Harry had been trained for all conceivable situations, including an encounter with other intelligent, space-going life. Automatically, he struck a specific button, and immediately a small torpedo shape leaped away to shift through alternate space and back to Earth with the information so far obtained.

And a pale, thin beam reached up and out from the pyramid below. Harry's emergency messenger component ceased to exist.

Shaken, but not yet really worried, Harry struck back instantly with all the power his official self could draw from the GO-type sun, nearby.

The power was funneled by some action below, directly into the pyramid itself; and it vanished there as indifferently as the single glance of a sunbeam upon a leaf.

Harry's mind woke suddenly to some understanding of what he had encountered. He reached for the controls to send the *John Paul Jones* shifting into the alternate universe and away.

His hands never touched the controls. From the pyramid below, a blue lance of light reached up to paralyze him, select the control-suit from among the other components, and send it tumbling to the planetary surface below like a swatted insect.

But the suit had been designed to protect its occupant, whether he himself was operative or not. At fifteen hundred feet, the drag chute broke free, looking like a silver cloth candle-snuffer in the sunlight; and at five hundred feet the retro-rockets cut in. The suit tumbled to earth among some trees two kilometers from the pyramid, with Harry inside bruised, but released from his paralysis.

From the pyramid, a jagged arm of something like white lightning lashed the ground as far as the suit, and the suit's outer surface glowed cherry-red. Inside, the temperature suddenly shot up fifty degrees; instinctively Harry hit the panic button available to him inside the suit.

The suit split down the center like an overcooked frankfurter and spat Harry out; he rolled among the brush and fernlike ground cover, six or seven meters from the suit.

From the distant pyramid, the lightning lashed the suit, breaking it up. The headpiece rolled drunkenly aside, turning the dark gape of its interior toward Harry like the hollow of an empty skull. In the dimness of that hollow Harry saw the twinkle of his control buttons.

The lightning vanished. A yellow lightness filled the air about Harry and the dismembered suit. There was a strange quivering to the yellowness; and Harry half-smelled, half-tasted the sudden, flat bite of ozone. In the headpiece a button clicked without being touched; and the suit speaker, still radio-connected with the recording tank in orbit, spoke aloud in Harry's voice.

"Orbit . . ." it said. ". . . into . . . going . . ."

These were, in reverse order, the last three words Harry had recorded before sighting the pyramid. Now, swiftly gaining speed, the speaker began to recite backward, word for word, everything Harry had said into it in nine weeks. Faster it went, and faster until it mounted to a chatter, a gabble, and finally a whine pushing against the upper limits of Harry's auditory register.

Suddenly, it stopped.

The little clearing about Harry was full of silence. Only the odd and distant creaking of something that might have been a rubbing branch or an alien insect came to Harry's ears. Then the speaker spoke once more.

"Animal . . ." it said flatly in Harry's calm, recorded voice and went on to pick further words from the recordings. ". . . best. You . . . were an animal . . . wrapped in . . . made clothing. I have stripped you back to . . . animal again. Live, beast . . ."

Then the yellowness went out of the air and the taste of ozone with it. The headpiece of the dismembered suit grinned, empty as old bones in the sunlight. Harry scrambled to his feet and ran wildly away through the trees and brush. He ran in panic and utter fear, his lungs gasping, his feet pounding the alien earth, until the earth, the trees, the sky itself swam about him from exhaustion; and he fell tumbling to earth and away into the dark haven of unconsciousness.

When he woke, it was night, and he could not quite remember where he was or why. His thoughts seemed numb and unimportant. But he was cold, so he blundered about until he found the standing half-trunk of a lightning-blasted tree and crept into the burned hollow of its interior, raking frill-edged, alien leaves about him out of some half-forgotten instinct, until his own body warmth in the leaves formed a cocoon of comfort about him; and he slept.

From then on began a period in which nothing was very clear. It was as if his mind had huddled itself away somehow like a wounded animal and refused to think. There was no past

or future, only the endless now. If now was warm, it had
always been warm; if dark—it had always been dark. He
learned to smell water from a distance and go to it when he
was thirsty. He put small things in his mouth to taste them. If
they tasted good he ate them. If he got sick afterward, he did
not eat them again.

Gradually, blindly, the world about him began to take on a
certain order. He came to know where there were plants with
portions he could eat, where there were small creatures he
could catch and pull apart and eat, and where there was water.

He did not know how lucky he was in the sheer chance of
finding flora and fauna on an alien world that were edible—let
alone nourishing. He did not realize that he had come down
on a plateau in the tropical highlands, with little variation in
day and night temperature and no large native predators
which might have attacked him.

None of this he knew. Nor would it have made any difference to him if he had, for the intellectual center of his brain
had gone on vacation, so to speak, and refused to be called
back. He was, in fact, a victim of severe psychological shock.
The shock of someone who had come to feel himself absolute
master of a universe and who then, in a few short seconds, had
been cast down from that high estate by something or someone inconceivably greater, into the state of a beast of the field.

But still, he could not be a true beast of the field, in spite of
the fact his intellectual processes had momentarily abdicated.
His perceptive abilities still worked. His eyes could not help
noting, even if incuriously, the progressive drying of the vegetation, the day-by-day shifting in the points of setting and rising of the sun. Slowly, instinctively, the eternal moment that
held him stretched and lengthened until he began to perceive
divisions within it—a difference between *now* and *was*, between *now* and *will be*.

III.

The day came at last when he saw himself.

A hundred times he had crouched by the water to drink and,
lowering his lips to its surface, seen color and shape rising to
meet him. The hundredth and something time, he checked, a

few inches above the liquid plane, staring at what he saw.

For several long seconds it made no sense to him. Then, at first slowly, then with a rush like pain flooding back on someone rousing from the anesthesia of unconsciousness, he recognized what he saw.

Those were eyes at which he stared, sunken and dark-circled under a dirty tangle of hair. That was a nose jutting between gaunt and sunken cheeks above a mouth, and there was a chin naked only because once an ultrafine laser had burned out the thousand and one roots of the beard that grew on it. That was a man he saw—*himself.*

He jerked back like someone who has come face-to-face with the devil. But he returned eventually, because he was thirsty, to drink and see himself again. And so, gradually, he got used to the sight of himself.

So it was that memory started to return to him. But it did not come back quickly or all at once. It returned instead by jerks and sudden, partial revelations—until finally the whole memory of what had happened was back in his conscious mind again.

But he was really not a man again.

He was still essentially what the operator of the pyramid had broken him down into. He was still an animal. Only the memory and imaginings of a man had returned to live like a prisoner in a body that went on reacting and surviving in the bestial way it had come to regard as natural.

But his animal peace was broken. For his imprisoned mind worked now. With the control-suit broken up—he had returned to the spot of its destruction many times, to gaze beastlike at the rusting parts—his mind knew he was a prisoner, alone on this alien world until he died. To know that was not so bad, but remembering this much meant remembering also the existence of the someone or something that had made him a prisoner here.

The whoever it was who was in the pyramid.

That the pyramid might have been an automated, mechanical device never entered his mind for a moment. There had been a personal, directed, living viciousness behind the announcement that had condemned him to live as a beast. No, in that blank-walled, metallic structure, whose treaded mechanical servants still prospected through the woods, there was something alive—something that could treat the awesome power of a solar tap as a human treated the attack of a mosquito—but something *living*. Some being. Some Other, who lived in the pyramid, moving, breathing, eating, and gloating —or worse yet, entirely forgetful of what he had done to Harry Brennan.

And now that he knew that the Other was there, Harry began to dream of him nightly. At first, in his dreams, Harry whimpered with fear each time the dark shape he pursued seemed about to turn and show its face. But slowly, hatred came to grow inside and then outside his fear. Unbearable that Harry should never know the face of his destroyer. Lying curled in the nest of leaves under the moonless, star-brilliant sky, he snarled, thinking of his deprivation.

Then hate came to strengthen him in the daylight also. From the beginning he had avoided the pyramid, as a wild coyote avoids the farmyard where he was once shot by the farmer. But now, day after day, Harry circled closer to the alien shape. From the beginning he had run and hidden from the treaded prospecting machines. But now, slowly, he grew bolder, standing close enough at last to touch them as they passed. And he found that they paid no attention to him. No attention at all.

He came to ignore them in turn, and day by day he ventured closer to the pyramid. Until the morning came when he lay, silently snarling, behind a bush, looking out across the tread-trampled space that separated him from the nearest copper-colored face of the pyramid.

The space was roughly circular, thirty yards across, broken only by a small stream which had been diverted to loop inward toward the pyramid before returning to its original channel. In the bight of the loop a machine like a stork straddled the artificial four-foot-wide channel, dipping a pair of long necks with tentacle-clustered heads into the water at intervals. Sometimes Harry could see nothing in the tentacles when they came up. Occasionally they carried some small water creature which they deposited in a tank.

Making a perfect circle about the tramped area, so that the storklike machine was guarded within them, was an open fence of slender wands set upright in the earth, far enough apart for any of the machines that came and went to the forest to pass between any two of them. There seemed to be nothing

connecting the wands, and nothing happened to the prospecting machines as they passed through—but the very purpose-
lessness of the wands filled Harry with uneasiness.

It was not until after several days of watching that he had a
chance to see a small native animal, frightened by something
in the woods behind it, attempt to bolt across a corner of the
clearing.

As it passed between two of the wands there was a waveriness in the air between them. The small animal leaped high,
came down, and lay still. It did not move after that, and later
in the day, Harry saw the indifferent treads of one of the prospecting machines bury it in the trampled earth in passing.

That evening, Harry brought several captive, small animals
bound with grass up to the wand line and thrust them through,
one by one at different spots. All died.

The next night he tried pushing a captive through a small
trench scooped out so that the creature passed the killing line
below ground level. But this one died also. For several days he
was baffled. Then he tried running behind a slow-moving machine as it returned and tying a small animal to it with grass.

For a moment as the front of the machine passed through,
he thought the little animal would live. But then, as the back
of the machine passed the line, it, too, died.

Snarling, Harry paced around outside the circle in the brush
until the sun set and stars filled the moonless sky.

In the days that followed, he probed every gap in the wand-
fence, but found no safe way through it. Finally, he came to
concentrate on the two points at which the diverted stream
entered and left the circle to flow beneath the storklike machine.

He studied this without really knowing what he was seeking.
He did not even put his studying into words. Vaguely, he knew
that the water went in and the water came out again unchanged; and he also wished to enter and come out safely.
Then, one day, studying the stream and the machine, he noticed that a small creature plucked from the water by the
storklike neck's mass of tentacles was still wriggling.

That evening, at twilight, while there was still light to see, he
waded up the two-foot depth of the stream to the point where
the killing line cut across its watery surface and pushed some
more of his little animals toward the line underwater.

Two of the three surfaced immediately, twitched, and floated on limply, to be plucked from the water and cast aside on the ground by the storklike machine. But the third swam on several strokes before surfacing and came up living to scramble ashore, race for the forest, and be killed by wands further around the circle.

Harry investigated the channel below the killing line. There was water there up to his midthigh, plenty to cover him completely. He crouched down in the water and took a deep breath.

Ducking below the surface, he pulled himself along with his fingertips, holding himself close to the bottom. He moved in as far as the tentacled ends. These grabbed at him, but could not reach far enough back to touch him. He saw that they came within a few inches of the gravel bottom.

He began to need air. He backed carefully out and rose above the water, gasping. After a while his hard breathing stopped, and he sat staring at the water for a long while. When it was dark, he left.

The next day he came and crept underwater to the grabbing area of the storklike machine again. He scooped out several handfuls of the gravel from under the place where the arms grabbed, before he felt a desperate need for air and had to withdraw. But that day began his labors.

IV.

Four days later the bottom under the grasping tentacles was scooped out to an additional two feet of depth. And the fifth twilight after that, he pulled himself, dripping and triumphant, up out of the bend of the diverted stream inside the circle of the killing wands.

He rested and then went to the pyramid, approaching it cautiously and sidelong like a suspicious animal. There was a door in the side he approached through which he had seen the prospecting machines trundle in and out. In the dimness he could not see it; and when he touched the metallic side of the structure, his fingers, grimed and toughened from scrabbling in the dirt, told him little. But his nose, beast-sensitive now, located and traced the outline of the almost invisible crack around the door panel by its reek of earth and lubricant.

He settled down to wait. An hour later, one of the machines came back. He jumped up, ready to follow it in; but the door opened just before it and closed the minute it was inside—nor was there any room to squeeze in beside it. He hunkered down, disappointed, snarling a little to himself.

He stayed until dawn and watched several more machines enter and leave. But there was no room to squeeze inside, even with the smallest of them.

During the next week or so he watched the machines enter and leave nightly. He tied one of his small animals to an entering machine and saw it pass through the entrance alive and scamper out again with the next machine that left. And every night his rage increased. Then, wordlessly, one daytime after he had seen a machine deep in the woods lurch and tilt as its tread passed over a rock, inspiration took him.

That night he carried through the water with him several cantaloupe-sized stones. When the first machine came back to the pyramid, in the moment in which the door opened before it, he pushed one of the rocks before the right-hand tread. The machine, unable to stop, mounted the rock with its right tread, tilted to the left, and struck against that side of the entrance.

It checked, backed off, and put out an arm with the grasping end to remove the rock. Then it entered the opening. But Harry was already before it, having slipped through while the door was still up and the machine busy pulling the stone aside.

He plunged into a corridor of darkness, full of clankings and smells. A little light from the opening behind him showed him a further, larger chamber where other machines stood parked. He ran toward them.

Long before he reached them, the door closed behind him, and he was in pitch darkness. But the clanking of the incoming machine was close behind him, and the adrenalinized memory of a wild beast did not fail him. He ran, hands outstretched, directly into the side of the parked machine at which he had aimed and clambered up on it. The machine entering behind him clanked harmlessly past him and stopped moving.

He climbed cautiously down in the impenetrable darkness. He could see nothing; but the new, animal sensitivity of his nose offered a substitute for vision. He moved like a hunting dog around the chamber, sniffing and touching; and slowly a clear picture of it and its treaded occupants built up in his mind.

He was still at this when suddenly a door he had not seen opened almost in his face. He had just time to leap backward as a smaller machine with a boxlike body and a number of upward-thrusting arms entered, trundled to the machine that had just come back, and began to relieve the prospecting machine of its sample box, replacing it with the one it carried itself.

This much, in the dim light from the open door, Harry was able to see. But then, the small machine turned back toward the doorway; and Harry, waking to his opportunity, ducked through ahead of it.

He found himself in a corridor dimly lit by a luminescent strip down the center of the ceiling. The corridor was wide enough for the box-collecting machine to pass him; and, in fact, it rolled out around him as he shrank back against one metal wall. It went on down the corridor, and he followed it into a larger room with a number of machines, some mobile, some not, under a ceiling lit as the corridor had been with a crossing of luminescent strip.

In this area all the machines avoided each other—and him. They were busy with each other and at other incomprehensible duties. Hunched and tense, hair erect on the back of his neck and nostrils spread wide, Harry moved through them to explore other rooms and corridors that opened off this one. It took him some little time; but he discovered that they were all on a level, and there was nothing but machines in any of them. He found two more doors with shallow steps leading up to them, but these would not open for him; and though he watched by one for some time, no machine went up the steps and through it.

He began to be conscious of thirst and hunger. He made his way back to the door leading to the chamber where the prospecting machines were parked. To his surprise, it opened as he approached it. He slipped through into darkness.

Immediately, the door closed behind him; and sudden panic grabbed him, when he found he could not open it from this side. Then, self-possession returned to him.

By touch, smell, and memory, he made his way among the parked machines and down the corridor to the outside door.

To his gratification, this also opened when he came close. He slipped through into cool, fresh outer air and a sky already graying with dawn. A few moments later, wet but free, he was back in the woods again.

From then on, each night he returned. He found it was not necessary to do more than put any sizable object before the returning machine. It would stop to clear the path, and he could enter ahead of it. Then, shortly after he was inside, a box-collecting machine would open the inner door.

Gradually, his fear of the machines faded. He came to hold them in a certain contempt. They always did the same thing in the same situation, and it was easy to trick or outmaneuver them.

But the two inner doors of the machine area with the steps would not open to him; and he knew the upper parts of the pyramid were still unexplored by him. He sniffed at the cracks of these doors, and a scent came through—not of lubricating medium and metal alone, but of a different, musky odor that raised the hairs on the back of his neck again. He snarled at the doors.

He went back to exploring minutely the machine level. The sample boxes from the prospecting machines, he found, were put on conveyor-beltlike strips that floated up on thin air through openings in the ceiling—but the openings were too small for him to pass through. But he discovered something else. One day he came upon one of the machines taking a grille off the face of one of the immobile devices. It carried the grille away, and he explored the opening that had been revealed. It was the entrance to a tunnel or duct leading upward; and it was large enough to let him enter it. Air blew silently from it; and the air was heavy with the musky odor he had smelled around the doors that did not open.

The duct tempted him, but fear held him back. The machine came back and replaced the grille; and he noticed that it fitted into place with a little pressure from the outside, top and bottom. After the machine had left he pressed, and the grille fell out into his hands.

After a long wait, he ventured timorously into the tube—but a sudden sound like heavy breathing mixed with a wave of a strong, musky odor came at him. He backed out in panic, fled the pyramid, and did not come back for two days.

When he came back, the grille was again neatly in place. He removed it and sat a long time getting his courage up. Finally, he put the grille up high out of reach of the machine which had originally removed it and crawled into the duct.

He crept up the tube at an angle into darkness. His eyes were useless, but the musky odor came strongly at him. Soon, he heard sounds.

There was an occasional ticking, then a thumping or shuffling sound. Finally, after he had crawled a long way up through the tube, there was a sound like a heavy puffing or hoarse breathing. It was the sound that had accompanied the strengthening of the musky odor once before; and this time the scent came strong again.

He lay, almost paralyzed with terror in the tube, as the odor grew in his nostrils. He could not move until sound and scent had retreated. As soon as they had, he wormed his way backward down to the lower level and freedom, replaced the grille, and fled for the outside air, once again.

But once more, in time he came back. Eventually he returned to explore the whole network of tubes to which the one he had entered connected. Many of the branching tubes were too small for him to enter, and the biggest tube he could find led to another grille from which the musky-smelling air was blasted with force.

Clearly it was the prime mover for the circulation of air through the exhaust half of the pyramid's ventilating system. Harry did not reason it out to himself in those intellectual terms, but he grasped the concept wordlessly and went back to exploring those smaller tubes that he could crawl into.

These, he found, terminated in grilles set in their floors through which he could look down and catch a glimpse of some chamber or other. What he saw was mainly incomprehensible. There were a number of corridors, a number of what could be rooms containing fixed or movable objects of various sizes and shapes. Some of them could be the equivalent of chairs or beds—but if so, they were scaled for a being plainly larger than himself. The lighting was invariably the low-key illumination he had encountered in the lower, machine level of the pyramid, supplied by the single luminescent strip running across the ceiling.

Occasionally, from one grille or another, he heard in the distance the heavy sound of breathing, among other sounds,

and smelled more strongly the musky odor. But for more than
a week of surreptitious visits to the pyramid, he watched
through various grilles without seeing anything living.

V.

However, a day finally came when he was crouched, staring
down into a circular room containing what might be a bed
shape, several chair shapes, and a number of other fixed
shapes with variously spaced and depthed indentations in their
surfaces. In a far edge of the circular room was a narrow
alcove, the walls of which were filled with ranked indentations, among which several lights of different colors winked
and glowed.

Suddenly, the dim illumination of the room began to
brighten. The illumination increased rapidly, so that Harry
cringed back from the grille, lifting a palm to protect his
dimness-accustomed eyes. At the same moment, he heard approaching the sound of heavy breathing and sniffed a sudden
increase in the musky odor.

He froze. Motionless above the grille, he stopped even his
breathing. He would have stopped his heart if he could, but it
raced, shaking his whole body and sounding its rapid beat in
his ears until he felt the noise of it must be booming through
the pyramid like a drum. But there was no sign from below
that this was so.

Then, sliding into sight below him, came a massive figure on
a small platform that seemed to drift without support into the
room.

The aperture of the grille was small. Harry's viewpoint was
cramped and limited, looking down directly from overhead.
He found himself looking down onto thick, hairless brown-
skinned shoulders, a thick neck with the skin creased at the
back, and a forward sloping, hairless brown head, egg-shaped
in outline from above, with the point forward.

Foreshortened below the head and shoulders was a bulging
chinline with something like a tusk showing; it had a squat,
heavy, hairless brown body and thick short forearms with
stubby claws at the end of four-fingered hands. There was
something walruslike about the tusks and the hunching; and

the musky odor rose sickeningly into Harry's human nostrils.

The platform slid level with the alcove, which was too narrow for it to enter. Breathing hoarsely, the heavy figure on it heaved itself suddenly off the platform into the alcove, and the stubby hands moved over the pattern of indentations. Then, it turned and heaved itself out of the alcove, onto the flat, bed surface adjoining. Just as Harry's gaze began to get a full-length picture of it, the illumination below went out.

Harry was left, staring dazzled into darkness, while the heavy breathing and the sound of the figure readjusting itself on the bed surface came up to his ears. After a while, there was no noise but the breathing. But Harry did not dare move. For a long time he held his cramped posture, hardly breathing himself. Finally, cautiously, inch by inch, he retreated down the tube, which was too small to let him turn around. When he reached the larger tubes, he fled for the outside and the safety of the forest.

The next day, he did not go near the pyramid. Or the next. Every time he thought of the heavy brown figure entering the room below the grille, he became soaked with the clammy sweat of a deep, emotional terror. He could understand how the Other had not heard him or seen him up behind the grille. But he could not understand how the alien had not *smelled* him.

Slowly, however, he came to accept the fact that the Other had not. Possibly the Other did not have a sense of smell. Possibly . . . there was no end to the possibilities. The fact was that the Other had not smelled Harry—or heard him—or seen him. Harry was like a rat in the walls—unknown because he was unsuspected.

At the end of the week, Harry was once more prowling around back by the pyramid. He had not intended to come back, but his hatred drew him like the need of a drug addict for the drug of his addiction. He had to see the Other again, to feed his hate more surely. He had to look at the Other, while hating the alien, and feel the wild black current of his emotions running toward the brown and hairless shape. At night, buried in his nest of leaves, Harry tossed and snarled in his sleep, dreaming of the small stream backing up to flood the interior of the pyramid, and the Other drowning—of lightning striking the pyramid and fire racing through it—of the Other burning. His dreams became so full of rage and so terrible that he woke, twisting, and with the few rags of clothing that still managed to cling unnoticed to him soaked with sweat.

In the end, he went back into the pyramid.

Daily he went back. And gradually, it came to the point where he was no longer fearful of seeing the Other. Instead, he could barely endure the search and the waiting at the grilles until the Other came into sight. Meanwhile, outside the pyramid in the forest, the frill-edged leaves began to dry and wither and drop. The little stream sank in its bed—only a few inches, but enough so that Harry had to dig out the bottom of the streambed under the killing barrier in order to pass safely underwater into the pyramid area.

One day he noticed that there were hardly any of the treaded machines out taking samples in the woods any more.

He was on his way to the pyramid through the woods, when the realization struck him. He stopped dead, freezing in midstride like a hunting dog. Immediately, there flooded into his mind the memory of how the parking chamber for the treaded machines, inside the base of the pyramid, had been full of unmoving vehicles during his last few visits.

Immediately, also, he realized the significance of the drying leaves, the dropping of the water level of the stream. And something with the urgency of a great gong began to ring and ring inside him like the pealing of an alarm over a drowning city.

Time had been, when there had been no pyramid here. Time was now, with the year fading and the work of the collecting machines almost done. Time would be, when the pyramid might leave.

Taking with it the Other.

He began to run, instinctively, toward the pyramid. But, when he came within sight of it, he stopped. For a moment he was torn with indecision; an emotional maelstrom of fear and hatred all whirling together. Then, he went on.

He emerged a moment later, dripping, a fist-sized rock in each hand, to stand before the closed door that gave the machines entrance to the pyramid. He stood staring at it, in broad daylight. He had never come here before in full daylight, but his head now was full of madness. Fury seethed in him, but there was no machine to open the door for him. It was then that the fury and madness in him might have driven him to pound wildly on the door with his stones or to wrench off one of the necks of the storklike machine at the stream and try to pry the door open. Any of these insane things he might have done and so have attracted discovery and the awesome power of the machinery and killing weapons at the command of the Other. Any such thing he might have done if he was simply a man out of his head with rage—but he was no longer a man.

He was what the Other had made him, an animal, although with a man locked inside him. And like an animal, he did not rave or rant, any more than does the cat at the mousehole, or the wolf waiting for the shepherd to turn in for the night. Instead, without further question, the human beast that had been Harry Brennan—that still called himself Harry Brennan, in a little, locked-away, back corner of its mind—dropped on his haunches beside the door and hunkered there, panting lightly in the sunlight, and waiting.

Four hours later, as the sun was dropping close to the treetops, a single machine came trundling out of the woods. Harry tricked it with one of his stones and, still carrying the other, ran into the pyramid.

He waited patiently for the small collecting machine to come and empty out the machine returned from outside, then dodged ahead of it, when it came, into the interior, lower level of the pyramid. He made his way calmly to the grille that gave him entrance to the ventilating system, took out the grille, and entered the tube. Once in the system, he crawled through the maze of ductwork, until he came at last to the grille overlooking the room with the alcove and the rows of indentations on the alcove walls.

When he looked down through the grille, it was completely dark below. He could hear the hoarse breathing and smell the musky odor of the Other, resting or perhaps asleep, on the bed surface. Harry lay there for a number of slow minutes, smelling and listening. Then he lifted the second rock and banged with it upon the grille.

For a second there was nothing but the echoing clang of the beaten metal in the darkness. Then the room suddenly blazed with light, and Harry, blinking his blinded eyes against the glare, finally made out the figure of the Other rising upright upon the bed surface. Great, round, yellow eyes in a puglike face with a thick upper lip wrinkled over two tusks stared up through the grille at Harry.

The lip lifted, and a bubbling roar burst from the heavy fat-looking shape of the Other. He heaved his round body off the bed surface and rolled, waddling across the floor to just below the grille.

Reaching up with one blunt-clawed hand, he touched the grille, and it fell to the floor at his feet. Left unguarded in the darkness of the ductwork, Harry shrank back. But the Other straightened up to his full near six-and-a-half feet of height and reached up into the ductwork. His blunt-clawed hand fastened on Harry and jerked. Off balance, Harry came tumbling to the floor of the chamber.

A completely human man probably would have stiffened up and broken both arms, if not his neck, in such a fall. Harry, animallike, attempted to cling to the shape of the Other as he fell, and so broke the impact of his landing. On the floor, he let go of the Other and huddled away from the heavy shape, whimpering.

The Other looked down, and his round, yellow eyes focused on the stone Harry had clung to even through his fall. The Other reached down and grasped it, and Harry gave it up like a child releasing something he has been told many times not to handle. The Other made another, lower-toned, bubbling roar deep in his chest, examining the rock. Then he laid it carefully aside on a low table surface and turned back to stare down at Harry.

Harry cringed away from the alien stare and huddled into himself, as the blunt fingers reached down to feel some of the rags of a shirt that still clung about his shoulders.

The Other rumbled interrogatively at Harry. Harry hid his head. When he looked up again, the Other had moved over to a wall at the right of the alcove and was feeling about in some indentations there. He bubbled at the wall, and a second later Harry's voice sounded eerily in the room.

"You . . . You are . . . the one I . . . made a beast . . ."

Harry whimpered, hiding his head again.

"You can't . . ." said Harry's voice, ". . . even speak now. Is . . . that so . . ."

Harry ventured to peek upward out of his folded arms, but ducked his head again at the sight of the cold, yellow eyes staring down at him.

". . . I thought . . . you would be . . . dead by now," said the disembodied voice of Harry, hanging in the air of the chamber. ". . . Amazing . . . survival completely without . . . equipment. Must keep you now . . ." The eyes, yellow as topaz, considered Harry, huddled abjectly on the floor. ". . . cage . . . collector's item . . ."

The alien revolved back to the indentation of the wall a little way from the alcove. The broad, fleshy back turned contemptuously on Harry, who stared up at it.

The pitiful expression of fear on Harry's face faded suddenly into a soundless snarl. Silently, he uncoiled, snatched up the rock the Other had so easily taken from him, and sprang with it onto the broad back.

As he caught and clung there, one arm wrapped around a thick neck, the stone striking down on the hairless skull, his silent snarl burst out at last into the sound of a scream of triumph.

The Other screamed too—a bubbling roar—as he clumsily turned, trying to reach around himself with his thick short arms and pluck Harry loose. His claws raked Harry's throat-encircling arm, and blood streamed from the arm; but it might have been so much stage makeup for the effect it had in loosening Harry's hold. Screaming, Harry continued to pound crushingly on the Other's skull. With a furious spasm, the alien tore Harry loose, and they both fell on the floor.

The Other was first up; and for a second he loomed like a giant over Harry, as Harry was scrambling to his own feet and retrieving the fallen rock. But instead of attacking, the Other flung away, lunging for the alcove and the control indentations there.

Harry reached the alcove entrance before him. The alien dodged away from the striking rock. Roaring and bubbling, he fled waddling from his human pursuer, trying to circle around the room and get back to the alcove. Half a head taller than Harry and twice Harry's weight, he was refusing personal battle and putting all his efforts into reaching the alcove with its rows of indented controls. Twice Harry headed him off; and then by sheer mass and desperation, the Other turned and burst past into the alcove, thick hands outstretched and grasping at its walls. Harry leaped in pursuit, landing and clinging to the broad, fleshy back.

The Other stumbled under the added weight, and fell, face down. Triumphantly yelling, Harry rode the heavy body to the floor, striking at the hairless head . . . and striking . . . and striking . . .

VI.

Sometime later, Harry came wearily to his senses and dropped a rock he no longer had the strength to lift. He blinked around himself like a man waking from a dream, becoming aware of a brilliantly lit room full of strange shapes —and of a small alcove, the walls of which were covered with rows of indentations, in which something large and dead lay with its head smashed into ruin. A deep, clawing thirst rose to take Harry by the throat, and he staggered to his feet.

He looked longingly up at the dark opening of the ventilator over his head; but he was too exhausted to jump up, cling to its edge, and pull himself back into the ductwork, from which he could return to the stream outside the pyramid and to the flowing water there. He turned and stumbled from the chamber into unfamiliar rooms and corridors.

A brilliant light illuminated everything around him as he went. He sniffed and thought he scented, through the musky reek that filled the air about him, the clear odor of water. Gradually, the scent grew stronger and led him at last to a room where a bright stream leaped from a wall into a basin where it pooled brightly before draining away. He drank deeply and rested.

Finally, satiated, he turned away from the basin and came face-to-face with a wall that was an all-reflecting surface; and he stopped dead, staring at himself, like Adam before the Fall.

It was only then, with the upwelling of his returning humanness, that he realized his condition. And words spoken aloud for the first time in months broke harshly and rustily from his lips like the sounds of a machine unused for years.

"My God!" he said croakingly. "I've got no clothes left!"

And he began to laugh. Cackling, cackling rasping more unnaturally even than his speech, his laughter lifted and echoed hideously through the silent, alien rooms. But it was laughter all the same—the one sound that distinguishes man from the animal.

He was six months after that learning to be a complete human being again and finding out how to control the pyramid. If it had not been for the highly sophisticated safety devices built into the alien machine, he would never have lived to complete that bit of self-education.

But finally he mastered the controls and got the pyramid into orbit, where he collected the rest of his official self and shifted back through the alternate universe to Earth.

He messaged ahead before he landed; and everybody who could be there was on hand to meet him as he landed the pyramid. Some of the hands that had slapped his back on leaving were raised to slap him again when at last he stepped forth among them.

But, not very surprisingly, when his gaunt figure in a spare coverall now too big for it, with shoulder-length hair and burning eyes, stepped into their midst, not one hand finished its gesture. No one in his right senses slaps an unchained wolf on the back; and no one, after one look, wished to risk slapping the man who seemed to have taken the place of Harry.

Of course, he was still the same man they had sent out—of *course* he was. But at the same time he was also the man who had returned from a world numbered 1242 and from a duel to the death there with a representative of a race a hundred times more advanced than his own. And in the process he had been pared down to something very basic in his human blood and bone, something dating back to before the first crude wheel or chipped flint knife.

And what was that? Go down into the valley of the shades and demand your answer of a dead alien with his head crushed in, who once treated the utmost powers of modern human science as a man treats the annoyance of a buzzing mosquito.

Or, if that once-mighty traveler in spacegoing pyramids is disinclined to talk, turn and inquire of other ghosts you will find there—those of the aurochs, the great cave bear, and the woolly mammoth.

They, too, can testify to the effectiveness of naked men.

THE CHILDE CYCLE SERIES

By Gordon R. Dickson

COLLECTIONS OF FANTASY AND SCIENCE FICTION